LITTLE BLUE ROOM

LITTLE BLUE ROOM

A NOVEL

by

DEANNA MACLAREN

LONDON
VICTOR GOLLANCZ LTD
1974

ISBN 0 575 01777 5

PRINTED IN GREAT BRITAIN BY
NORTHUMBERLAND PRESS LIMITED
GATESHEAD

To J.G.

ACKNOWLEDGMENT

The poem on pages 184 and 185 is "Dream in the
Park" by David Pownall. It first appeared in his
collection of poems, *An Eagle Each*, published
by Arena (Carlisle, 1971).

One

I SHOULD NEVER have come, Vivienne panics, as they drive down the hill from Brighton Station. I look like a petrified frog, she decides, glimpsing her stricken reflection distorted in the taxi window. Why didn't I make an excuse, say my mother was ill, anything to get out of it? But then I *wanted* to come; I've been longing for today, counting the hours, almost delirious with excitement, and now it's here I want to go home. I'm obviously not cut out for this sort of thing. Look at me, trembling with nerves in a pool of cold sweat on the edge of my seat, too scared even to light a cigarette in case my hands shake and give me away. Anyway, I smoked so many on the train coming down I feel sick now. No, not sick, please don't let me be sick, not in front of Alex. Quick, take your mind off it, think of something to say. Anything.

Swallowing hard to try and control her lurching stomach, Vivienne turns wildly to the man lounging beside her.

"What's the hotel like?" she croaks, whispering so the taxi driver won't hear.

"I haven't the faintest idea," Alex says, in a normal voice that to the overwrought Vivienne sounds like a shout. "I just picked it out of the AA book with a pin."

"After all, darling," he yells urgently, as if it is important that she believe him, "I don't do this sort of thing every weekend, you know."

Neither do I, Alex. In fact, you're the first man I've ever

spent a weekend with and the reason for my maniacal grin
is that I'm practically blacking out with the effort of trying
to look poised, even slightly amused at the whole situation.
It is very hard, Alex, for a girl to look poised when, in the
frantic rush to catch the train, she packed the wrong knickers
and was forced to wear the ones that didn't dry overnight:
the result is like being encased in two clammy slabs of wet
haddock. God, Alex, what a sensational advert for swinging
London I am. It was terrible meeting you at Victoria this
evening. My legs always seize up when I'm nervous, so I
couldn't seem to walk properly and I felt like a clothes peg
strutting along stiff-legged with that glaring red weekend
case bumping against my knees. I kept telling myself I wasn't
doing anything particularly unique, after all, and it wasn't
Crippen I was meeting but Alex, the man I love and who
loves me. You do love me, don't you? And then I was all hot
and damp with my top lip drenched in sweat so I was sure
when you kissed me you'd notice ... No, for heaven's sake,
don't stick your hand up there, you'll get a horrid shock.

Quickly she grabs his hand which has been moving dangerously up her thigh, and shows him the ring on her wedding
finger.

"I borrowed it from Stella; you know, the girl in the flat
next door. She even offered me engagement and eternity rings
as well but I didn't want to overdo it." Alex laughs, and
Vivienne feels more confident. At twenty-two she is still young
enough to think that she has to make people laugh in order
to make them love her.

Alex says, "Stella sounds a very organised girl. What's she
like?"

"Blonde, a few years older than me, about twenty-five I suppose. Very talkative and energetic."

"I mean is she good looking," he says.

"Oh, yes, in a modern, very *awake* way: lots of false eye-lashes and shine, you know. She told me she used to go out with a millionaire but gave him up because she got sick of drinking champagne all the time."

Alex scoffs: "I bet she really ditched him because he was a lousy fuck. Does Stella work or is she kept by a succession of rich boyfriends?"

"No, she works. She's got a very good job as manageress of the Miss London department at Wallis and Steadman's, that rather stuffy store in Wigmore Street."

"Mmm, I know the place," Alex says, "Claire has an account there."

Yes, Claire *would*, Vivienne thinks, pulling on her gloves as they arrive at the hotel. To her relief it is quite unimposing, just a large converted private house: no doormen or liftboys for her to face and imagine sniggering behind her back. As they enter the tiny lobby she lingers behind Alex, wondering anxiously if it would be more natural to leave her gloves on or take them off to (casually) reveal the ring. What was it she'd read that some famous ex-Head Doorman had said about weekending couples? You can always tell the ones who aren't married because while the man signs the register the girl hovers nervously in the background with her eyes glued to the local bus time-tables on the notice board.

Vivienne leaves the gloves on and draws level with Alex, peering round his shoulder to watch him sign his name and her address: R. A. Mallender, 18 Kirton Road, Chelsea.

The faded middle-aged woman behind the high reception desk lays down her grey knitting and slides across a small key attached to a huge plastic disc.

"Room twelve, second floor. Is there any luggage, Sir?"

"I can manage it, thanks."

*　　*　　*

Room twelve is yellow, in a heavy-handed way. The prim-rose walls and ageing lemon curtains fight a losing battle with the dark gold bedspread and mustard carpet, while two small canary and gold striped towels hang on a washbasin the colour of sour cream. Wedged unhappily in the corner is a thin pine wardrobe and in the middle of the room hangs a fluted lampshade in mustard coloured plastic. On the bedside table squats a chipped yellow glass ashtray and a Gideon Bible, inexpertly covered with sun-flowered Fablon.

"Not too bad, is it?" asks Alex absently, busy unpacking his canvas hold-all.

"No," Vivienne lies. "And at least they've given us a double bed."

Alex looks up and embraces her. "You lovely natural girl," he says, kissing her face and gently stroking her long hair. "Vivvy, I know so many women who'd be scared to make a remark like that because it doesn't sound sophisticated or clever."

Sophisticated and clever like Claire, she thinks. And how many "many women" *does* he know?

"But you're so refreshingly straightforward about every-thing, Vivvy, it's marvellous. It's just so ... so honest, some-how."

It's just plain nerves, she thinks. He doesn't understand how depressingly young and completely ill-at-ease I feel walking into a hotel room like this for the first time with a man. Worse, a married man I've only known a couple of months. Everything is so blatant: here's The Room and there's The Bed. That's what we're here for, Bed. It's a double bed and takes up most of this insane room so it seems silly to try and pretend it isn't there and make polite comments about the colour of the curtains instead. Alex doesn't seem to feel awk-ward at all. He's unpacked, made four funny jokes about the

Gideon Bible and now he's off to have a bath ... while I've been standing here staring blankly out of the window pretending to be fascinated by a view of a Brighton back street.

Vivienne moves across to the handbasin and washes her hands, gazing critically at her face in the mirror, her large grey eyes hunting, as usual, for spots. She is quite unaware of the sensuality of her face, the lively quality which makes so many other faces seem dull and dead in comparison. To Vivienne, her nose is too blobby, her mouth too big and her teeth too crooked, while her eyes, though an attractive colour, lack the depth that comes, she hopes, with experience. Vivienne is desperate for experience. Her hair, she feels, is all right. Long and glossy, a dark rich brown, the colour, Alex once remarked, of barley wine. She dries her hands on the striped yellow towel, promising herself that after this weekend she really will stop biting her nails, and lifts the shiny new red weekend case on to the bed.

The case, she decides, taking out a dry pair of knickers, is a mistake. Too obvious. Next time use one of those airline hold-alls, as Stella suggested. But there were so many things Stella *hadn't* told her, that no one ever told you about the first few hours of a weekend away with a man you don't really know very well. It's different at the flat when he always leaves around midnight. Here, in this odd yellow room everything is so unfamiliar: his things on the dressing table, his underpants and socks in the top right drawer; that must be where he keeps them at home. I don't know which side of the bed he usually sleeps on so I don't know on which side to put my neatly folded nylon nightie. I don't normally wear nighties but this is a hotel and I'm here with a man and its different. Everything is different. I don't know if he uses a deodorant or if he snores or if his feet smell or if he has bad breath in the mornings like me ... all these silly domestic sort of things that make you feel so strange and diffident with a person, however much you love them. That's probably why I made that remark about the bed. Sex is the only familiar ground I've got at the moment.

And some time over the weekend the bathroom won't be free and I'll have to use that sink and wash myself in front of Alex. It won't occur to him that I'm embarrassed because it *never* occurs to him that I could be shy. Even when I take my clothes off in front of him I'm terribly aware of him looking at me. People you read about are always so wildly confident, undressing and jumping in and out of one another's beds as easily as hopping on a bus, but I'm just not used to it. Alex thinks women like being looked at by men, that they are forever inviting it, but he forgets that if you aren't used to it you imagine the man is criticising your tits or comparing your figure to somebody else's. Like Claire's.

Alex comes back, wearing just a bath towel, looking virtuously pink and scrubbed. Had she been older, Vivienne might have found it endearing the way Alex has obviously spent some time carefully touselling his thinning brown hair and arranging the towel round his waist to hide the slight spare tyre. But at twenty-two, Vivienne, looking only for that which she wants to see, doesn't notice such things, seeking simply the reassurance in his blue eyes that tells her he loves her.

"The bathroom's horrific," Alex announces, "but I've run you a bath. Are you hungry?"

"Starving."

"Good. Well hurry up and we'll go and eat. I'll find the bar downstairs and meet you there."

Half an hour later Vivienne nibbles the cherry from her sweet Martini and asks: "Alex, what were you thinking about when I came into the bar just now?"

Alex smiles. "How beautiful you looked."

Months afterwards, when Vivienne reminds him of their romantic weekend in Brighton, Alex confesses that in fact while he sat waiting for her he had downed four large scotches very quickly and decided he must be mad. With a wife like Claire at home whom he loved, and, let's face it, had no intention of leaving or anything crazy like that, what on earth was he doing carting a girl twelve years his junior off to Brighton for a dirty weekend? Sex? Yes, of course, but they could have that any time at Vivvy's grubby little flat without all the upheaval and lies involved in a weekend drama. And *Brighton* of all places. How corny could you get? He should have outgrown this sort of thing years ago.

Still, at least in Brighton there were plenty of things to do. Vivvy might want to stay in bed all the time but he knew he hadn't got that sort of stamina; he was thirty-four, for heaven's sake, not twenty-four like the creatures she'd associated with before. No, if you were going to do this at all, Brighton with its shops, the pier and even those bloody dolphins was a much better bet than some lonely hotel deep in the country where your only diversion was a tramp through muddy fields in a howling March gale. And knowing Vivvy, the whole rustic scene would probably turn her on and she'd demand a knee-trembler up against an oak tree. At least in Brighton with all these people about she couldn't do that. Could she?

And, Alex thought, it would be good to be by the sea again. He and Claire had avoided it for the last four years, ever since the accident. Quickly, Alex pushed the thought away as Vivienne appeared in the doorway. Don't think about Claire now. Concentrate on Vivvy. Lovely Vivienne who's so much in love with you it hurts. Lots of sex, loads of food, drink and the sea air this weekend. Perhaps it wasn't such a mad idea after all.

Fresh from her bath, Vivienne feels elated as they leave the hotel. Alex is so funny, tender and entertaining and it's such a luxury to be together like this with two whole glorious days in front of them. It has been raining and as the lamp-light shines on the damp cobbled back streets Vivienne feels she could almost reach out and touch all the magic and happiness that surrounds her. They find a pub with a restaurant next door and later Vivienne remembers it as an evening when they laughed and talked and loved and felt very pleased with themselves.

For Vivienne, accustomed to sleeping alone, it is a strange experience waking up in the morning to feel a naked man instead of the usual cold hot-water bottle beside her. There is something rather shocking, she thinks, about the sheer physical size of a man, warm and rough, taking up such a large amount of the bed. Uneasily aware of Alex propped up on one elbow, looking down at her, she stretches, moving carefully so as not to touch him, as if she were lying beside an unexploded bomb.

"Did you sleep well, my love?" he asks.

"Oh, yes." Please, she prays, let me look all right. Don't let there be bits of last night's mascara still gummed to my eyes. "Yes, like a log."

Alex laughs. "Darling, you are funny. You look like a little angel lying there with your hair all curly and your face puffy with sleep and then you wake up and make such a very un-angelic remark!"

"Well, I was tired," Vivienne protests. "It was late you know, by the time you finally let me get to sleep."

"Lying bitch, *you* kept attacking *me*."

"I didn't—"

"Shut up and come here," he says, drawing her close. "I've been waiting ages for you to wake up."

They are late for breakfast but it doesn't matter, for the dining room is still full, populated exclusively with elderly people, mainly women, all of whom stop eating and gaze at the newcomers with undisguised interest.

"Morning!" breezes Alex.

Twenty grey heads bend to twenty bowls of soggy sunshine breakfasts; no one responds. Alex and Vivienne give their order and talk in whispers until the food arrives, served at speed by the faded receptionist in a gravy-stained apron; she clearly resents the time she's having to spend away from her knitting. They start to eat, but with the elderly residents following the progress of every forkful from plate to mouth they are made to feel, Vivienne says afterwards, like gatecrashers in a geriatric ward, cruelly intent on stealing the inmates' food.

Alex stirs the tea. "I'll pour," he says, and childishly Vivienne feels slighted. I can do other things apart from fuck, you know. She tries a reproachful look but Alex, teapot in hand, is smiling engagingly at the old lady at the next table. She stares back challengingly, her square mouth deliberately working over a fugitive piece of toast lodged in a crevice in her gums. Alex is fascinated.

"Milk first," Vivienne hisses irritably.

"What?"

"I said I always have the milk in first."

"Don't be silly, darling. It really doesn't make any difference. Hey, have you noticed how the door to the kitchens makes a noise like someone crunching a radish?"

Vivienne giggles and scoops away the grease from her rub-berised fried egg. She feels hot and uncomfortable.

"Vivvy, you're very flushed all of a sudden. Are you sure you're OK?" asks Alex, concerned.

Miserably, Vivienne realises she cannot delay matters any longer. She pushes back her chair. "Actually Alex, I, er ... I do feel a little sick. Would you excuse me a moment?"

Confidence, she reflects, once safely ensconced in the Ladies, confidence is a grammar-school-educated, nicely-brought-up middle class girl like me being able to say over breakfast to her fairly new lover: "Hell, I feel like a crap. See you in fifteen minutes and don't hog all the toast." Simple and straightforward. Not all this, oh, I feel a little sick nonsense. Let's face it, Vivvy, you can't go through the rest of your life stammering out shy excuses every time a big egg and bacon breakfast gets you going.

The inevitable notice on the lavatory door is also, she sees, displaying middle-class origins.

"Please," it urges, "put used towels in the incinerator, not down the lavatory, as these toilets are cleaned BY MEN!"

Underneath, another typewritten note implores users to "leave this lavatory as you would wish to find it," under which is the scrawled explanation: "i.e. WARM."

Vivienne tugs furiously at the roller towel. Alex is human, after all. He craps as well, you know. Once, maybe *twice* a day. He's thirty-four and married. He *knows* about things. He *expects* you to have normal body functions. Now go back into the dining room, walk normally, not woodenly across to the table, smile and be quite open and honest about it all. After all, he has this mistaken idea that you are an open, honest sort of person.

As Vivienne returns the silence in the dining room is, if possible, more stifling than before. She runs the gauntlet of

inquisitive eyes and sinks with relief into her chair. Alex takes
her hand.

"Are you all right, angel?"

All chewing stops, hearing aids are adjusted and twenty
greying heads crane to hear her answer. Vivienne takes a
deep breath.

"Oh *fine*, yes, quite all right. What it was, actually, was
that well, I ... I think, really, it must have been the egg you
know. Eggs always make me feel queasy first thing in the
morning."

Later, as the lift lurches upwards, she asks: "By the way,
where are you this weekend?"

"Where am I? ... Oh, I see what you mean. Yes. Well
oddly enough I am supposed to be in Brighton; there's a
public relations conference on here. They choose a different
place each year and have dull seminars with even duller
speakers. If you don't mind, angel, I think I ought to look in
for a couple of hours this afternoon, just to show my face."

"Oh."

"You could go and look at the dolphins, and afterwards I'll
meet you and we'll find a real English tea shoppe and have a
proper tea."

"Mmm! Buttered scones!"

"And toasted teacakes!"

"And seed cake and chocolate biscuits and—"

"Vivvy, you are a greedy little bitch, you've only just had
your breakfast. Come on now, get your coat and we'll go for
a good bracing walk."

"That sounds horrible. It looks cold out there."

"There's just a healthy March wind," he laughs.

"I love you."

"We were lucky," Alex says. "Finding a typically English

tea shoppe in a typically English seaside town is not easy. Steak bars and fish and chip shops, yes. Indian and Chinese, yes. Jellied eels, yes. But tea shoppes, no. And once you've found your shoppe, it's inevitably closed—according to a typically English handwritten sign—or overflowing with tourists from the monstrous coach that's blocking the quaint cobbled side street."

"But this is ideal," says Vivienne happily. "Chintzy curtains, oak beams, copper kettles and real teacakes!"

"Yes, I wondered how long it would take you to mention the food. Still, you're looking much better than you were this morning. I was quite worried about you."

To change the subject, Vivienne hastily asks him about the conference.

"God, I don't know why they bother," Alex says, gulping down the scalding tea. "All these posturing PR blokes invite a crowd of equally idiot journalists to discuss how we can achieve a better relationship between same PR men and journalists. They then proceed to spend two solid hours shouting the odds at one another."

"Did you say anything?"

"Hell no," Alex grins. "I repaired to the bar. If anyone was looking for me that's where they'd expect me to be."

"You used to be a journalist, didn't you?"

"I was made redundant, along with a couple of hundred others. After that I decided I'd had enough of Fleet Street— well, to be honest, I couldn't get another job at the right money, so I used my redundancy pay to form my own PR outfit with a couple of other guys. And then of course I wrote my book."

"I thought it was awfully good," says Vivienne on cue. "How's the new one coming along?"

"It's what is known as 'stuck', and has been for some time

now. The thing about the first one was its topicality. Fleet Street was news at that time, and of all of us who started books when the paper folded, I was lucky enough to be the first to get mine finished and published. The new one's more difficult—a sort of psychological thriller. Claire thinks it's going to be better than *Street* but I'm not sure."

Vivienne has, of course, heard all this before, but when she can't think of anything entertaining to say she always takes refuge in asking questions. It's relaxing watching Alex talk and not having to make any particular effort herself and anyway she is sure Alex's conversation is far more interesting than her own. Vivienne envies people like Stella who are never at a loss for words, but when she mentioned this once to her, the older girl had said she only wished she had some of Vivienne's restraint.

"When I meet someone new I yak on and on about myself so much that it takes me weeks to get round to finding out what *he's* like and then I usually discover he's painfully boring and curse myself for wasting all that time."

Vivienne lights a guilty cigarette. Alex doesn't smoke and disapproves of her admitted twenty a day. In fact, she thinks, it's nearer thirty, but with women cigarettes are like birthdays, always lied about after twenty-five.

"By the way," Alex says, "I'm afraid we'll have to leave immediately after lunch tomorrow. I completely forgot I'm giving a drinks party in the evening and I ought to get back in time to organise booze and arrange cheese straws artistically on plates."

"Oh," says Vivienne. "Yes, of course." Why, she wonders, does he always say "I" when he means "we"?

"Do you have many parties?" Vivienne asks later, in the pub. After wine with dinner and now on her third Martini, she feels immunised enough to want to talk about Claire.

"Quite a few, yes," Alex replies. "It's part of my job up to a point, and Claire arranges a lot of them, invites people from the publishing world she thinks might be useful to me. It was through her that I got *Street* published so quickly: she knew the right people to go to. But this whole party thing used to be worse before I left Fleet Street. She used to have a crowd of do-goody friends who came round to drink large quantities of sherry and plan further good works."

"What sort of things?" Vivienne wonders whether to risk another cigarette and decides to wait until the next drink.

Alex says, "Well, Claire has a tremendous social conscience you see. She had one of those rather strict religious childhoods, with Duty as the watchword. Her father owned an educational publishing business in Bristol—Claire runs the London end of it now—and turned out gloomy moralistic tracts in between eating bagfulls of Sharps toffees. I never saw him without a toffee in his mouth. Anyway, all this washed off on Claire rather, and she and a crowd of hen friends used to get together and have a lost cause a month. We used to get them homeless, drugged, incontinent, pregnant and unmarried, married and wanting divorces, married and resisting divorces. Whoever they were they all seemed to end up in my house with my wife's smart friends drinking my sherry. I must say, though, Claire was very good and put a stop to it all when I started working from home on my book."

Vivienne wishes Alex wouldn't be so bloody decent about Claire all the time.

Alex smiles. "Don't look so serious, angel. How about another drink?" He waves unsuccessfully at the barmaid.

"I thought," says Vivienne, "that people with strict childhoods tended to rebel."

"Claire did," says Alex. "She married me."

The barmaid notices Alex's wave the second time. He is, Vivienne thinks admiringly, the only man she knows who doesn't pretend to be coughing or smoothing back his hair when he can't attract a barmaid's attention. Seeing Alex pay for the drinks nags her into worrying if she should offer him some money for this weekend. She knows she can't afford such a gesture, but does he? Will he think she's mean and grabbing if she doesn't make the offer? It's lovely coming away like this, she thinks, but it's such a strain forever trying to avoid looking gauche. I'll have to ask Stella about the money angle when we get back to London.

The pianist, with three pints ranged on top of the piano, is thumping out "Apple Blossom Time", and the little gang of residents in the corner is noisily joining in.

"I was taught to play the pia—"

"I've got a marvellous Andrews Sisters record," says Alex. "One time when Claire's away you must come round and I'll play it for you."

"What's Claire doing while you're away?" Has she got a lover?

"Oh, visiting her old school friend Joyce, I expect. She's married to a wealthy Canadian called Maxwell who refers to everybody as 'hunne'."

"Stella used to go out "

"Vivvy, you do look beautiful." He leans forward and strokes her hair. She wishes he would stop interrupting her all the time. It makes her feel like that newspaper advertisement that starts: WHY ARE YOU BORING? However, he *is* saying loving things to her, telling her how much he loves her, how much he thinks about her when they are apart. Reassured, she is able to stop dwelling on Claire. Poor old thing, if she doesn't know how to hold on to her husband, why should she, Vivienne, care?

Softly, Alex tells her to hurry up and finish her drink. He wants to make violent love to her. Vivienne slips off her shoe and rubs her foot up his thigh. "Why are you whispering?" says.

"Darling! Put your foot down! You'll get us thrown out."

"I thought we were leaving anyway."

"Somehow, I think we'd better."

Hand in hand, they run back to the hotel, past the furiously knitting receptionist, up the stairs into the mad yellow bedroom, where they make very wild love for hours.

Two

THE FOLLOWING SATURDAY Vivienne has arranged to meet her mother at Sloane Square. Or rather, her mother has arranged to meet Vivienne.

"We can have a look round the shops and then have tea at your flat," Mrs Tyler said firmly over the telephone. "You've never invited me to see where you live, you know."

"You wouldn't like the shops here, mum. They're all trendy boutiques with loud pop music and dim lights so you can't see what you're buying. Not your style at all." And you won't like my flat, Vivienne thought.

"Nonsense, dear," Mrs Tyler's voice was crisp and antiseptic. Vivienne could imagine her swabbing out the telephone mouthpiece with Dettol after each call. "Nonsense. There's Peter Jones which is an excellent store. It's allied to the John Lewis people you know: 'never knowingly undersold'." Mrs Tyler purred her approval.

"All right," Vivienne agreed, ungraciously. "I'll meet you at half past two at the flower stall in Sloane Square. Don't expect my flat to be the Ritz, that's all."

Vivienne lives in one room on the first floor of a red brick Victorian house just off the King's Road, sharing the bathroom and kitchen with Stella who has the room next door. It costs her £9.50 a week, which she can't really afford. The flower stall is her favourite rendezvous. She avoids arranging for people to call for her at the flat, hating the awkward business of having them hang around while she makes strained remarks to cover the fact that she isn't ready, and can't even offer them the glass of sherry she is sure they expect.

She is late now as she hurries to meet her mother. Vivienne feels a desperate sense of compassion and sadness as she regards the anxious matronly figure in her sensible camel coat and round brown felt hat. Sloane Square on Saturdays belongs to the young, the elegant, the eccentric, not the middle-aged suburban housewife looking like a misplaced Oxo cube.

"Dear mum," thinks Vivienne with a rush of affection, "she can't help being like she is."

"You look hot and untidy," announces Mrs Tyler, managing in five words to banish Vivienne's new-found compassion. She watches the girl's face harden, and cries a little inside. Why does she always say the wrong thing? It hurts seeing Vivienne like this, her face rebellious and withdrawn. She used to be such a happy child, rushing into the kitchen after school, laughing as she spilled out the story of her day. They were close then, she and her daughter, her child, the fruit of her own body she had suffered to be born into this world. And how she had suffered. Lillian Tyler shudders inwardly as Vivienne leads the way into the big department store.

Strangely, it is not the act of intercourse which bothers Mrs Tyler. In a way, *That* is not too dreadful. Vaseline makes it easier and you don't have to look, because it's always done under the bedclothes with your eyes shut tight. Very cosy and familiar, really, and quite clean too because she always has her wash afterwards and insists that Stanley does too. She would never admit it, but in her quiet, comfortable way, she quite enjoys it. Not too often, of course, just once every three weeks or so, now. Anyway, it is her duty, in the same way that it was her duty to give Stanley a child. But only one, thank you. My word, what an embarrassing, messy affair. Male doctors rummaging round inside you, and then having to lie with your legs in stirrups while all those people, including strange *men* peer at you. And that unspeakable afterbirth! No, it had all been too revolting ever to be undertaken again. One was enough. Yet Mrs Tyler loves her daughter and wishes with all her heart she could be closer to her. Sadly, she doesn't know how.

Vivienne, oblivious to her mother's private reflections, is gloomily steering them towards Electrical and Light Fittings. She dreads taking her mother back to the flat afterwards, but it is clear that Mrs Tyler will not be put off; in spite of the stated purpose of buying a new shade for the standard lamp, Vivienne is sure the main reasons for her mother's visit are to poke round the flat, pick it to pieces, tell her how wonderfully her ex-boyfriend Doug is getting on, and pry into her sex life.

Three hours later Vivienne unwillingly ushers her mother into the dark, drab hall at 18 Kirton Road and gently closes the heavy front door. "Please do not slam the door" instructs a notice above the letter box. Mrs Tyler sniffs and Vivienne quickly urges her up the long flight of stairs before she has time to make her usual comment about people whose houses have a musty smell, like that of moulting animals.

Vivienne's room is on the first floor, facing out over the road. She settles her mother into the only armchair, feeds 10p into the meter and lights the small gas fire.

"What's in there?" asks Mrs Tyler, pointing to a blue-painted door at the opposite end of the room to the window.

"That's the kitchen I share with Stella, the girl next door. You can have a look after we've had some tea; I won't be a minute." She doesn't want her mother prowling round the kitchen until she's had a chance to tidy up a bit.

Left alone, Mrs Tyler studies the room, her sharp eyes picking out the darns in the faded blue carpet, the scratched brown wardrobe and the crumpled cover thrown over the divan bed. Brought up under a system of separate rooms for each activity, dining, living, sleeping, Mrs Tyler is disturbed by this, her first glimpse of bedsitter living. Most upsetting of all is the presence of a bed in the room: a permanent reminder of *That*. Not that there is anything wrong with *That* if you are married, of course, but it just doesn't seem right for a single girl to be reminded of *That* all the time, not to mention any single men that might come here. She must question Vivienne about it, and *That*.

Vivienne returns with a tray of tea, Stella's best cups, cucumber sandwiches and some almond slices she bought last week and hopes are still fresh. She is tense, waiting for her mother's acid comments on the flat, but Mrs Tyler has arranged her mouth in a tight wavy line and, miraculously, says nothing. Looking at the five pathetic anemones struggling in a glass jar on the dusty mantelpiece she feels sorry for her daughter living in what is to her such a shabby way. She makes a mental note to send Vivienne a little parcel of, perhaps, a pretty flower print to brighten up the walls and a proper vase to use instead of that common jam jar. For the rest of her life Mrs Tyler will send Vivienne "proper" vases which her daughter will give away, continuing to use glass jars which reveal the patterns of the stalks in the water.

But Mrs Tyler hasn't come to tea to talk about vases. As Vivienne guessed, it is Doug and his promotion she wants to talk about, and does talk about, until Vivienne, tired and angry, says:

"Look mum, I don't want to know anything about Doug any more, so stop going on will you? I'm glad he's getting on well and being promoted. Great. But it's pointless you thinking everything is going to come all right and in the end I'll come home and Marry Doug and live in a house just up the road so you can pop in with treacle tarts and advice, because I'm not. It's not what I want, I've told you that before."

"Is this what you want, then?" asks Mrs Tyler, looking round the dreary room.

"It's not a question of surroundings," says Vivienne passionately. "At the moment I don't regard them as particularly important. I don't mind things being untidy and run down, worn out or even dirty. It's *me* I'm interested in, mum. I went to find out who I am and what I can do. I want to stretch a bit, find out what my limits are—"

"I don't understand why you can't do all that at home, Vivienne. We've been good to you, given you the best education, a year's secretarial course and the eighteen months in Paris you wanted to perfect your French. I would have thought you'd be glad to come and live at home after all that time abroad. And..."

Vivienne sips her tea, telling herself she knows this record by heart ... a good home, good education (failed A Levels), secretarial course and the exciting opportunity of some time in France with her mother's sister, Aunt Rose, and family. Wonderful, except that it wasn't really Paris. It was a provincial town twenty miles outside the capital and Vivienne quickly discovered that French suburbia was ten times more stultifying than the English variety she had just left. Worse, she was chaperoned most of the time by Aunt Rose who even imposed a rigid nightly curfew of half past ten. Vivienne sighs at the thought of all that lost opportunity and tunes in again to her mother.

"...only forty minutes on the train to Victoria so you could easily live at home and keep your job in town."

"Mum I do appreciate all you've done for me, don't think I don't. But at home I'd be bumping into Doug all the time and people would accidentally on purpose invite us to the same parties, and there would be all this pressure on me to get married like all the other good little girls in the town. I don't *want* to get married; and in particular I don't want to marry Doug. It's better for me to be completely away from it all."

"I don't see what you've got against marriage. Your father and I have been very happy."

Vivienne pours some more tea and reserves judgement on her parents' marital harmony. "I just don't think I'm ready for marriage yet, that's all."

Mrs Tyler can contain herself no longer.

"Well, I must say, Vivienne, I don't like the idea of you living in *Chelsea*" (she makes it sound like Sodom) "all alone with a bed in the room and picking up all sorts of strange ideas. And no doubt," she adds with heavy menace, "all sorts of strange *men*."

"Oh, for God's sake, mum," Vivienne says wearily.

"You're my daughter, Vivienne, and I trust you. So does your father. But it's only natural that we should worry."

"Well don't worry. I'm perfectly all right."

Mrs Tyler hesitates, then reaches across and takes Vivienne's hand. Vivienne tries not to flinch, recognising it as a remarkably demonstrative gesture from her mother.

"Now Vivienne, tell me the truth. I am your mother, you can confide in me. Have you ... are you ... are you still a virgin?"

Vivienne has a vision of herself last weekend, kneeling on the bed waving her naked backside at Alex, screaming with delight as he fucked her from behind. She controls her rising hysteria and somehow utters the words her mother wants to hear.

"Yes, mum," she says kindly. "Of course I am."

*   *   *

When her mother has gone unwillingly in a taxi to Victoria because Vivienne insisted she would get crushed to death on the Tube, Vivienne washes up the tea things and thinks about Doug. It was her mother's parting shot as they kissed awkwardly through the taxi window, with Mrs Tyler firmly clutching her new lampshade on her knee.

"What message shall I pass on to Doug, dear?"

"No mess— Oh, I don't know, mum. Say what you like. No, just say I hope he's well. Something ordinary like that."

Doug, she reflects, swishing Stella's tea cups round the chipped enamel bowl in the sink, is such an *ordinary* person. A nice chap. A good bloke. Steady, reliable and depressingly mature. He was middle-aged from the day he was born, and when he was aged something like five he realised that his vocation in life was to be a solicitor so from then on he arranged his life accordingly. He did all the right subjects at school when everyone else did all the wrong ones because they didn't know what they wanted to do when they left, and eventually he pitched up in her father's firm. Where he Did Well. Naturally, the next sensible step would be to marry the boss's daughter, just back from France, and live in a nice little semi with an orderly garden, two quiet, neat children and a Vernon Ward print over the mantelpiece. It went without saying that his carnal lust for the boss's daughter would remain repressed and she would be delivered up to him, swathed in pure white, unsullied and untouched by human hand, to be borne away to a secret place where it would be his fortunate duty to rifle the goodies.

It was partly to thwart these ideas that Vivienne seduced him. At least that was the word Doug always used—she supposed it made him feel extra wicked. Ambushed was how Vivienne always thought of it. With her parents out for the evening, and Doug out of the room making coffee, Vivienne had turned out all the lights, taken off all her clothes and lain down on the floor in what she hoped was an alluring pose.

Douglas came in, and with quite exceptional self-control did not drop the coffee cups, scream or faint. Instead, he put the coffee down carefully on the table, making sure it didn't spill and then went systematically round the room turning on all the lights, after which he sat down on the settee and looked down at the by now very chilly Vivienne. When he had studied every inch of her he sat back, stared at the wall and drank his coffee.

After a moment, Vivienne sat up and drank hers too. To cover the fact that she was feeling increasingly silly, she said belligerently:

"What's the matter? Don't you want me?"

"Of course I want you," he said, still staring at the wall.

"Well let's—"

"I think I'd better go," said Doug, standing up and switching his gaze to the door. Vivienne jumped to her feet and put her hands round his face, forcing him to look at her.

"You're not going anywhere. You're going to stay here and make love to me!" she shouted romantically. Vivienne pushed him back on to the settee and sprawled on top of him, breaking her nails in her struggle to undo his trousers. Trust Doug to have all these difficult buttons and zips in strange places. Passive, his eyes closed, he let her remove his clothes. Vivienne turned out the lights again and wondered what to do next. She had eleven-and-a-half stone of naked man lying on her settee, physically quite obviously wanting her but mentally conscience-stricken and she just didn't know what to do. Really, it was too bad of Doug to lie there like a pound of mince when she was offering him what her mother would call Woman's Most Priceless Gift. God, this was no time to think of her mother. Angrily she shook his shoulder.

"For God's sake, don't just bloody lie there! What's the *matter* with me? I thought you wanted me!"

Doug caught her close and whispered miserably, "I do want you, Vivvy. I just don't think it's right, that's all."

"Oh don't be silly, Doug. I want to, you want to..."

He hadn't, he said, got any—you know—things on him but Vivienne said authoritatively that he could take it out just before he came. She pulled him to the floor where he lay beside her, not touching her, with his head turned away.

"Well what's the matter now? Why won't you touch me?"

He was afraid, he said. He'd never done it before and didn't want her to be disappointed. She had turned his head towards her and said encouragingly: "Well I've never done it before either, so we'll help one another."

Vivienne throws the tea leaves down the sink and laughs out loud at the memory. God it had been awful. At first she had guided him:

"Down a little bit ... that's right. Now push, ow! not too much! It hurts, you'll have to do it gently. Now push a bit more, gently, and a bit—"

And then he had lost control and come all over the place, leaving her to clean up the mess on the carpet and wonder if she had lost her virginity at all. Not surprisingly, their love-making never improved over the next six months. Douglas still felt guilty about it and this dampened her own ardour; and with neither of them knowing much about it, it really was a case of the blind leading the blind, with most unsatis-factory results. And then Doug had passed his final exams and was pressing her to get married. Her parents and friends were pressing too. Her parents adored Doug; he was hard-working, respectable and clean, said Mrs Tyler. Of course, Vivienne thought, he would have to be clean. If she had told her mother Doug had made love to her, or attempted to, at least three times a week, her mother would have called her a liar and threatened to wash her mouth out with soap.

So Vivienne was relieved when the offer of this translating job gave her an excuse to leave home. It wasn't really too far to commute but she made out a good case. Then her parents and Doug ganged up on her so she flounced out one morning, went into London and accepted the first flat she could find at a rent she knew she could barely afford. Anything to get away. Her father, surprisingly, helped to move her things, patiently loading up the car and tactfully saying nothing about the dreary appearance of the small flat.

It was all over very quickly. One week she was at home, the daughter of the centrally-heated house, handing round tinned salmon sandwiches to her parents' friends, who watched with approval and sly winks her courtship by an up-and-coming young solicitor. There were wall-to-wall carpets, regular meals, endless supplies of freshly-laundered clothes in the fitted cupboards in her bedroom, and church and "Family Favourites" on Sundays. The next week she was installed in her one-roomed flat. It was cramped and cold but it was hers and she was excited at the thought of stamping on it her own personality (whatever that might turn out to be).

But Vivienne found it hard living alone for the first time in her life. Stella was kind and helpful but was out most of the time with one of her string of boyfriends, and often had to work late at the store. She was young at twenty-five she said, to be manageress of the Miss London department; all the other Buyers in the store were knocking on and disapproved of her trendy department with the dolly-bird salesgirls. She felt she had to work doubly hard just to make sure they could never do the dirty on her.

So, for the first time, Vivienne cooked her own meals in the small ill-equipped kitchen. Meat was totally beyond her

budget: she learnt to like vegetables, eggs, cheese, nuts and
yoghurt. After three weeks, when she ran out of fresh clothes
she had to force herself to visit the launderette. Another
"first" and she despised herself for feeling nervous about
going. She had often passed it, a bright bustling place in
the King's Road. Once she had seen a boy and a girl, both
with identical shoulder-length hair, run out of the launderette and dash across the road carrying a big round basket
overflowing with washing. The girl slipped and, as everything
tipped on to the pavement, the couple stood and laughed at
one another while passers-by stopped and helped scoop up the
clothes. Vivienne had envied them their shared laughter, as
she envied the young, weirdly dressed people in the launderette their chirpy, easy confidence.

Sometimes she revelled in being alone. When she came
home from work it was such a pleasure to make a cup of tea
and stretch out on the unmade bed with a cigarette and know
there was no one to nag her to tidy up, lay the table for
supper, marry Doug. She would lie back and look round her
little room, planning a painting for that wall, or a fresh glass
of yellow flowers to be set against the mirror above the mantelpiece. Every week she bought the *Radio Times* and circled in
red the programmes on Radio Three and Four she wanted to
listen to; Stella often invited her to watch her portable television but it reminded Vivienne too much of home.

One of her main discoveries at this time was that she wasn't
robbed, raped or laughed at if she went to a cinema or con-
cert by herself. She found it was quite painless and hundreds
of other people did it too. The worst part was standing in the
queue when everyone else seemed to be with someone, and
being convinced that they were all whispering about her,
especially when she asked for a single ticket.

Because she knew so few people in London, Vivienne was

especially excited when she was invited out. Getting ready
became a ritual: emerging from the bathroom, her skin soft-
ened with baby lotion and soothed with cheap talc, to the
chaos of her room ... heated hair rollers, her make-up strewn
all along the mantelpiece, coffee getting cold in a brown-
stained mug, her reflection in the big mirror with the ornate
golden frame. A last cigarette. Then she was off, running
away from the drab room down the dark stairs into the light,
then along the back streets to Sloane Square and the flower
stall. As she drew away from the flat, she would feel increasingly excited, her senses totally alert to all the scents, sounds
and colours of London, and full of anticipation, with a child-
like certainty that something wonderful was about to happen.

A few times she met an old school friend for lunch. They
ate in the Chelsea Kitchen with her friend acting out her
fantasies as the heroine of a modern novel about the frustrated
mind and wayward body of an intelligent woman bound by
her wedding ring to the barren confines of her newly-painted
Wimpey house, with a sickly toddler son and a husband
whose main ambition was to come top of his current man-
agement-training course. Vivienne listened and drank most
of the carafe of red wine paid for by her friend, before they
went shopping in Peter Jones where the friend gravitated to
the soft furnishing department, emerging triumphant with
some remnant material, just what she wanted for new kitchen curtains. And she happily caught her train back to
Coulsdon, vaguely wondering while planning the evening
meal, what on earth was to become of poor Vivienne.

In January, five months after she left home, Vivienne joined
a literary society and was taken out a few times by earnest
young men who wanted to write. She didn't find any of the
young men attractive, but went to bed with one out of pity,
and a terrible sense of obligation because he was poor and

had bought her an unexpectedly expensive dinner. It wasn't any more inspiring than it had been with Doug, but she continued to see him, for company. Simply for the sake of being with someone, she put up with his moods, the way he was intense about everything, and his poverty which was worse than her own. She tried not to dwell on not having much money, in case it made her start thinking she might be better off at home.

It was with a tremendous sense of relief that she met Alex.

"He was invited to speak at the literary society I belong to," she said when Stella asked.

"And it was love at first sight!"

"Don't be so bloody cynical, Stella. No it wasn't. We were all chatting afterwards and I had flu and felt dreadful, so he offered to run me home in his car. I was rather impressed, because he didn't just drop me at the door, he came up, made me sit in the warm and fetched me a hot lemon drink. Then about a week later he phoned up and said he happened to be in a pub just round the corner and would I like a drink."

Stella had groaned. "Vivvy! Men don't just *happen* to be in pubs just round the corner..."

Alex was so attractive she was sure he would be marvellous in bed and show her what to do. And he was intelligent without making an issue of it, and amusing and *fun*. She felt she would never understand why he was attracted to her, but thank God he was. She found she was right; he was marvellous in bed and he did show her all sorts of new things to do. He knew when to be tender and when to be aggressive; they even played silly animal games, growling and romping round the bed. But above all she was so grateful for his control, his complete expertise. He made her feel good in bed. "Vivvy, I've never felt like this before," he said, and she was sure he meant it. It was ridiculously important to her to be thought of as good in bed.

She didn't tell the aspiring writer about Alex but he sensed the opposition and drifted out of her life. Years later he turned up on a BBC2 chat programme, interviewing successful writers and embarrassing them with his obvious envy.

Three

"WHAT TIME WILL Claire be back?" asks Vivienne.

"Oh, not till lunchtime," Alex says. "We've got a few hours yet."

"I think it's most considerate of her to go away like this. I really appreciate it."

As Claire had gone to visit her head office in Bristol, Vivienne and Alex seized the opportunity to spend a night together at the house in Highgate. Now they are lying happily in bed watching the birds in the almond tree outside the open window. It is a beautiful May morning, sunny and fresh and Vivienne feels very glad to be alive.

"Is this a guest room?"

"Not really," says Alex, propping himself up, his hands behind his head. "It used to be Robin's room, but after he was drowned we took all the nursery things out and painted it this blue colour; it was pink originally because Claire was sure she was going to have a girl. She wanted to call her Margaret after her mother. Anyway, after he died we didn't want to use this room any more so we just shoved this spare bed in for use in emergencies."

"Darling, I've never been called an emergency before!"

Alex laughs. "Idiot. You know what I mean. The proper guest room is across the hall but I didn't want to use that last night as it's full of Claire's tapestry paraphernalia. Really, this damn house is too big for us but Claire isn't willing to sell it." He sees the surprise on Vivienne's face. "Oh yes, it's her house. Her father left it to her. The only thing that's wrong with it, apart from its size, is that it hasn't got a garden, but as we haven't any children that doesn't really matter."

"Don't you mind living in Claire's house?"

"Not at all! I think it's an excellent arrangement."

"Oh." Vivienne rolls over on to her stomach. "What effect did Robin's death have on Claire, then?" She knows Robin was drowned four years ago, just after his fifth birthday.

Alex says neutrally: "She became an alcoholic."

"She *what*?" Alcoholics, to Vivienne, are people who lie sprawled under the arches at Charing Cross: you read about them in the Sunday papers.

"Not many people know. She felt responsible for his death, you see. We were on holiday in Cornwall and as we'd had quite a lot of wine with our lunch, I went to our room and flaked while Claire took Robin down to play by the sea. Well, what with the wine and the heat, Claire fell asleep and when she woke up Robin was dead; he'd tumbled into a rock pool and knocked himself out. After the funeral we both hit the bottle pretty hard, and I just didn't realise how much Claire was drinking, until one day her mate Joyce suddenly took charge and insisted on Claire going to a special clinic in Switzerland to dry out. She did that painting of the horses while she was there."

Vivienne remembers the painting: stark, in black and white, showing two horses grazing in a paddock, it hangs downstairs in the sitting room.

"Claire moves it about the house," Alex says, "because she says if you keep pictures in the same place all the time you stop noticing them. I think it's brave of her. Most people would want to forget it all, but Claire says it's important that she *is* reminded. She can't drink any alcohol at all now, of course, but thank heaven she's strong-minded enough not to mind me drinking."

"Yes, you do drink rather a lot, Alex."

"Well, I enjoy it, and it's my only vice, because I don't smoke. Anyway, I haven't noticed you refusing drinks when you're offered them."

"No, I'm delighted to say you encourage me to indulge myself. Do you realise we made love absolutely everywhere last night except in bed?"

"Oh God, you are a wicked woman. Leave me alone ... No, don't leave me alone ..."

"Vivvy, we *must* get up. We've got to clean up downstairs, remember, and I must put in a token appearance at the office. Some of us have to work on Spring Bank holidays, you know."

Vivienne, who has been lying on top of him, reluctantly rolls back on to the bed and stretches luxuriously. "You are wonderful, Alex! I feel marvellous. I feel as—"

"Oh *hell*," Alex swears, "you've made a mess on the sheets." He sweeps aside her indignant protests. "Look, get up quickly Vivvy and pass me some tissues, there's a good girl."

"I don't see what all the fuss is about," she sulks, as Alex dabs vainly at the sheets.

"Because this room is rarely used and if Claire comes in and sees the bed not made the way she does it, I can always explain it away by saying I had a nap in here or something. But if she sees the sheets in this state ..." He shrugs.

"Are you afraid of Claire?"

"It's not a question of being afraid. I just don't want to upset her. Use your head, Vivvy."

"I'll use the bathroom instead," she says pettishly, realising too late that it's impossible to stalk with dignity out of a room when you've nothing on.

Later, bathed, dressed and better-humoured, she discovers Alex in his own bedroom wearing only a pair of red briefs and perched dangerously on a chair at the open window.

"You've forgotten your parachute," she laughs.

"Very funny."

"Well what on earth are you doing?"

"I should have thought it was obvious that I'm hanging the sheets out. I had to give them a quick wash and I want them to dry in the sun."

"For heaven's sake, darling, it's ridiculous draping them out of the window like that. You look like Smythe of the Fourth engaged on a dare-devil escape from the dorm. Whatever will your neighbours think?"

"Fuck the bloody neighbours."

"What's wrong with the spin dryer?"

"Broken."

"The radiators?"

Alex sighs. "They. Aren't. On," he says, with icy deliberation. "These are nylon sheets and they should dry quickly in the sun. Now instead of standing there with your mouth open, why don't you go down and start clearing up?"

Controlling her rising resentment, Vivienne marches down the green-carpeted stairs and into the large living room, where she has to smile at the sight that confronts her.

Cushions, empty bottles of wine, glasses and coffee cups are strewn all over the expensive beige wool carpet. A full ashtray has overturned on to a chair and records lie out of their sleeves in piles all over the floor. The dress Vivienne wore yesterday is unaccountably draped over an elegant standard lamp and on the marble coffee table lie the shredded remains of her black panties. Vivienne giggles and thinks of Alex upstairs hanging pink sheets out of the back window. "Oh, how I'd love dear Claire to walk in now!"

By the time Alex appears, dressed and shaved, the room is just about back to normal again. "You are a marvel," he says. "I'm afraid I'm not much good round the house. Look, I'm going to have to shoot off to the office. Can you finish all the clearing up and everything on your own?"

"All right. I shouldn't think you'd be much help anyway." He kisses her, and she thinks what a refreshing change it makes that for once she is the one who's in charge, who can cope with a situation when he can't. Then he adds, "You've got about two hours before she comes in, and the sheets should be dry long before then—the sun's very strong today. Oh, by the way angel, try not to leave bits of hair from your hairbrush in the wastepaper basket upstairs."

"For heaven's sake, Alex," Vivienne explodes, "stop making me feel like an old sweaty sock you only wear when no one's looking!"

The outburst amazes both of them and they make up quickly before her bitterness has time to take root in more angry words. She's been so understanding, he says, and he knows it's difficult at the moment, but he loves her, will always love her. She must believe him. He holds her face in his hands.

"I can't hurt Claire, Vivvy, but I'm not letting you go, angel. Last night was wonderful ... something I shall never forget. I'll ring you later at the flat, OK?"

When he has gone Vivienne discovers that feeling alone, and lonely are not the same thing, for now she is feeling both in this still, silent house. She puts away the vacuum cleaner and makes herself some coffee, rattling the spoon unnecessarily against the cup just for the sake of making a familiar noise.

I am in Claire's house, and these are all Claire's things, she thinks, looking round her. A practical kitchen, big enough to

hold a fashionable pine dining table and a beautiful matching dresser. A washing-up machine, spin dryer, Kenwood
mixer; lovely natural stone jars with cork stoppers, marked
tea, flour, oil, in large copperplate handwriting. Vivienne can't
help but compare this kitchen with the muddle she shares
with Stella; piles of greasy plates, dirty coffee cups and a teapot permanently half-full of cold tea. Occasionally they have
a purge, usually after a row about who should have emptied
the mound of putrid rubbish decaying in the cardboard box
under the sink. Claire, Vivienne notices, has a tidy swing-top
bin.

Gingerly she opens a cupboard and stares at the orderly
rows of tins, bottles and packets. Like soldiers, she thinks,
guarding this tiny part of Claire's empire. As she shuts the
door she realises that she is afraid of touching anything; she
has not picked anything up to examine as one would in most
kitchens. It was like going up to the altar in a church and
touching the cross. You looked, perhaps you even worshipped,
but you didn't touch.

Everything seems to be looking at *her*. The lustrous dark
brown pottery on the dresser, even the big, shiny, copper
saucepan hanging by the window, they are all daring her:
We belong to Claire. Claire chose us and uses us, and you are
an intruder. If you touch us, she will know.

Vivienne turns abruptly and retreats into the sitting room.
On each side of the big bay window hang heavy olive curtains,
framing a huge bowl of lilac standing on a polished table.
Outside is the almond tree they had watched from the little
blue bedroom. The elegant room is flooded with May sunshine, but Vivienne shivers and stretches out on the settee in
front of the fireplace with its big gas fire. The mantelpiece is
completely clear of ornament, except for an exquisite onyx
cigarette box. As Vivienne lights one of her own cigarettes

she realises that the room is full of carefully chosen things in onyx, alabaster and malachite, that she hadn't noticed last night.

Now she knows its history, she stares curiously at Claire's painting hanging in the alcove. There are two thin black horses nibbling hay in a fenced paddock, the fencing drawn in harsh black lines and leading to a broken-down shed, with a door opening on to more blackness. The only relief is in a tree, with no leaves, just bare stark branches, where a bird sits, pathetically outlined against sharp triangular-shaped grey clouds in a dead white sky. The black horses seem unaware of, or perhaps resigned to, the implied menace all around them.

Looking at the sane, sunny room it seems extraordinary to Vivienne that its creator could once have been in such distress as to paint something so depressing. She wishes, suddenly, with a stab of jealousy that there was something in this room she could dislike or laugh at. But apart from the painting, which disturbs her, there is nothing she can fault.

In front of the painting, to the right of the fireplace, is a rocking chair in dark, almost black wood, with dark olive green cushions; a washed Chinese rug is spread across the fireplace area to the opposite alcove, which is full of books, records and stereo equipment.

She studies the books. Alex's is there, of course, placed optimistically next to Steinbeck and Fitzgerald. The biographies would be Alex's too, Vivienne decides. *The French Lieutenant's Women*, annoyingly, turns out to be Claire's: it is one of Vivienne's favourites. The row of French translations, Zola, Mauriac, Voltaire, are also Claire's. The little poetry section is interesting: Shakespeare and Masefield are Alex's while the volumes of Spender and Auden have Claire's maiden name written inside. Claire M. Ross, 1959. Vivienne wonders what Claire M. Ross looked like in 1959. There are no photographs anywhere in the room.

She looks at her watch. 11.30. Claire will be home in about an hour and Vivienne still has the sheets to organise. She carries the ashtray through to the kitchen, empties it, carefully puts it back in the sitting room and goes upstairs to Claire's room. Of course, she realises, it is Alex's room, Alex's house, too, but instinctively one thinks of everything as Claire's. Quite apart from knowing that she owns the bloody place, it reflects her taste, it tells you who she is without having met her. At times it positively screams her name.

In Claire's room everything is white ... the carpet, walls, bedspread, curtains, everything except the ceiling and the silken scatter cushions on the bed which are pale apricot. The immaculate conception, Vivienne sniffs, yanking in the dry sheets from the window.

Then on impulse she opens the sliding louvred doors of the fitted wardrobe. Claire's clothes. She picks out a well-cut navy gabardine coat and sees from the label that it came from Stella' shop. Expensive, Vivienne thinks, trying it on. It is too short and slightly too small. Claire must be about five foot three then, and size ten, smaller and slimmer than Vivienne. Pleased with her detective work, she riffles through the rest of the clothes; they are all smart and well-tailored, in beiges, blues, green or a startling burnt orange colour. Some of the things Claire has made herself and they are meticulously finished and lined. At the bottom of the wardrobe is a row of shoes, arranged by colour, black at one end, beige at the other.

Suddenly feeling guilty, Vivienne closes the door. Alex's clothes are presumably in the other cupboard. Apart from some general clutter, again there is very little evidence that he occupies the room at all. Hurrying, she picks up the sheets and goes to make the bed in the little front bedroom before wandering downstairs to pick up her bag from the sitting room. She is about to leave when she notices her gold charm bracelet behind the cigarette box on the mantelpiece.

Thoughtfully, she lights a cigarette and stands looking at the bracelet, imagining herself as Claire walking in and finding it. She would look round the room trying to visualise what had been happening and what this unknown woman was like. Then she would have to think what to do. Ring Alex and cause a scene? Confront him with the evidence when he returned home? Or would she say nothing, put the bracelet away somewhere and play a cool waiting game? Vivienne remembers a television play where a woman had a huge tallboy crammed with unwanted souvenirs of her husband's mistresses. Well, what would be to my advantage? Vivienne wonders. To let her find the bracelet and get all worried and nervous wondering who I am, or to leave no sign at all that I've been here, to leave her completely ignorant. Reluctantly, she decides it is best that Claire does not know. Otherwise she might start making it difficult for her and Alex to meet. She picks up the bracelet and pushes it into the overnight bag. Then she takes one final look round the bright sunlit room. Everything seems to be in order. She smiles, thinking of what they did in here last night, then stubs out her cigarette, empties the ashtray and leaves the house.

It is 12.15. Perhaps, she thinks, I shall meet Claire coming along the road. She feels tense and slightly excited at the thought.

Four

CLAIRE KNOWS AS soon as she enters the house. From
the road she has noticed the open window of the little blue
bedroom, and now she walks slowly upstairs, closes the window and studies for a moment the freshly-made bed. Then
she returns to her own room, hangs up her coat and tidies
away the trail of Alexander's things.

Claire Mallender is thirty-five, a year older than her husband, a petite woman, whose short, well-shaped, chestnut
hair now touched with grey frames a rather grave face with
what everyone admires as good bones. It is a strong face, but
what people notice first are her eyes. Bright, sharp, hazel
eyes, they look out on the world with interest, compassion,
sometimes with disgust but rarely with humour. A quick,
alert mind and fine intelligence save her from appearing
dull; Alexander once described her as one of the most aware
women he has ever known.

She is aware now, strongly aware, of the presence of another woman in her house. It is not, she reflects, a feeling
totally new to her: she knows her husband too well for that.

In the bathroom she picks up the wastepaper basket and
lifts out two crumpled tissues. They are pink, whereas the
box of Kleenex in the bathroom is white. She takes the pink
tissues downstairs and throws them into the kitchen bin; it
doesn't need emptying but she takes out the white plastic
liner and carries it outside to the dustbin. There she is not

at all surprised to see, carefully stuffed down at the bottom, two empty wine bottles and a small whisky bottle. Claire firmly replaces the lid and returns to the kitchen, conscious that she is delaying going into the sitting room. Not hurrying, she makes herself some coffee, moves the tea towel from the edge of the draining board where Vivienne had left it, back to its rightful hook near the window; then she goes into her sitting room.

She puts on a Bach record, rearranges the Sinatra LPs in order as she had left them and straightens the book Vivienne was looking at an hour before.

"Well," Claire says aloud, wryly, "at least this one can read."

She settles in the rocking chair with her coffee and, leaning back against the olive-green cushions, rocks in rhythm with the music. It soothes her.

Men are so incompetent, she thinks, at keeping their squalid affairs to themselves. Perhaps it is because they are so vain that subconsciously they *want* you to find out. But I really do not see how any intelligent woman can fail to realise when there is another woman in the offing, particularly if she has been in your home. Not that there is ever anything so obvious as lipstick on a glass or a glove left behind. Alexander is careful to remove that sort of evidence. But even without those pink tissues or the bottles in the dustbin, I would know. One's things are slightly out of order ... objects have been picked up, admired and put back in the wrong places.

Above all, there is the smell. Someone has been smoking in here recently and Alexander does not smoke. The bathroom, too, smells wrong: there is an alien aroma of strange talcum powder, while the blue bedroom has a lingering, bittersweet scent of sex. Of course, it never occurs to Alexander that when he has been with a girl I can smell her on him.

The essential thing, Claire decides, is to work out what stage Alexander has reached with this girl. He has brought her to the house, which means she can't be a "one-off" affair. The wine bottles and the Sinatra records point to it all being fresh enough for sex still to be the main interest.

Claire sighs. She has no objection on sexual grounds to Alexander's having a mistress. She is realistic enough to appreciate that even in the best of circumstances, no woman can be all things to a man, and after ten years of marriage circumstances are hardly at their best. Passion is not, Claire knows, in her nature, and after Robin's death and the ensuing drama, sex has become relatively unimportant to her.

What is important is the quality of her life and her relationship with her husband. Claire's publisher father was, in her eyes, a successful and worthwhile man and she is fully conscious of seeking the same qualities in her husband—through his books. Working in Fleet Street was all very well, but to Claire writing novels, good ones, is a more worthwhile occupation.

And I am not prepared, she decides, to allow Alexander's sexual adventures to interfere with his new book. His first one showed such enormous promise and I really thought he was well on the way to something brilliant. But he is such an infuriating man: he has tremendous talent and imagination and he wastes it all. If only he would channel some of his energy into his writing, instead of frittering it away on ego-boosting affairs with stupid girls. Or even intelligent girls.

Claire gets up and crosses the room to the small study where a bulky manilla folder lies on top of the typewriter.

He's done nearly half, she thinks, sifting angrily through the manuscript, and it's *good*. If only he would give up some time from this ridiculous PR firm, the other two can carry it perfectly well, he doesn't need to spend all this time at the office, he could have this book finished in a few months. And I would encourage him and support him. He knows that.

The phone rings.

"Hello," Alexander says, "just ringing to make sure you got back OK."

"Oh. Yes, I had a good journey, thank you."

"You answered the phone quickly. Am I clogging up the line for a call you were expecting?"

"No, darling, not at all. As a matter of fact I was in the study taking a look at your novel. It *is* very good, you know."

Claire pictures her husband's exaggerated eye-rolling at the other end of the phone.

"Claire—"

"Listen Alexander, I just think you should give yourself a proper *chance*," Claire says quickly. She hurries on: "When you first started the firm it was agreed that the others should do most of the day-to-day work and you would go in just one or two mornings a week, spending the rest of the time at home, working on your book. But recently you've done nothing but PR work, week after week. Why don't you tell them you're taking a few months off to write? You could take a cut in salary if they were difficult about it, and we could use my money for a bit—"

"Claire, for Christ's sake," Alex snaps, "I don't want to use your bloody money. It's bad enough living in your bloody house."

"But what does it *matter* whose money it is or whose house?" Claire persists. "Surely the important thing is your book, to get it finished."

"It will get finished, Claire. I'm just bogged down with it at the moment, that's all. It's quite common for writers to get blank periods, you know; even Hemingway was convinced at one stage that he'd never write another word."

"Of course you're bogged down, trying to write for a few hours in the evenings after a day in the office, and promising yourself you'll do some more at weekends and then never getting round to it. Nothing gets done that way." Particularly if you're trying to fit in a girlfriend as well.

"Claire do we have to go into all this just now? I've got a client to see and I just phoned to make sure you got home OK."

"Well, I'm fine, thank you," Claire says quietly.

"Good. I'll see you later then. Quite a bit later, probably, as I have to brief some photographers, but I'll try not to let it drag on."

Which is why you phoned, Claire thinks, as she replaces the receiver. And it will, inevitably, drag on.

Accurately foreseeing another lonely evening ahead she decides to invite her friend Joyce round, praying as she dials the number that Max isn't home to take the call with his wince-making greeting of "Hiya hunne". But it is Joyce's teen-aged daughter who answers.

"Mummy is out shopping, Aunt Claire."

"Please don't call me Aunt, Belinda. It makes me feel so old."

"Sorry. Can I get her to phone you?"

"No, it's all right. I have to go out myself in a moment to deliver some posters I've had printed for the Camden Community Centre..." She talks on but finally senses the girl's restlessness and reluctantly rings off.

I suppose I am old and boring to Belinda, Claire thinks. Thirty-five is unbelievably ancient to a seventeen-year-old and I expect I would appear old to Alexander's girlfriend, too. Interesting that I automatically assume she's very young, brainless and incredibly sexy ... I wonder what she's really like, or where she lives. If I knew just that I would know quite a lot about her.

Earls Court is easy: she would have to be Australian or New Zealand to live there, while Chelsea of course attracts the trendy, dolly type. Knightsbridge girls are upper-middle-class horses in large silk headscarves, and further west, around Ealing, they are all air hostesses, teachers or art students. In Russell Square and Bloomsbury they pose as intellectuals with strong overtones of Virginia Woolf and Saturday afternoons in the British Museum. If she lives in South Kensington she shares a flat with a gaggle of girls who are all husband hunting. Those who fail pretend marriage doesn't matter anyway and move to Hampstead, if they can afford it, where they live on tranquillisers and the reflected glory of NW3. Those who can't afford it take their tranquillisers down the road to less fashionable Camden and just pretend they are living in Hampstead.

Camden. God, the posters! Quickly she picks them up, checks them for error and slips a heavy elastic band round, telling herself that whoever this girl is and wherever she lives, if the affair runs true to form it should all be over by the end of the summer.

Five

"COME ON, VIVVY! Get a move on or I shall run off with both these dishy men I've got in here!"

This is Stella banging on the door while Vivienne struggles into her only long dress, a fussy printed affair that looks, like most of her clothes, slightly too old for her.

She tugs crossly at the zip. God, in this heat you'd think I'd lose weight instead of putting it on. And dishy men, ha bloody ha. Podgy Bob, an old flame of Stella's, re-kindled since he inherited Daddy's money, and his acolyte, Richard, who is "something in cocoa". A lump probably.

It is the last Saturday of a hot, sticky August and Vivienne is making up a four for dinner; she accepted the invitation ungraciously, only agreeing because it was Stella's twenty-sixth birthday celebration and, more important, because she hoped to make Alex jealous. He was, however, rather patronising about it, merely saying: "Well, have a good time with your pals, darling, and be a good girl."

And then, she thinks bitterly, he went waltzing off to France for two weeks with Claire. How could he do that after the time we've had in the last few months?

It was a magic, golden summer for Vivienne. Sometimes she met Alex for lunch at the little Greek restaurant in Charlotte Street, where they sat outside in the sun with kebabs, lemon-soused salad and a big carafe of warm white wine. The hot sun, the scent of the lemon, the persistent Greek music mingled with the gentle babble of voices ...

drowsily she would close her eyes and daydream about Greece, then waking up once more, enjoy watching tanned young men stroll by, chatting to lithe, alert girls with bouncing bra-less breasts. This was London, this was what she had left home for ... the heavy scent of strawberries laden on street stalls; a taxi-driver opening the door for a glowing redhead in a singing pink dress, a glimpse of white knickers and rounded tanned thighs before the door slammed provoking a murmur of appreciation; but no one whistled, leered, or made a fuss because this was London and all around were lovely girls showing legs, arms, breasts, bums, everything ... and here she was, lucky Vivienne Tyler sitting in the sun drinking wine with the most marvellous man in the world, who was making her laugh and telling her he loved her. "I love you," they said, a hundred times a day, for surely it was impossible that anyone else had ever been so deeply in love as they? Vivienne envied no one that summer, happily convinced that the world belonged to her and Alex, and pitying everyone who wasn't, couldn't be, as loved as she.

In the long lingering evenings they walked by the river, and held hands under countless gingham cloths in countless tiny bistros; they went to the zoo; they fed the ducks in the Serpentine and joked with the mad Scotsman at Speakers' Corner. But mostly they shunned other people; engrossed in themselves and their love, they were their own favourite topic of conversation. And above all, of course, they made love. Usually in Vivienne's flat, sometimes by moonlight near the river and once, laughing because they couldn't wait, in a dark shop doorway off Regent Street.

Twice when Claire was away they went to the house in Highgate, but Vivienne felt increasingly uneasy there. Except in the little blue room with the almond tree outside that she came to think of as "her" room, in the rest of the house she still had the impression of being watched, and judged. And all the time there was the fear that Claire might walk in unexpectedly, to confirm Vivienne's nightmares of being hurled, naked, out on to the road, quickly followed by her clothes and embarrassing abuse.

All through the summer the lovers managed to see each other for some part of every day, except weekends. Vivienne came to dread waking up on Saturday morning to face two whole days without Alex, yet he was firm about it.

"Darling, I see you all the time I can in the week. But at the weekend Claire often invites our friends round and it's only fair I should be there, and spend some time with her. I'm also supposed to be writing a book, you know."

"What do you do at weekends, then?"

"Usually make excuses not to write my book—and think about you instead."

She believed him. She *had* to believe him.

Vivienne tried to occupy herself over the weekends, carefully planning every moment to keep busy. Meeting the married girlfriend from Coulsdon for lunch, shopping and a film; going to the inevitable concerts and art galleries. Or she would paint, read, or go for long walks. But she was lonely, and all the time her thoughts would stray back to Alex and Claire.

With a sense of defeat she would stop inventing things to do and lie instead on her bed, listlessly chain-smoking, imagining *them* having Saturday lunch together, Alex telling Claire about his week, laughing and joking about the people he worked with. On Saturday evening perhaps they would be invited to a dinner party. "Oh, good, here's Alex and Claire," these fabulously elegant people would say, and Alex would be popular and amusing while Claire ... what would Claire be like? Vivienne didn't like to question Alex too much about her. Small and petite, she knew, and terribly well-organised, working at her office most mornings, doing charity work, running the home, giving parties. Cool and sophisticated, probably, never at a loss for the right thing to say. Many times Vivienne was tempted to ring the house, just to hear Claire answer and listen to her voice. It was childish and ridiculous of her, she knew, but deliriously, the idea obsessed her.

She saw Claire moving through her house, laying the big pine table in the kitchen, setting out the brown, glazed pottery, laughing and talking with Alex. It would all be very easy, very familiar. They would have their own private jokes, Alex and Claire, and at parties they would look across the room at one another in a special way to say, "this man is a bore—darling, rescue me!" or "you look gorgeous" or "let's go home now".

Home. Home to bed. This was the height of Vivienne's self-torture, imagining, in painful detail, her lover in bed with his wife. Time and again Alex had reassured her, but Vivienne could not understand how any woman could *not* want him. What was Claire like in bed? God, please don't let her be better than me. Vivienne thought of them asleep and waking up with their arms round each other as she and Alex did; it was such a delight on the rare occasions when she could open her eyes and find Alex beside her, instead of an empty space, a memory of him rushing home with ill-concealed haste in the early hours of the morning.

And now he had taken Claire to France.

"Darling I'm sorry, but I can't avoid it," he had told her. "We usually go away in August and Claire hates London when it's hot and unbearable like this. She also says she's been feeling a bit run down—she hasn't been looking too well, actually. It's only a couple of weeks, angel, and I shall miss you and think of you all the time."

Vivienne would not be consoled. She sulked, pouted and put on the special little-girl face that worked so well on her father. It had no effect on Alex.

"Look, Vivvy. Every year we go away in August. She's going to think there's something very funny going on if I suddenly start making excuses about not going."

She pictured them care-free and sun-tanned on the beach. No, not the beach; Claire wouldn't go near the sea now. Well, strolling hand in hand through the countryside then; they were touring round, Alex said. Perhaps it would even turn out to be a second honeymoon? Vivienne drove the knife in deeper, seeing them embracing passionately, making promises, sharing secrets, renewing old bonds.

And, the sod, he hadn't even *minded* that she was going out to dinner with another man.

"Vivvy! What the hell are you doing?" yells Stella.

Vivienne gives her hair a last few vigorous strokes and bangs the hairbrush down viciously on to the mantelpiece, chipping the yellowed paint.

"Just coming," she calls.

"Well, Stella," oils Richard massacring a bread roll, "I'd no idea you had such an attractive neighbour. It's very naughty of you not to have introduced me to Vivienne before."

Vivienne fakes a smile. She has met so many Richards in her short time in London. Rent-a-Richard. They are all aged between twenty and twenty-five, and they are all something in advertising or PR, cocoa or computers. If pressed to describe the "something" they reveal titles like Client Liaison Officer, Account Executive or Trainee Assistant Deputy Under-Manager. Their ill-fitting dark suits are bought on subscription accounts from chain tailors along with their daring, coloured, nylon shirts, conscientiously drip-dried over the bath once a week; and while they will agonise for hours coaxing their hair into the latest required style, they will forget to clean their shoes, or have them repaired.

Once lured into non-jobs in large companies, they are then courted by big banks, wooed by advertisements for cigars, alcohol, fast cars, aftershave and underwear ... buy me and four bikinied blondes will appear ... smoke me and you will have instant boardroom power and success ... drink me and you will immediately be surrounded by an admiring group of the smart, trendy people. Where, the Richards must ask as they stand in a bank queue in their lunch hour, waiting fifteen minutes to draw out £5, where is this fantastic scene I've been promised? What am I doing wrong? Have the in-crowd passed me by, the swinging set with busty birds begging to be laid, the men who sail and shoot and do things? Men of action. Where are they, all these people? Not in the office I'm dashing back to, that's for sure, with its unapproachable women, and men who can talk only of the mortgages on their lawnmowers. Except for Greene, in Sales, perhaps, with his yellow corduroy jacket. Is Green the in-scene? Is *he* pulling the birds?

Poor Richard, Vivienne thinks, watching him watching Bob. Somehow, he's latched on to Bob, and Bob's money, and this for him is living. This plush restaurant with its red velvet and bendy waiters handing each woman a long stemmed rose as she comes in. The place, she realises, is full of bewildered women awkwardly clutching roses and eyeing everything else for a lead on what to do with them. Strange, she thinks, how we never learn the art of carrying flowers gracefully: brides are the worst, bearing their bouquets too far in front of them like bunches of freshly-dug carrots.

The menu is very long, very French and very expensive. Vivienne had planned to order the second cheapest dish but Stella, her rose snapped short and pinned in her blonde hair, gaily orders caviare for them all to start with. She allows no protracted deliberations over the wine. The murmuring wine-waiter, slick like a stick of liquorice with teeth, is dismissed with a flourish and a cry from Stella of: "Champagne, of course! Lots of champagne for my birthday!"

Then she whirls Bob off to dance on the minute dance floor. Vivienne, left with Richard, is informed that she is by far the most beautiful woman in the room, in fact one of the loveliest women he has ever met. She is also intelligent, different, marvellously full of character and obviously an extremely independent, liberated woman.

"I can't stand these stupid dolly birds," Richard confides.

No, I shouldn't think they can stand you, either.

"I much prefer women like you who know their own minds."

I am not going to bed with you.

"Now I know you won't mind me saying this, Viv, but you are mature enough to be able to say to yourself, yes, I like this man X. He attracts me. I want to sleep with him. And you do just that, without any hang-ups. Don't you?"

No.

"You sound as if you know a lot of girls, Richard. Do you meet them all through your job—it is cocoa, isn't it?" And don't call me Viv.

Richard's run-down of the girls in cocoa is mercifully interrupted by the arrival of champagne followed by Stella and a breathless Bob, back from the dance floor. Like a bright, bossy nanny Stella automatically takes charge of the conversation in a way that Vivienne would find infuriating in anyone else, except Alex. But Stella's enthusiasm is so disarming they are content to let her bubble on as, in answer to Richard, she tells them how she came to be living next to Vivienne.

"I used to live in this ra-thah posh block in Maida Vale, as you know. Well, I was having an extremely torrid affair at the time. It really was all go, you know, with this guy leaping on me all the time, and all through the night as well. It was tremendous, and I really let myself go, shouting and screaming encouragement. Anyway, next thing was I had a letter from the landlord's agent, asking me to go and see him; so I toddled along in my best clerical grey suit all sober and respectable and there he was all po-faced and serious.

"'Miss Caxton,' he said, 'we have had some complaints from some of the other residents in your block.'

"'Oh, I'm sorry to hear that,' I said politely, 'what seems to be the trouble?'

"'The other residents have been complaining of noise, Miss Caxton. Noise emanating from your flat rather late at night.'"

Stella's china-blue eyes bulge. "I nearly had a fit on the spot, I can tell you, especially as the maggot of a man then demanded an explanation. I had to think fast. 'Oh well,' I said at last, in what I hoped was a comforting sort of voice, 'I think now I come to think of it, that I have had the television on rather loud recently. And personally I absolutely *deplore* all the violence they have on the box nowadays. Nothing but murder and rape and people screaming with terror ... Yes, I'm positive it must have been the television the other residents heard.'

"I looked at the agent hopefully, and he looked back at me with barely-disguised malice. 'Television, Miss Caxton?' he said disdainfully. 'Television? Not, surely, at three o'clock in the morning?'"

Stella takes a mouthful of duck and gulps some champagne while the others shout with laughter. Vivienne stares at her plate, uncomfortably aware of Richard, wet-lipped and thoroughly excited by this story, poised to leer as soon as he can catch her eye. Now he's wondering if *I'm* like Stella, Vivienne realises, wishing Stella had never started to tell this anecdote.

Stella goes on: "Oh, it gets worse. You see, lover boy and I had been mucking around a bit with some leather belts and things, just for laughs you know, and the noise of all that had carried upwards and outwards too. The agent gleefully announced that there had also been reports 'that sounded, Miss Caxton, as if someone was being *beaten* and was in severe pain. Have you any idea what this could have been?'

"I said no, I hadn't a clue and then he started creating about what *nice* people they had as tenants at the flats and how it would be such a *pity* if anything should disturb them and how some of them had young children you know, home from expensive public schools."

"Why didn't you suggest that the little beasts from public schools were probably quite used to that sort of noise?" says Bob placidly. He looks a little flushed, but otherwise, Vivienne decides, is showing no signs of minding Stella's laying her past exploits with other men over the table for them all to pick at. Richard's mouth is hanging open.

Stella says: "I was tempted, but by now the wretched man was moving in for the kill. Surely, he said, I could offer *some* explanation for these mysterious sounds. *Was* there, in fact, anyone being beaten in the flat? He was obviously secretly quite thrilled with the idea. He went on and bloody on and it was obvious he had me, so in the end I said I'd been very ill recently, with terrible nightmares, crying out with fear in my sleep. What a pity, he said, that I wasn't in good health, perhaps the air in that part of London didn't agree with me; and perhaps it would be a good idea for me to look round for another flat. So that was that."

"And now you live next door to the adorable Viv!" says Richard silkily, running his hand down the length of Vivienne's bare arm. She flinches, cursing Stella and Bob who desert her to dance again.

"It's Vivienne, or Vivvy. Not Viv."

"Adorable, but just a little remote," Richard presses on, fingering his glass in the same way that he has just fingered her arm. "Come and dance and we'll see if we can relax you a little."

Imagine Richard's clammy body pressed hard up against yours. "No thank you Richard, I'm really a dreadful dancer. My feet get all tangled up. Anyway, we don't want to steal Stella's limelight."

Vivienne points at the floor where Stella, now well into her stride is fizzing madly, followed by the unhappy Bob, hurling himself after her like a round potato chip sent berserk by hot fat.

After the meal there is brandy, and coffee that tastes of stewed acorns.

"Champagne and lots of brandy," Richard murmurs to Vivienne. "The things I've seen the most well-brought-up young ladies do after that combination!"

Vivienne, drowning in alcohol, wishes she had come right out at the beginning and admitted she did not like brandy. But it is too late now.

"Twenty-seven pounds, fifty," announces Stella, scrutinising the bill over Bob's shoulder. "Considering all the booze, that's not at all bad for four, is it?"

Vivienne is appalled. Richard turns a delicate sage green and makes a token gesture of reaching for his wallet, but Bob waves him aside and ladles five-pound notes on to the silver plate while Stella prattles on, "Of course, it's better value at Danny's, or even that new place near Curzon Street. We went there recently and the bill was only twenty-two pounds for four and the dance floor was bigger than this, too." Bob, to Vivienne's surprise, doesn't seem at all put out by any of this but just smiles indulgently, almost proudly.

"Well folks," he says, "we can go to La Valbonne, or the 007 or the Saddle Room. Stella, it's your birthday, it's up to you."

"Why don't we go to the 007 and then on to the Saddle Room," she suggests. "They're nearly next door to one another anyway. Vivvy, have you ever been to the Hilton? No? Well you must get someone to take you to lunch at the Roof Restaurant one day. It's absolutely superb."

"I prefer Trader Vic's myself," announced Richard. "That marvellous drink with the gardenia floating on top..."

You liar, thinks Vivienne, you can't possibly afford that sort of thing on your rotten salary. Someone probably paid for you, like Bob is paying tonight. But they are away, the three of them. Is the Hilton here better than the Hilton there ... has Club Chantel gone down again ... did you catch Tony Bennett at the Talk of the Town...

What the hell am I doing here in this gaudy place, thinks Vivienne, her head spinning. Oh Alex, I want you so much, I want you *now*. I love you so desperately but I can't remember what you look like any more. Why aren't you here? What did you have to go away for? Please still love me when you come back. Please don't fall in love with *her* again.

"Darling you're very quiet. Are you all right?" says Richard.

"I can't face a nightclub," she whispers. And you probably can't afford it anyway. "Could you just take me home?"

Richard is delighted. "Don't worry, Stella, I'll look after her. Tuck her up nicely in bed!"

It starts in the taxi, when his arm round her waist keeps accidentally nudging her breasts. Vivienne, feeling queasy, hasn't the energy to protest.

"I'm so pleased you wanted to duck out, darling," he says, drawing her closer and nibbling the back of her neck, leaving it wet and cold.

"I feel a bit sick," Vivienne confesses, hoping the news will put him off. "I don't usually drink brandy."

Richard is undaunted. He will make her a nice cup of coffee when they get to the flat, he says. Then she'll feel heaps better.

God, better for what? she wonders wearily.

Two hours later Richard has reached the belligerent stage.

"Well, why not?" he shouts. "What's wrong with me?"

"*Nothing's* wrong with you, Richard. I simply don't want to go to bed with you, that's all."

"Why did you lead me on then?"

"I didn't lead you on."

"Look, *you* got us to duck out from the restaurant. You didn't have to invite me up here for coffee, you didn't have to let me kiss you and you didn't have to let me touch you up."

"Richard, I'm sorry. I invited you in for coffee partly because you practically invited yourself and partly because it seemed the polite thing to do."

"And what about the rest of it?"

"What rest of it?"

"The cockteasing bit."

"Don't be horrible. I let you kiss me and everything, because there seemed no harm in it and I suppose because you wanted to so much." I was too tired, she thinks, to stop you.

"Look Richard, do we have to go through all this? I'm not going to bed with you and that's that."

"Why not?" Richard says again, whining this time, changing tactics and putting on his best wounded-animal look.

Vivienne wants to say, "Because I don't fancy you," but it seems too unkind. And Richard knows enough about women of Vivienne's type to be sure she would never come straight out and say that. A cockney girl would, but no one as suburban as Vivvy.

"Why not?" he goads.

Vivienne flounders: "We don't know one another well enough."

"We could get to know one another in bed." It comes out pat, stock answer number 114. Vivienne lights another cigarette, Richard changes the record. Then he comes back and starts to kiss her neck and arms.

"Richard, please stop it."

"Vivvy, you're so lovely, don't be so hard on me. Please Vivvy."

"No!"

Another change of tack. "What's so bloody special about you, anyway? So you're having an affair with a married man and no one else is good enough, is that it?"

"It isn't a question of being good enough. I simply prefer one man at a time."

"That didn't stop you coming out with me tonight, did it?"

"Just because I go out to dinner with you it doesn't mean I have to go to bed with you as well."

"But can't you see you're just making a fool of yourself with this married guy? He's using you, Vivienne. You're a great big boost for his ego: he boasts about you to his friends and they all laugh at you—"

Vivienne slaps his face as hard as her weakened state will

allow. It leaves a red mark. Equally embarrassed, for the next few minutes they both pretend to be engrossed in Frank Sinatra's "September of my Years". Richard recovers first. He is, after all, more used to this kind of situation. He takes her hand, murmuring, "I'm sorry. That was unforgiveable."

"No," protests Vivienne, feeling tired and sick, "I shouldn't—"

He puts his hand lightly over her mouth. "You must think I'm a totally insensitive oaf," he says. "Now I'm going to make us a last cup of coffee, and then I shall go quietly home to my lonely little bed."

When they have drunk the coffee and smoked more cigarettes he reaches across to her. "No, don't shy away. Please, let me have one goodnight kiss to show you forgive me."

She lifts her head, and suddenly he is on top of her, pressing her down on to the floor, his mouth firmly on hers, his hand inside her dress, his knee grinding up against her groin. Furious, she yanks at his hair, forcing up his head but he has freed her left breast and is torturing the nipple. Yelling with pain, she pulls viciously at his hair, but he twists and tears at her breast until at last she digs her only two unbitten nails into his face and scores hard down to his neck. He screams in agony and anger, but releases her. As she rolls, sobbing, on to her stomach, she hears the door slam. Then as the room starts to go into orbit she drags herself to her feet, runs to the bathroom and is sick for a long time, before reeling back into her room and blacking out on her bed.

She wakes twelve hours later feeling as if a pair of garden shears have run amok in her head; her mouth tastes of baked rope and there is also a terrible noise, a combination she realises sluggishly, of heavy rain beating on the window and the phone ringing. She stumbles out of bed and gazes disgustedly round: overflowing ashtrays, stained coffee cups, the record player still switched on and an acrid smell that makes her want to retch. Also her left breast is bruised and swollen. Thank you Richard, she thinks, blearily stretching out a shaking hand to the telephone.

"Hello," she says dully, unable to remember the number or read it off the dial. Her voice echoes in her aching head as she makes the first of countless lifetime vows: never to drink brandy again.

"Hello, is that Vivvy?" says a man's voice.

"I think so. Who's that?"

"Darling, it's me! Alex. Thank heavens you're in. I thought you'd never answer."

"Alex!" Dazed, Vivienne subsides to the floor, knocking over the sugar bowl. "When did you get back?"

"Yesterday evening. I tried to phone you—"

"No, I went to Stella's birthday party. I told you—"

"Yes," Alex cuts in. "Look angel, lots of things have happened. I can't explain everything now but Claire and I had a terrible row last night and I told her all about you."

"Oh Christ. What did she say?"

"Took it all very calmly, really. Said she'd known for ages that there was someone. But the important thing is, she said she wanted to talk to you."

"Oh Alex, I really don't think—"

"That's why I'm phoning. I'm sorry, but she's on her way now. I couldn't stop her."

Six

THE HOLIDAY IN France had not been a success. Claire had hoped that a couple of weeks by themselves would get their relationship back on to its old footing but now, edging the car through London's Sunday traffic, she realises that she had miscalculated the effects of separating Alexander from this girl. She had been wrong, too, to suggest that they tour Brittany, an area she and Alexander had visited years before and loved. Inevitably, it had not been the same. It had been almost unbearably hot, so she had had little energy for sightseeing, preferring to sit somewhere cool and sip iced drinks, but Alexander was restless, forever wanting to push on somewhere else in the sun-baked car. Then something had gone wrong with the brakes so they had been forced to spend three precious days in a complacently dull village while infuriatingly slow French mechanics ferreted under the bonnet and muttered dourly about the difficulty in obtaining spares for English cars. Alexander had refused to have anything at all to do with them and sat and drank all day until, with the car at last repaired, he had developed stomach trouble. Something not unconnected, Claire felt, with the large quantities of whisky he'd been consuming.

She had hoped that, away from the strain, the rush of London, they would be able to relax and talk to one another again. But this Alexander seemed determined to avoid. In the car he concentrated over-zealously on his driving, commenting that it was a long time since he'd driven on the right and these narrow twisty lanes made things even more hazardous. When they stopped for a cool drink or a meal he would turn on the charm with the result that soon they were the centre of a noisy group with Alexander, deliberately she was sure, making more row than everyone else. Evenings, too, were hopeless, intimacy being washed away by the mob rule of wine and whisky. Claire refused to allow herself to nag, moan or complain; she would sit with their new-found "friends" for a while until the everlasting coffees and orange juices made her want to gag, and then she would go to bed early, with a book instead of Alexander.

That part of it did not worry her unduly. She had long ago accepted that as a non-drinker, an ex-alcoholic married to a man who very much enjoyed drinking (as she herself had done at one time) it was ridiculous to expect him to sit and drink orange juice with her all evening. In company Alexander was always charming and gregarious, so however small or sullen the crowd he would have a good time, and his enjoyment was usually infectious.

He would, she knew, have preferred a holiday by the sea, somewhere a little more lively than the pretty little villages of Brittany. But he understood, he said, her cold terror of the sea, the sick, guilty memory of their son's small body lying face down in the water . . .

It is beginning to rain hard now and Claire switches on the car wipers, cursing because the little gadget that squirts water on to the windscreen is empty. Why can't he take *care* of the car? Alexander is, she reflects, a basically lazy man who likes to think of himself as someone who works hard and plays hard. The trouble is, as he gets older, it is either one or the other and recently it has been one long playtime. Although he is capable of sustained, concentrated effort—he proved that by writing *Street*—he is the type of man who has to be goaded into it. He had been really shocked when the paper made him redundant, and wrote *Street* in something under four months, in a state of bitter fury.

His new novel had remained untouched, of course, throughout the summer, and this was something else Claire had wanted to talk about in France; she considered that she had been extremely patient during the last few months. Increasingly, Alexander had come home late, often after midnight, two or three evenings a week and Claire had lost count of the times she had caught him out over stupid little things. But she had said nothing, hoping that this affair, like the others before it, would burn itself out.

What had alarmed her in France, however, was her realisation of the extent to which she and her husband had grown apart. For the first time, Claire felt frightened for her marriage. His other affairs had never radically affected their own marital relationship; they had been short-lived passions, leaving the pleasant pattern of their life together undisturbed. Now, she and Alex were still married, still formally inhabiting the same house, but it was as if increasingly they were living apart: it was like being with someone who would never look you fully in the face. They were polite and considerate to one another, doing everything to avoid a row or argument in case they broached the one subject that would force them to look honestly at one another and inflict mutual, lasting scars.

They had both been glad to come home a day early, Claire thought. The ferry was cramped and the drive back to London interminable. Then Alexander was booked for speeding. The hot weather was breaking up and there was thunder in the air, giving Claire a headache. Once home, they had slumped down in the cool sitting room, feeling too irritable to unpack. She went to make some tea to revive them, but of course they were home a day early so there was no milk. Usually when they returned from holiday they were both quite happy to be home again amongst their own familiar things, reading aloud to one another from the backlog of mail and sitting back with relief to enjoy some good English eggs, bacon and tea.

This time, however, she felt strange and uncomfortable with her husband. He offered to drive down to the corner shop and buy food and milk and she knew he would make a phone call at the same time. But he was back quickly. Then after they had eaten, as she was washing up she heard him dialling on the phone in the study. After a short pause the receiver was quietly replaced.

It is almost, she reasoned, as if subconsciously he wants me to know.

As if he wanted her to force the issue. In the past, although she had usually guessed about his affairs, he had gone to all sorts of comical lengths to prevent her finding out. He would never, for instance, have tried to phone a girl while she, Claire, was in the house! If he was being as obvious as this, then the next stage would be all the things she couldn't possibly pretend to ignore, all the corny, True Romance things like *her* photograph falling out of his library book, finding a love letter in the suit he left out to be cleaned, or even the ubiquitous lipstick stains on his shirts.

I must not let that happen, Claire thought, swallowing two aspirins. I will have to do something, I have no choice any more. It is too much of a strain living like this, forever tensed up waiting for him to tell the next lie, make the next excuse. I hate seeing Alexander squirming about in this manner, prowling round the house, itching to get out away from me. Each time he closes the front door behind him on his way to see her, there is relief in every line of his body, a jauntiness in his walk that he thinks I do not notice; or perhaps he does not even notice it himself.

Claire made the coffee and took it through into the sitting room where Alexander was scanning the television programmes in the evening paper. She settled herself in the rocking chair and picked up some sewing.

How to begin?

"Alexander, would you mind telling me what is going on?" ... "Darling, I want to talk to you. You know what about." ... "Look, I don't think you are behaving very well about this girl." ... "Alexander, do you want a divorce?"

Claire shuddered as the words screamed round her head. God, it all sounded so melodramatic. But she would have to do something quickly or he would turn on the television. She cleared her throat.

"Alexander," she began nervously, her voice low, "I'm afraid it really is getting too obvious, you know."

He must have been thinking about the same thing because he didn't look surprised, or ask what she was talking about.

"Yes I know," he said quietly. "I'm sorry, Claire."

As he slowly folded up his newspaper and put it in its usual place on the table beside him, Claire thought, how odd, the way we cling to the familiar in an unfamiliar situation. You would think, tonight of all nights, he might have flung the newspaper down in a crumpled heap; and why am I sitting here sewing as if my life depended on it? Because I do not want to hear what he is saying, that's why. Because I do not want to admit to myself how disappointed I am.

Bleakly, Claire realised that deep down she had hoped he would laugh it off, take her in his arms and tell her yes, he'd been having a stupid affair but it didn't mean anything and was all over now ...

But he hadn't. He was sitting on the other side of the fireplace, his back to the fading evening light, leaning forward and looking at her wretchedly. He was wearing some old grey slacks and his thin blue cotton shirt had damp patches under the arms. He was nervous. She knew, because the hairs on his arms were standing up slightly, in spite of the heat, a sure sign of anxiety with Alexander. And he has odd socks on, she thought. What a strange thing to notice at a time like this.

Almost reluctantly, then, Claire began to ask her questions, trying to sound reasonable and unaggressive. How long has this been going on? what is her name? where did you meet? how old is she? do you want a divorce? Then, gaining strength from his firm "no" ... what have I done wrong? where does she live? what does she look like? what does she do for a living? do all our friends know? am I the last to learn about it?

Alexander admitted that yes, they had been seen around together by various people and had even had dinner a few times with some mutual friends of his and Claire's. Claire kept her head down, stabbing angrily at her needlework. Now that the threat of divorce had receded, this was what really hurt, she thought, the fact that people pitied her. "Poor Claire," she heard them say, "left at home to grow old while Alex touts around a younger, fresher model."

"I suppose," Claire said, "you take her out for intimate candlelit dinners, and go for walks along the Embankment before taking her back to her little bedsitter?"

Alexander poured himself another drink, moving deliberately, saying nothing, and she saw her words had gone home.

"Really, Alexander, it is so *trivial*," she burst out, sewing cast aside, her hands gripping the smooth arms of the rocking chair. "A quick affair is one thing, but this sort of romanticised nonsense is cheap and irresponsible. You are thirty-four years old, intelligent and gifted and you are throwing it all away on some mindless girl—"

"She's not mindless, Claire. She's—"

"Well I want you to stop seeing her."

"I can't," he said at last. "Claire I love you and I think the world of you. You are the only solid factor in my life, you give it a rock-hard centre. You are like an oasis of peace and understanding for me; I need you, I love and admire you. But Vivienne has added another dimension. She's not better than you or intended as a replacement. She's just different. And for a few hours a week I find her company refreshing."

More than a few hours, Claire thought. "But it interferes with your writing."

"I can't help it. I can't help the way this girl has got under my skin. I love her, Claire, I must be honest with you. In a way it's a relief to be able to talk to you about it."

"But you *can* help it, Alexander! You know perfectly well this is an infatuation based on pure sex, pure animal appeal. It is lust you feel for this girl, not love for heaven's sake! I've told you, I don't mind you going to bed with someone else, but at least be honest with yourself and realise the attraction for what it is. Believe me, you do not love her."

"Claire I *do*. I'm sorry but I do. And it's not just sex. I know it started out like that but now it's something much more."

"Does she have other boyfriends or is she, er, faithful to you?"

"I don't think she sleeps with anyone else, or goes out with anyone else for that matter. I've told her she should, but she says she finds kids of her own age brash and boring."

Claire sighed.

"Well of course she does. You are ten times as sophisticated, amusing and experienced as a boy of twenty-three. You're being totally unfair to the girl. Don't you see that all the time she's infatuated with you she won't go out with anyone else, or if she does they won't measure up to you in her eyes. Don't you think you're spoiling her chances of meeting someone she could grow to love and maybe marry?"

Alexander refilled his glass. He looked tired and, in spite of herself, Claire felt sorry for him. We should go to bed, she thought.

"I don't know," he said, "what is going to happen or where we are all going to end up in this situation. I'm glad you know, Claire, and I'm glad we can talk about it. I do know I love you and I don't want to break up our marriage. I also know I love Vivienne."

"Would you marry her if you were free?"

"I don't know. I think she would marry me. I'm sorry, Claire, but I suppose in time it will all sort itself out. Please give it time."

And so they went to bed and lay fastidiously not touching one another. Alexander immediately fell into an exhausted coma, but Claire lay awake, dry-eyed, thinking.

Alexander woke at eleven in time to see Claire dressed, picking up the car keys from the dressing table.

"I am going to see Vivienne," she said, forestalling his question. "I know the address," and then she was gone, leaving him to struggle awake, gulp a Bloody Mary and phone Vivienne.

Now Claire has reached Sloane Street, and now the King's Road, cheerless and totally unswinging on this dismal Sunday morning. She turns right into the row of red, narrow Victorian houses and brakes smoothly outside number 18. This is not the first time she has been here. One day in the summer when she grew tired of waiting at home for her husband she found Vivienne's address scrawled at the back of his address book. She went all the way by Tube, and discovered their car outside a dingy Victorian house. For a long time she studied the house, as if it would give her some clue to its occupants. Then she went home.

Claire looks down the row of bells: Lambert, Caxton, Tyler. Three rings for Tyler. Claire rings three times and waits.

Seven

CLAIRE HAS TO wait several minutes while Vivienne, panic-stricken, flies around the room trying to restore some sort of order after the fracas of the previous night. Sod you Richard, and sod you Claire, Vivienne curses. What a bloody time to pick. The room looks worse, too, with the murky daylight filtering in through the rain. The bell rings again.

She'll think I'm not going to answer because I'm afraid of her, Vivienne thinks, shoving shoes underneath the divan and half-heartedly blowing dust off the mantelpiece. God, it's still a shambles but it'll have to do. And I *am* afraid of her, she admits, running down the brown-painted stairway to the front door. She feels dreadful. Sick, feverish, hung over and not at all in the mood for what is sure to be a difficult confrontation with Alex's wife. She pauses in front of the mirror in the dark hall to rub the sleep from the corners of her eyes. Oh well, at least now I'll know what she bloody well looks like.

Vivienne swings open the door and sees a small woman in a green dress. Round her shoulders Vivienne recognises the navy gabardine coat she once tried on in Claire's room.

"I'm Claire Mallender," Claire says gravely. Stella dubs it later the most unnecessary announcement of the year.

Vivienne says: "Oh yes. Do come in ... Claire." I'm damned if I'm going to call her Mrs Mallender. Vivienne tries what she hopes is a friendly smile but there is no response from Claire. She tries again as she leads the way up the stairs, her voice strained and pitched high: "Horrid day, isn't it?"

Claire ignores this and says, "I expect Alexander telephoned to say I was coming?"

"Yes he did," replies Vivienne, wincing at the stale smell in her room. In spite of the rain, she should have opened the window to clear the air. "Do take off your coat and sit down," she says, wishing her voice would stop shaking. "Would you like some coffee or tea? I was just going to make some," she lies.

"No thank you," says Claire, who is extremely thirsty.

"Well I think I will. I shan't be a moment." Vivienne makes an awkward escape to the kitchen. Now calm down, Vivvy, she tells herself, heaping instant coffee into an unwashed mug. Stop sounding so terrified. You haven't done anything criminal, and Alex loves you. He's told you he loves you and he's told her he loves you. Hang on to that, Vivvy, because that's what's important. You've got a minute before the kettle boils and you've got to go back and face her, so take some aspirins and a few deep breaths and (catching sight of her face in the mirror) comb your hair, it looks like a year-old Brillo pad.

In the frantic half hour following Alex's phone call she barely had time to scramble into blue trousers and matching top, splash cold water on her face and clear a passage through her room.

Claire, meanwhile, is looking round with secret amusement at a brave imitation of her own sitting room. (For Vivienne's taste has undergone a not-too-subtle change in the last six months.)

Of course, Claire thinks, it is less tidy than her own sitting room, with a lumpy, hastily made divan-bed and piles of dross everywhere; but if you have to live in one room it must be difficult to keep everything in order. No, apart from that, it is the way things are arranged which remind Claire of her own home. The jar of flowers by the window, the beautiful green alabaster thinking stone (a present, she guesses correctly, from Alexander) even the shade on the bedside lamp is exactly the same as one of her own. And in this cluttered room, the mantelpiece is completely clear—a special feature of Claire's. As in the house at Highgate, all the books and records are grouped in one corner of the room, but here the records are out of their covers and strewn all over the floor. Sinatra again, she notices. Behind her is the kitchen door and a big wardrobe enlivened by a Toulouse-Lautrec poster. Now if it were my room, Claire muses critically, I'd paint the wardrobe white to lessen the bulky effect and bring down that high ceiling with a coat of dark paint...

Vivienne returns, holding the coffee and one of the kitchen chairs, as Claire is seated in the only armchair. Usually when Vivienne has visitors she sits on a cushion on the floor, but today she feels Claire has quite enough going for her without poor old Vivvy kneeling at her feet as well. She sits down opposite Claire on the other side of the fireplace, clutching the big mug of coffee in both hands. Claire is perfectly still, her hands, emerging from the big dolman sleeves of the green lawn dress, cupped calmly in her lap. She stares steadily, but not unpleasantly, at the younger girl.

In a moment, Vivienne thinks, she will ask me if I'm sitting comfortably, and then she'll begin. Well, let her begin. She's the one who wants to talk to me; let her get on and say it then.

"Vivienne," Claire says, "I've come to see you because I wonder if you have any idea at all what you are doing. I wonder if you realise how serious this situation is that we all find ourselves involved in?"

Vivienne studies the grey-brown liquid in her mug and

refuses to respond. This isn't school, she tells herself, you aren't obliged to leap politely to your feet and answer every question that's put to you.

Claire goes on, earnestly: "You see, Vivienne, my marriage is the most important thing in the whole world to me, and my husband is the most important person. My whole life, my whole being, my whole reason for existing is built round Alexander and has been for the last ten years. That's a long time. And I'm afraid I really cannot allow you to spoil something we have so carefully built up together over all these years of marriage."

"But I'm not deliberately setting out to spoil anything!" Vivienne cries, stung by the injustice of Claire's words. "I can't help the fact that I love Alex and he loves me."

"He also loves *me*," says Claire quietly.

Vivienne looks up resentfully.

"Yes he does, Vivienne. I'm his wife and he loves me. He told me so last night. And having loved him for so many years I *know* the man I love. You have been acquainted with Alexander for a matter of months and the things you think you love are just certain qualities you see in him at the moment. Perhaps qualities you lack yourself. You do not love the whole man because you do not know the whole man. You cannot know him in such a short time. But I do know him and he knows me. I love him as he is and I need him too. Our only child, our son, was drowned you know, and I cannot have any more children. Alexander is all I have, Vivienne, and I need him. Please don't try to take him away from me."

Vivienne listens to the dull insistent beat of the rain on the window, mesmerised by the direct gaze of the bright hazel eyes, the pale intense face and the still, calm body in the soft, green dress. She finds Claire's voice utterly compelling. Later she realises that this is because the older woman speaks very precisely, giving full weight and emphasis to every word and syllable, with the effect of making everything she says seem tremendously important.

Vivienne is beginning to feel hypnotised. With an effort, she drags her eyes away and lights a cigarette to break the spell.

"Would you like one?"

"No thank you."

Vivienne is annoyed to see her own hand shaking. She feels at odds with the whole situation. She is losing her grip. It is bad enough feeling groggy and dizzy (the cigarette, she realises) without having Claire score all the points a well.

"Claire, I need him too," she says, her head reeling with the cigarette smoke and her stomach still rebelling from last night's brandy. God, please don't let me have to make an un-dignified dash to the loo.

Claire seizes her chance. "I think it's a question of degree, Vivienne. Remember you are young and single and you will meet someone else whom you can love. But I am thirty-five and Alexander is the only man I've ever wanted, *could* ever want. I am familiar with him, and it would be extremely difficult for me to start all over again with someone else. Its easier for you to find another man."

"I don't *want* anyone else, Claire, and I'm not trying to take him away from you. But Alex and I do have a very special love, a special feeling for one another which would be almost ... well, quite sinful to deny. I think if you find someone you can love as we love each other then you must hang on to it because that is one of the most important things that life is all about," Vivienne speaks passionately, if ungrammatically, Claire thinks. "And they're not my words, Claire, they're Alex's. That's what he said to me a few weeks ago and I know he's right. This is one of the most important experiences in my life and in his and it would be morally wrong to put a premature end to it. Alex is special, quite unlike any other man I've ever met and I know I could never ever meet anyone else I could love as much." She stares earnestly at Claire. I mean it. Believe me. It's true.

Claire says slowly, "He is special, Vivienne. He is also very talented. Yet in the last six months he has not written a word of his new novel and his agent and I have been extremely worried. I'm afraid you have been distracting him away from his work and that just will not do."

"Well," says Vivienne crisply, "I think you ought to look a bit nearer home. If he prefers being with me to being with you and writing his novel I would suggest there is something seriously wrong with this marriage you're trying to hold up as being so perfect."

Claire still holds her hypnotic gaze, but her hands stiffen slightly in her lap. "No marriage is ever perfect, Vivienne. They all have rough patches, sometimes, and believe me, the eight months or so you have known Alexander is but nothing over the space of our ten years of marriage. Marriage inevitably brings problems and difficulties, and perhaps I have not been as good a wife to Alexander as I could have been. Last night I cried myself to sleep worrying about it. But it means I shall have to try harder in future, that's all. And we shall have to have a great deal of faith in you."

"What do you mean, faith in me?" Surely, Vivienne thinks, she's not going to appeal to my better nature?

"Faith that you will come to see that what you are doing is wrong, and that you must give up seeing my husband."

The woman's mad, Vivienne decides.

They look at one another, Claire remaining straight and still, her face pale and grave. She is trying to assess the effect of her words but it is difficult as the girl's eyes are expression-less, almost glazed.

Vivienne grinds out her cigarette, her face still completely blank, then gets up and walks slowly to the window, her back to Claire. She can't even see to the other side of the road, the rain is coming down in such a torrent.

Claire stares at Vivienne's back.

She's very cool about it all, Claire thinks. She's much harder than I had imagined. I came prepared for shouts, rages, accusations. A scene. Alexander had said the girl was pas-sionate and forthright, and Claire had lain awake half the night planning what she was going to say, how she would sit, the way she would look. She was prepared for a stormy scene or drawn-out argument. But this long, stony silence, this blank face, this awkward gangling figure of periwinkle blue against the grey rain, this unnerved her.

Vivienne doesn't feel at all cool, stony, or unemotional. She is trying very hard not to cry. On top of the events of the previous night and her queasy hangover, the shock of Alex's suddenly coming back from France and Claire's visit are all, she thinks, a bit much. She wishes she knew more of what Alex thought of all this. It's so confusing. They had had the most wonderful summer, then he had gone to France with his wife leaving her feeling not only lonely and bereft but slightly cheap. She had been so proud in the summer when he had introduced her to his friends and they had gone to parties together, Alex and Vivienne, that it had seemed like a slap in the face when he had taken Claire on holiday. Then the sudden return, the phone call and the next thing here is Claire herself sitting in her best, her only, chair, going on about faith as if she were a Mother Superior reprimanding a wayward novice.

Through the haze inside her head Vivienne is suddenly aware of Claire's grave voice again.

"You know, I think it would make you much happier if you stopped seeing Alexander. It can't be very satisfactory just seeing him on the odd evening and then under rather unnatural circumstances ... it must be difficult for a relationship to develop fully like that. Surely you would be happier if you had the chance to develop a more natural relationship with someone of your own age, who isn't married?"

Vivienne can't reply. She knows if she tries to speak she will burst into tears. How humiliating to let Claire know she has made her cry! Claire seems so controlled, so possessed while she, Vivienne, is pathetically about to blub. Grief, how wretched it all is!

After a moment of indecision Claire decides against getting up and joining the silent Vivienne by the window. She is beginning to feel very tired and depressed. How to get through to this hard girl? Perhaps she is hoping that if she says nothing for long enough, Claire will give up and go home. So Claire soldiers on, her bird-like eyes boring into Vivienne's back, willing her to respond.

"I expect you find the young men that you meet a little unsophisticated—"

She is interrupted by a loud hammering on the door and Stella's gay voice: "Open up Vivvy! I've rescued a man from drowning on the doorstep who says he's looking for you. I'd half a mind to claim him myself but—"

Vivienne rushes to the door and flings herself, sobbing, at a drenched Alex. He has come by Tube and is, Claire can see, furious. She looks up at him across the head of the hysterical Vivienne.

"Alexander, will you please drive me home?"

"For heaven's sake, I've only just arrived! I'm wet and cold and—"

"I'm sorry Alexander but I've got a headache right across my eyes and I really don't think I can see to drive. And I honestly don't think Vivienne and I have any more to say to one another. I'll wait for you in the car downstairs."

Vivienne is still wailing and making incoherent sounds into his mackintosh.

"Claire, I can't leave her, not in this state. The poor kid's completely hysterical."

Claire picks up her coat and walks to the door.

"No, darling, what you can't do is leave your wife sitting alone in a car for an hour in the rain while you comfort your mistress. I'm upset too, and I need you too. I'm sure this young lady can do whatever is necessary for Vivienne."

She turns to Stella standing riveted, intrigued, in the doorway.

Alexander hesitates and Claire watches his quick, inward struggle—the decision based on which of these two women will make his life more unbearable if he doesn't give in to her. Vivienne is still clinging to him helplessly.

He looks at Claire, his eyes dull, his face sad.

"I'll see you in the car in five minutes," he says.

Eight

FOR WEEKS AFTERWARDS Vivienne is unable to look at her moulting armchair without seeing Claire sitting there, straight backed, her hands quietly in her lap, half hidden by the soft folds of the green lawn dress. She hears again the grave voice with its distinctively precise diction, so reasonable and controlled. Controlled. Vivienne feels particularly bitter about that. Claire had been completely in possession of herself, totally adult and civilised while she, Vivienne, had been incoherent, stupid and childish.

She had looked such a mess for a start, her face blotchy and blurred from the night before. Thinking about it, a gauze screen comes down in front of her eyes, making the scene float hazily before her in colours ... the green of Claire's dress, her own cornflower blue outfit, the beautiful soft purples and reds of the anemones by the window where the slate-grey rain was beating down. The colours and shapes float round and blend with the smells ... stale cigarettes, coffee and, over it all, the fresher note of Claire's perfume. Vivienne remembers the bottle of Madame Rochas on Claire's dressing table and if she by chance catches this scent on another woman the events of that Sunday morning will come flooding back to make her feel again, sharply, the frustration of it all, the anger at her own inadequacy and lack of experience.

It is years later, however, before she realises the significance of the perfume Claire had worn. One day, when she is nearly thirty, Vivienne will take out her memories and comfortably sift through them, cushioned now by time and distance from any hurt or pain.

No woman, she will realise, who, after a row with her husband about his mistress and a sleepless night sobbing her heart out, decides to be the brave little wife and go and confront the mistress, no woman in that sort of emotional state dreams of putting on perfume. If you're that upset you grab any clothes, shove a hat on to hide your hair and off you march, full of fervour and righteous indignation. Vivienne will remember Claire's well-brushed hair, the soft, ultra-feminine dress, the trace of lipstick, the perfume ... every trick of the trade, right down to the slight victimised tilt of the head, all carefully calculated for maximum effect. Clever Claire. Not that it matters now.

But to Vivienne at twenty-two it does matter. Above all, Alex matters. Through September and October they continue to see one another, though less obviously than before and Vivienne is sad that her golden summer seems to be fading now into a tarnished autumn. Alex says Claire was so upset he thinks it is only fair to calm things down for a while. He is sure Vivienne will understand. Now she begins to hear, for the first time, all the phrases that are going to become dauntingly familiar to her:

"Remember I love you, Vivvy. You are part of my life, part of me. The love I have for you is like a current, going on and on. You can't switch it off like an electric light. You are bright and alive like sunshine in my life. I can't let you go. In time Claire will accept that I need you as well as her, but obviously this isn't an easy concept for her. So you must be strong, angel, and patient. Give me time, will you, to work it all out. Understand if we can't be together as much. It will only be for a little while, I promise."

They still meet for lunch sometimes and for a brief couple

of hours after work when he comes round to the flat and they make love like people quenching a great thirst. Once she decides to take an afternoon off work and cook him a meal, a new venture for Vivienne. She has little natural flair for cookery but reasons that she is intelligent and can read so therefore should be able to follow and apply the instructions in a cookery book. The only one she has was forced upon her by her mother. A condensed Mrs Beeton, it is in small type with no helpful pictures and Vivienne has never used it.

"You must be mad," Stella says, watching Vivienne assemble bowls, mixing spoons and other, to Stella, weird paraphernalia.

"I know. Where's the egg whisk?"

"I don't think we've got one. You'll have to use a fork."

"And I need a collander."

"We haven't got one of those either," says Stella cheerfully. "This isn't the bloody Ritz, you know."

"Don't worry, I *know*. Shouldn't you be at work?" says Vivienne nastily.

"No, it's my half day in lieu of Saturday afternoon."

"Oh. Well honestly Stella, I don't see how you manage to give dinner parties when this kitchen is lacking in what seems to be totally basic equipment." Vivienne is agitated at the thought of cooking the meal, and consequently snappy. "Can you actually cook?" she raps.

"Actually, no," Stella admits happily. "But I have a clever girlfriend who is a Cordon bleu and together we make a formidable team. When a guy called John was hopelessly in love with me and wanted to marry me but couldn't bring himself to propose because he was afraid of my, ah, reputation, a friend bet me ten pounds I couldn't actually get him to pop the question. So I invited John to dinner and summoned a select band of friends."

Stella wedges herself comfortably against the door out of the way of Vivienne who is rushing about banging pots and pans, bowls and lethally sharp knives.

"So come the evening of the great dinner party, the unsuspecting John is greeted by me in a fetching frilly apron and introduced to Sally who is 'just giving me a hand' in the kitchen. I didn't, of course, mention to him that she was a Cordon bleu. Then he meets Brenda and Mike, our Happily Married Couple and how wonderful, they have brought their sweet baby along too. Fortunately the little beast remains sweet by sleeping the whole time, because, thank God, Brenda has the good sense to ram a couple of aspirins into its milk. All Brenda and Mike have to do is act Darby and Joan all evening and nod agreement to everything Phil says."

"Phil?" Vivienne asks, wondering how many potatoes she should peel.

"Sally's fiancé, but again we didn't tell poor John that. Phil's job was to promote Stella and allay John's fears. I disappeared into the kitchen, Mike poured them all some sherry and Phil waded in and did his stuff. Area one was what a home-loving girl Stella is, and what a lovely job she's made of this flat, so homey and cosy. Area two was Stella the family girl. How my father lived just down the road (he did at the time) and how every weekend I went home to see dear daddy."

"Doesn't sound much like you," says Vivienne. "Look, this recipe says black pepper and I bet we haven't got any."

"The last girl left some red pepper, if that's any good," suggests Stella. "I should use that; there can't be all that much difference. Anyway, the reason I went home so often was simply to clear up the stinking mess of bottles the drunken old fool left lying around. That's why my mother walked out on him. Brenda whispered to John that my parents were separated and I had been so *brave* about it all. Such a shock, you know. Meanwhile, every five minutes or so when I could control my rising hysteria, I would pop out of the kitchen prettily holding a mixing bowl—"

"While Sally slaved away on all the food?" Vivienne laughs.

"She didn't have to do *all* of it. My mother does a beautiful chilled chocolate sweet, so she brought that up for me the day before, Sally did the main course and I did the melon myself."

"Big deal," Vivienne says, concentrating anxiously on the separation of egg whites from yolks.

"It was, you've no idea. At one point John admired my flash flower arrangement and everyone choked because I'd had them specially done by a friend at Constance Spry. Meanwhile, Phil plodded on with the campaign ... Stella anti-Women's Lib, Stella who is really looking for the Right Man to settle down with. It all sounds very obvious, you'd have thought poor old John would have cottoned on the way every topic started with the word Stella, but as Mike said, the poor nutter was so much in love with me he was delighted to talk about me all the time. The only anxious moment came when Sally emerged from the kitchen, steam and sweat running down her face, hair all limp, and without thinking flopped into a chair. I was the one who was supposed to be cooking and I was as cool as a cucumber! But the moment passed. After the meal everyone was full of praise, and Sally, quite dead-pan, said I must give her the recipe for the marvellous glazed ham. A week later John proposed."

"Obviously you didn't accept."

"God no. I was a bit sorry really, after the effort everyone had made so I spent my ten pound reward on taking them all out to dinner. John meanwhile buggered off to New Zealand where he was quickly snapped up by a widow nine years older than him and with three children."

Howling with laughter Stella moves across to inspect the contents of the big saucepan Vivienne has just heaved on to the cooker.

"I'm doing coq au vin followed by lemon meringue pie. Do you think it'll be all right?"

"Sounds delicious. You could save a bit of the lemon meringue, shove it in a brown paper bag and give it to him to take home to wifey. I'm sure she'd be delighted."

"Oh, shut up Stella."

"Or perhaps," Stella goes on, waltzing round the kitchen table, "perhaps she'll just turn up, and having just driven all the way down from Highgate she will immediately want to go home again. 'Alexander, will you please drive me home,'" she mimics.

"God, don't remind me," Vivienne says, carefully separating egg yolks from the whites. "It was awful."

"Frankly, Vivvy, I thought it was hilarious. There's poor Alex standing on the doorstep like the proverbial drowned rat so I bring him upstairs and the door bursts open and there's you gushing more water like an overflowing soda fountain and in the midst of all this sodden mess appears this refined, miraculously dry-eyed lady who demands that Alex turn right round and drive her home. It's not as if *she* offered to drive him!"

"Look it was all very fraught and emotional for all of us, Claire included. Alex said she wept all the way home."

"Oh well, I suppose if you must go in for these complicated affairs. I've had enough of them myself. Dear Bob is so sweet, uncomplicated and kind—"

"And moneyed."

"And moneyed, you're so right. Actually that's what I

popped in for, you've just reminded me. Can I borrow a 10p piece for the meter? Thanks."

And she disappears into her own room, chanting, "Guess who's coming to dinner?" over and over and over. Instead of screaming, Vivienne vents her anger on the egg whites, beating them furiously with a fork while cursing the landlord, the previous tenants, the world and finally God for not supplying her with a whisk.

By the time Alex arrives, a little late and smelling of scotch, she is exhausted. She's cleaned the flat so it now has an overpowering aroma of lavender polish. All the books, papers, shoes, clothes and underwear have been tidied away. Her new Sinatra record is ready and waiting on the player and she has lit some special red Danish candles to make the room look festive and welcoming. She has bathed, talced and perfumed herself, and put on a new burgundy-coloured dress with crossover shoulder straps that shows a lot of back. It will be cold to wear as it has no sleeves, but no matter, she knows it is a style he likes. The dress, the new record, the expensive candles and the food for the evening have made an enormous gash in her small salary but she refuses to let that bother her just now. This is her first dinner party and everything must be perfect.

At first it is all right. Alex has brought some wine and they sit cosily in front of the gas fire, the candlelight casting the right romantic shadows and Sinatra murmuring appropriate noises in the background. The coq au vin is passable, though difficult to eat off plates on their laps. Alex doesn't seem to mind. He tells her the chicken is gorgeous but says nothing about the lemon meringue, for which she can't blame him; the oversweet lemon has sunk soggily into the pastry, while the meringue lies limp and helpless on top.

The fork wins, Vivienne concedes sadly, dumping the

dishes in the sink, and hoping Alex isn't comparing this with the efficiently organised meals he has with Claire. Please God, let the coffee be absolutely perfect.

As it happens, the coffee is extremely ordinary because in the middle of making it the lights go out. "That *fucking* meter," she hisses. Stella took her last 10p piece and has now gone out. Alex assures her, rather wearily, that he has no small change so she has to run up to the flat above and beg a couple.

The mood broken, Alex seems withdrawn, while Vivienne, tired and a little defeated by the day, yearns for comfort and reassurance. He tries to make love to her, but for the first time in their relationship, he fails. He apologises, saying he wanted to make love to her so much; he had been thinking of her all day, planning what he would say to her that evening, and all the ways he would make love to her, looking forward to it.

Then at five thirty, just as he was leaving the office, Claire had phoned. He had told her he had to go to a boring Press party. She was just phoning, she said, to say she might be late herself as she was taking Joyce and Belinda out to supper, but if he felt hungry when he came home there was some garlic chicken in the fridge. Oh, and she hoped the party wasn't too dull, and he would remember, wouldn't he, that she loved him very much?

"Crunch," says Vivienne dismally, lighting a cigarette.

To try and cheer themselves up they embark on a minor pub crawl until it is time for Alex to catch the last Tube home. Vivienne walks back down the King's Road, her bare arms goose-fleshed inside her big winter cape. Unbearably lonely, she is unwilling to return to the flat, knowing it will make her feel worse; but there is nowhere else to go.

A couple of French boys follow her for a while, making

vulgar comments in their own language which they think she can't understand, and then a braver Australian tries to pick her up. He is drunk, but looks lonely too, she decides, hurrying away down the side road that leads to her flat. Perhaps I should have taken him home with me, that big rough Aussie. We would have lain in my bed together and comforted one another. I wonder how many Londoners go to bed together just for comfort. Just to have someone there when you wake up in the night, someone to laugh and say don't be silly it's only the wardrobe creaking when you sit up, paralysed with fear that there is a man in the room who is going to strangle you. She had tried to tell Alex about this fear once, but he had been most insensitive, telling her that all women enjoy secret fantasies about being raped.

Vivienne sees Stella's light on and creeps in silently, unable to face her brash, bubbly humour. In her room the candles are still burning but because she is alone the effect is no longer romantic; it is ghostly now, with shadows stretching into frightening shapes on the wall.

Quickly, she undresses and, rare for Vivienne, takes the trouble to hang up the burgundy dress on a hanger filched from the hotel in Brighton. Then she arranges the curtains closely over the window and blows out the candles. If she can't see anything at all in the room she won't feel so afraid; it is the odd chink of light shining in and making the familiar objects of the room look strange that scares her. She slots her body into the friendly grooves in the bed and thinks back over the evening. It had not been worth it, somehow. She wants her evenings with Alex to be glowing, happy occasions, particularly now when she sees him so seldom. It was hateful if he was thinking of bloody Claire all the time.

Today is Wednesday, she thinks. Tomorrow she has her Italian evening class and Friday she is to work late to make up for taking time off this afternoon. And then the sodding weekend. She will see Alex for lunch on Friday and then a great big blank two days with absolutely nothing to do. She hears Alex:

"Rubbish, there's always something to do in London! Concerts, cinemas, theatres, parks, the zoo, art galleries! God, I wish I had the time..."

Well you can cut out things like concerts, cinemas and theatres, Alex darling, because they cost money and I haven't got any; and I know Hyde Park is just up the road but it's really no fun tramping round by yourself in late October. Most of the art galleries aren't free any more, and anyway they're half full of lonely people like me trying not to look at the other half who are all in jolly laughing pairs.

She thinks of Claire hurrying home from her evening out, sharing a cup of coffee with Alex. Sitting comfortably with one another, Alex sprawled in his chair, his face strained and weary. Occasionally she will look across at him and smile in a way that says, I understand. Then they will go upstairs to bed. Together.

"You will remember, won't you, that I love you very much?"

Vivienne curls up into a tight, miserable little ball and sobs. Great shuddering sobs of pain and self pity that shake her body and leave her weak, wide-awake and utterly wretched.

Claire's tears, that Sunday afternoon when Alexander grimly drove her away from Vivienne's, were not of sorrow. They were a mixture of anger and fear, both unfamiliar emotions to Claire.

Anger at herself for mishandling the situation. In Alexander's eyes she is sure she appeared hard. He had arrived, exhausted and wet and she, stonily ignoring the weeping girl (whom he would suppose Claire had upset) had stubbornly demanded to be driven home. Anger too, because Claire considered that Vivienne had been the hard one that afternoon, refusing to speak, or discuss the issue. Anger because everything she had planned had gone wrong. The girl was determined not to communicate, and then as soon as Alexander had arrived she had flung herself at him, oh so feminine, so vulnerable, so helpless. Poor little Vivienne. It was a quite masterly performance which made Claire furious.

She was also frightened. Realising how little she understood this girl and her relationship with Alexander, she was afraid for her marriage, for the world she had so carefully established for herself and her husband. If she could only understand, she would be one step closer to controlling the situation, but Vivienne had not been what she expected. She hadn't been glamorous or trendy or dumb and it was clear the girl really believed in her love. The difference being, Claire thought, that she loves him because of and I love him in spite of.

Afraid of what he would say, she avoided talking to Alexander about it, but they both knew the issue had to be faced. He was kind and considerate to her at this time, insisting that she stay in bed for a few days, stopping home from the office, and bringing her badly-cooked but well-meant meals on trays, always forgetting the salt. Once or twice she heard him murmuring on the telephone and tortured herself imagining it was Vivienne he was talking to. Even to say her name was an effort for Claire. She felt as if she had just lost an important battle, and now lay wounded while the victors were especially consoling to her.

After a few days she discussed it with Alexander, distantly, as if they were talking about someone else. He volunteered not to see Vivienne any more, saying he hadn't realised how much it had upset Claire. But they both knew he didn't mean it.

"Don't you think it's important," he said to Claire, "that you're the one I come home to?"

Yes Alexander, but I can hear you tell her: "Remember I'm with you because I want to be, not because I have to be."

Over the next couple of months Claire finds Alexander courteous, kind and remote. He makes love to her occasionally, violently, and she knows he is thinking of Vivienne. She can sense his restlessness; and his novel remains untouched. Soon, she knows, he will become resentful and bitter with her. She knows, too, that as long as he is still able to see Vivienne at lunchtimes, and for the occasional evening, the fire will still be there, warming the lovers and burning her.

Nine

"Vivvy, what the hell are you doing down there?"
"Nothing!"
Vivienne slithers back guiltily on to the worn leather of the car seat. She can't very well tell Alex she was checking to see if she had any shoes on. If they weren't on, it would confirm her hope that she was dreaming: often in her dreams she found herself walking along the road where she had lived as a child, feeling blissfully happy until she looked down at her bare feet. Then she knew it was only a dream and would wake up, bad tempered and disappointed.

But there they are on the floor, two blobs of imitation patent leather, carefully chosen to match the brown shoulder bag she is clutching between damp fingers. Deciding what to wear had been agony. She had wanted something smart enough to boost her failing confidence but casual enough to make it look as if the occasion wasn't important enough to merit a big effort. The attempt to look effortless had quite worn her out. Unable to afford anything new, the evening before was spent repairing her old orange wool two-piece, dashing to the chemist for oil of eucalyptus to clean the grease stains from her winter cape, and polishing the shoes and handbag to a high shine.

In fact, thinks Vivienne, staring at her reflection in the car window, everything about me is shiny today. My hair, meticulously washed in herb shampoo; my face, gleaming with slicky glossy gleamers on all the strategic areas like it said in Stella's *Vogue*. My poor bitten nails glisten with pearl-ised polish and the bright gold buckle on my belt is digging into my spare tyre and hurts.

I feel like a child on my way to a posh party, with instruc-tions from my mother not to crease my dress, scuff my shoes, get my nails dirty and to remember to thank them for having me. Except I am not a child and instead of going to a party I am going to spend the weekend with Alex and Claire. My mother would have a fit.

Alex had been quite off-hand about it. It was Claire's sug-gestion, he said. She had suddenly announced that she was tired of this underhanded way of going on, tired of watching Alexander tell lies about why he would be late home when they both knew quite well where he would be.

"There is no point in trying to sweep Vivienne under the carpet," she had said. "However much I resent it, the fact is that she exists and you want to continue to see her. Well let's face it and have it all out in the open. Why not invite her here for the weekend?"

Seeing Alexander's aghast expression, Claire hurried on in case she should allow herself to be talked out of the idea.

"Well, why not, darling? You say it isn't just a sex thing, that you want her to be part of your life, that you need both of us in different ways. I'd much rather you were here with Vivienne than sneaking off to phone her when you think I won't know, along with all the rest of the hole-in-the-corner secrets and lies."

"It's all very well, Claire," Alexander had said, "but she's young, and rather scared of you. She might not want to come."

"Well what does she usually do at weekends?"

"I don't know, she doesn't talk about it very much. I think she gets a bit fed up, though, being on her own."

That had decided it. Alex gave Vivienne an edited version of his conversation with Claire, and said casually that the whole thing was up to Vivienne. He didn't want her to feel pressured.

"Do *you* want me to come, Alex?"

"Yes, I think I do. After all, Claire knows about you and accepts you so there's no reason why all three of us shouldn't get along very well. You'll like Claire when you get to know her, I'm sure. You're quite alike in some ways. And I must say I have to admire Claire for taking this attitude. She could be raging with jealousy, issuing stormy ultimatums to stop me seeing you and generally acting the injured little wife, which I suppose some people would say she had every right to do. But instead she's taking a much more mature and adult line, when it can't be easy for her to accept that I want to bring you home."

Whether intentionally or not, in "mature" and "adult" Alex had chosen the two words most calculated to sway Vivienne. It was agreed that Alex should pick her up in the car on Saturday morning and they would arrive in Highgate in time for an informal lunch.

"Shall we stop for a quick drink?" Alex says, watching Vivienne extinguish her second cigarette in fifteen minutes. She agrees gratefully. The nearest pub is a brash, noisy place in Kentish Town which she knows Alex hates but he takes her there all the same, to the Alpine Bar, crammed with young people: thin, delicate boys squiring girls with pale faces and large unsurprised eyes. Alex gives her an enormous schooner of sweet sherry and tells her funny stories about all sorts of strange people he's met in pubs, while Vivienne dutifully doles out automatic bursts of laughter. Reluctantly, she drains her glass.

"Ready?" he says.

"Yes, fine." The dentist will see you now, Miss.

She wants to prolong the journey for ever, but too soon they are in Highgate, turning off from the gushing stream of traffic into the comparative peace of Ambassador Drive, with its big houses, blue-enamelled number plates and bold brass doorknockers. Vivienne looks sadly at the almond tree outside number 31. Last time she had been here it was summer and the tree had been green and full of birds. Now the birds have gone, and the tree is damp with November mist.

Somehow she had expected Claire to be at the door to meet them, but they find her instead in the kitchen looking slightly overwhelmed by a very large striped apron. The two women manage to smile stiff greetings without actually looking at one another. Vivienne observes that the kitchen has been re-painted since her last visit and Alex, as if reading her thoughts and afraid she will voice them, quickly suggests a drink.

"There's some Veuve du Vernay and fresh orange juice in the fridge," says Claire. "If you pour it, darling, I'll show Vivienne round."

What's she talking about, thinks Vivienne. I know my way around, and she knows I bloody well know.

Claire conducts Vivienne up the green-carpeted stairs to the little blue bedroom, considerately pointing out the bath-room on the way.

"I thought you'd like it in here," Claire says, straightening the bedcover that is straight already. "It's cosier than the proper guest room and rather pleasant with the almond tree outside."

I *know*, Vivienne wants to scream.

"Yes. Thank you," she says, slipping off her cape and drap-ing it on the bed. Claire picks it up and hangs it neatly in the little white-painted wardrobe. Vivienne cringes. God, don't let her notice the shredded lining.

"I put some hangers in here for you and there's a drawer in the bedside table for your bits and pieces. I'll leave you to tidy up now. Lunch will be in about twenty minutes. If you want anything just say, won't you?"

She smiles briefly, the warmth not reaching her eyes, and disappears.

Vivienne rummages in her handbag for her mirror and studies her face. What did Claire mean, tidy up? I *am* tidy. And I went to the loo in the pub. Hanging up the spare dress and shoving undies into the bedside drawer takes seconds. How long am I supposed to stay here? She sits down carefully on the bed and stares round the room where she and Alex had so happily made love. They won't be able to this weekend that's for sure.

"I don't really think it would be quite the thing, do you?" he had said uneasily. "I mean, it's very good of Claire to agree to this weekend and we can't very well barge off to bed whenever we feel like it. We have to think of her feelings too."

Vivienne had been unreasonably disappointed and he had comforted her, saying, "Let's just enjoy being together, angel."

She gives herself ten minutes and then wanders downstairs to the kitchen. It is empty. She stares challengingly at the rows of brown china, remembering how afraid she had been of them before. How silly.

"Oh there you are Vivienne!"

Claire, holding out a glass, looking at her quizzically. "I took your drink upstairs for you. I didn't realise you had come in here."

Vivienne takes the drink, wondering why she feels like a naughty girl caught with her hand in the cake tin before tea-time.

They don't have lunch round the big pine table in the kitchen as Vivienne had imagined, but sit instead round the fire in the sitting room. Alex sprawled in the big leather chair, Claire in the rocker and Vivienne between them on the long settee. There is delicious home-made soup with huge chunks of warm garlic bread and sharp cheddar cheese. For a while they chat about France, as Vivienne has lived there and the others were there in the summer, talking like strangers at a wedding, not wanting to offend, politely listening and agreeing and saying, "Sorry, what were you going to say? No, please, after you."

Until at last Claire says, laughing, "Poor Alexander! He's being terribly good, Vivienne, sitting here making conversation like this. He's really dying to immerse himself in the newspapers as usual to gen up on all the sport on television this afternoon. Go on, darling, I'm sure Vivienne won't mind."

"No of course not," says Vivienne, dismayed. Surely he isn't going to watch the box all afternoon? What are she and Claire supposed to do then, hold hands and swop stories about how good he is in bed? Claire catches her glance. "I usually closet myself in the kitchen on Saturday afternoons and do some good old-fashioned baking. I should warn you, though, the level of Alexander's temper for the evening is dependent on the success or otherwise of a football team called Rovers, or something equally doggy."

"That's a bloody lie," says Alex good-humouredly from behind his paper. "And I want a chocolate cake please." He switches on the television.

"Oh. I was thinking of a fruit one."

"But we haven't had chocolate for ages."

"No, I suppose not. All right then. I'm not sure if I've got all the ingredients, though. I need a bar of plain chocolate and I think you ate that last weekend."

"You can pop out and get some more, can't you?" he says as the commentator begins his breathless rundown of the afternoon's events. Wrestling, racing, a rugby international and a swimming gala.

"It hardly seems worth it, darling, when I've got all the ingredients for a fruit cake. Still, I'll have a look round. I'll probably find some chocolate hidden away somewhere."

"I must confess I ate the bar you hid at the back of the larder," Alex grins.

Claire makes a mock exasperated face at Vivienne who has been listening, amazed, to this banter. Claire mustn't joke with Alex. That's not fair, it's against the rules.

"Shall I give you a hand with the washing up, Claire," says Vivienne, as if prodded by her mother.

"No, no. I'll just load up the dishwasher and it will do itself. I'll bring you in some coffee in a minute."

"Are you sure you don't mind, Vivvy?" says Alex. "I don't want you to be bored. We could do something else if you like, if there's anything you'd like to do?"

"No, of *course* not, Alex. I'll just curl up here with some magazines and be perfectly happy."

"Oh dear," says Claire, concerned. "I'm afraid I don't read magazines." She makes it sound like, I'm afraid I don't drink Brasso. "Perhaps we could—"

"Not to worry," Vivienne cuts in breezily, "I'll have a quiet browse through your bookshelf. I'm sure I shall find something I've been longing to read for ages."

Claire picks up the tray. "Oh that's good. I'm sorry to appear unsociable, shutting myself away for the afternoon, but I'm one of those people whose cakes will only rise if they are left severely alone to get on with it!"

That's all right, Claire dear. Do fuck off. The longer the better. Vivienne looks at the bookshelves and sees they have all been rearranged since she was here last. She had asked Alex why he and Claire scribbled their initials in all the books and learnt that it was because he always liked to make pencil marks in them, a habit Claire deplored. Vivienne chooses a volume of short stories by a currently fashionable woman author and wanders back to the settee, smiling at Alex to show she is perfectly happy. Without looking for the CMM initials, she knows the book is Claire's. Alex is unreasonably prejudiced against women authors. "They always write about things like 'the listening horizon'," he scorned. "How the hell can a horizon listen?" And a big argument would start, leading inevitably to Women's Lib and ending with one pretty female chirping, to the accompaniment of male cheers, "I don't understand what all the fuss is about. I don't *want* to be liberated."

Claire returns with coffee in the most beautiful pot Vivienne has ever seen, brown with an unusual cherry design.

"Yes, isn't it lovely," says Claire, pleased, as Vivienne exclaims. "I bought the set in Switzerland when I was convalescing and the design, apparently, is over six hundred years old. Cream and sugar? Good. Well, I'll take mine into the kitchen and leave you to it. Are you sure you are all right?"

"*Fine*, thanks!"

As soon as Claire has gone Vivienne desperately wants to touch Alex for reassurance, but he just smiles briefly at her, mouths "I love you," and returns to Cardiff Arms Park.

She sips the very good coffee and basks in the warmth and comfort of the room. She has known it as a sunny summer room; now it glows with autumn colours. Where Vivienne once remembered lilac by the window Claire has arranged a huge mass of beech leaves in a big stone honey jar. Claire is, Vivienne thinks drowsily, the sort of person who *would* know how to preserve beech leaves. With anyone else they would just wither and die ... "We wi-ther and per-rish but nought changeth Thee-ee-ee" and any girl who dares open her eyes during the Lord's Prayer will get one hundred lines ... the sharp thrill of peeping through half-closed eyes at the newly-wed science mistress. One imagined she looked different. Surely there had to be some outward sign ... some people said you put on weight. After all, she had been married eight weeks and *she knew now what it was like*! Did it hurt? Was there lots of blood all over the bed?

Eyes open now, listen to the portly Head Girl read the lesson. Good old Hilary, a fine Head Girl. Good speaking voice (thank-you-on-behalf-of-the-school speeches), conductor of school orchestra, soloist in choir (now Hilary our Head Girl will lead the girls in the school song). Clever (I am delighted to announce that Hilary our Head Girl has won an open scholarship to Oxford!) and popular (the governors wish to mark Hilary's scholarship achievement by awarding the school an extra day's holiday). Three girlish cheers for Hilary with her apple-red face and fat sausage legs in thick sensible stockings. Would Hilary ever know what it was like? No, Hilary would never have time to find out. It was hard work winning scholarships, and in her spare time Hilary was Brown Owl and leader of the church youth club and choir. It looked good on university application forms.

Hilary wouldn't lie in bed on Saturday nights and listen to her mother in the next room padding to the cupboard for the vaseline, then creak into bed, silence, then a build up of rhythmic creaks for two and a half minutes followed by patter patter slippered feet into bathroom, mother washing all the nasties away, pat dry on own special towel; murmured words, then a slower, more reluctant patter, father unwillingly to bathroom for a quick sluice on orders from ma.

Still, probably Hilary wasn't interested in finding out what it was like, it was obviously fulfilling enough being the sensible popular head of the school. Not sulky and unco-operative like Vivienne who failed exams and slouched against the wall bars during prayers, looking in awe at Janet West in Form Five who had definitely done it. She had told her riveted clique of friends about it one lunch hour and en-thralled the rest of the class with throwaway lines like, "Well, Tony's really got the hang of my new bra now." Breathtaking stuff. Occasionally word would go round that Janet West was a week *late*, and tension would mount as Janet disappeared down to the boys' school in lunch hours for worried confer-ences with Tony until finally, to everyone's secret disappoint-ment, they would learn that Janet had *started*. "All quiet on the Western front," Vivienne had written wittily in her diary.

"Really, it doesn't matter at *all*. I can soon get another sent over from Switzerland," says Claire as Vivienne apologises for the tenth time.

"It was just that I was dozing and then Alex screaming like that I was so startled I just forgot I was holding the cup."

"Never mind," says Alex. "We'll blame it on the evil Welsh, as it was their try I was so excited about."

"It's not possible to mend it, I suppose?"

"No, I'm afraid it shattered as it hit the marble-topped table," says Claire, absorbed in sponging coffee stains from the oatmeal fabric on the settee.

"Oh dear, I am sorry."

"Please don't worry about it, Vivienne. I can soon order another one through my friends in Vevey."

"Darling surely we could find something nearer home? What about the Swiss Centre?"

"No, I know you can't, Alexander, because I've made enquiries before. It's a very old Swiss design and there are only two people in Switzerland licensed to do it. They don't make enough for export so you have to buy it locally or not at all."

"Look please let me have a go at those coffee stains—"

"Oh it's all right, Vivienne, it won't take a minute."

"I hope you'll let me pay—"

"I wouldn't dream of it. It was an accident and that's that. Anyway, it wasn't your fault, it was Alexander's."

"Agreed!" says Alex cheerfully. "And to atone I shall take you both out for a meal tonight. How about an Indian? We know a very good place in the Finchley Road, don't we Claire?"

"Oh, I'd love that!" Vivienne exclaims, glad to be able to say something positive at last.

"There is that other place, of course," suggests Claire carefully, "further up towards the station. Why don't we try it for a change?"

"Right, I'm easy. Now Vivvy sit down, stop looking guilty and try to stay awake this time. Your snoring disturbs my concentration."

"I don't snore!" Vivienne wants to add that she doesn't grind her teeth, either, like he does but stops herself in time and goes instead to open the door for Claire who is carrying out the tray with the offending shattered pieces of cherry cup.

Driving back from the restaurant Vivienne unreasonably resents having to sit in the back of the car. Although she couldn't really have expected Claire to give up the front seat she does consider that the older woman might have been courteous enough at least to offer it to her guest, particularly as Claire had virtually ignored her throughout the entire meal. It doesn't occur to Vivienne that after eight undiluted hours of her company, Claire might be feeling the strain; unable to say what she really thought to Vivienne, Claire had turned waspishly on her husband.

"The trouble with you Alexander," she had said, neatly dissecting the tandoori chicken, "is that you have a completely untrained mind. If only you'd been taught a modicum of self-discipline you might have achieved something worthwhile by now."

"Claire you know I have always envied and admired your strength of will and the way you discipline yourself. Unfortunately, I do not possess those qualities to any great degree. I am the sort of person to whom things have always come fairly easily and I hope to God they will continue to do so."

"If you had the sort of upbringing that I had—"

"What you're really saying, *dar*ling, is that you're jealous, because I had an indulgent mother who encouraged me to be a lazy bastard and when my father came back from India and whisked me off to school to toughen me up, they discovered I was naturally brilliant at English and Rugby so of course I was regarded as a star pupil. You on the other hand now try to make a virtue of the fact that because you were average at everything you had to work yourself practically into the ground to get a scholarship to some backwoods university and the Head Girl badge."

"Were you Head Girl?" asked Vivienne curiously, remembering Hilary.

"Yes," said Claire shortly before again addressing her husband. "It's not that I'm jealous, Alexander, it's just that I think you should have been made to work harder at the subjects you didn't like—that's where the discipline comes in. It's good training for later years when one has to get on and do all manner of things every day that one doesn't care for. And don't try and pretend this doesn't happen to you, Alexander, just because Vivienne is here. You know you have awful battles with yourself."

"I know you've got a mind like a bloody electric carving knife."

Feeling left out, Vivienne tried to joke her way back into the conversation by commenting that Indian food always seemed to take on the appearance of something else: the tandoori chicken resembled a fugitive from the lobster pot, while the sticky Gulabjaman sweet tasted remarkably like treacle pudding.

But no one appeared to be listening.

Now, after a silent drive back to Highgate, Claire has regained her self control and organised them into the sitting room while she goes to make a bedtime drink. The glow of the fire provides the only light in the room, flickering on Alex's face across from Vivienne on the other side of the hearthrug. Her enforced isolation in the restaurant makes her yearn now for physical contact. She needs to touch Alex, to feel his hands on her, caressing, loving, demanding. Desperately, she wills him to look at her and obediently his eyes travel slowly up her body to her face. Surely he can see, surely he must know how much she wants him! Beneath her clothes her body is tense, waiting. God, if only he'd reach across and devour her here in front of the fire, his hard, strong body crushing hers...

Vivienne nearly faints with disappointment as Claire appears with the hot chocolate.

"Goodness, how cosy you are in here! Let's not turn on the light, it's much more beautiful like this. Shall we have some music?"

"What would you like?" Alexander sounds strained.

"Oh, Palestrina, I think darling. Something to feed the soul."

God, thinks Vivienne, watching Alex resume his seat opposite her as the glorious music fills the room, it isn't my bloody *soul* that needs feeding. Her skin is tingling with longing and expectancy. Surely he will arrange something! Perhaps after Claire has gone to sleep he will come to her tonight. In the darkness Vivienne knows he is looking at her with the same intensity ... there are fearful waves of desire between them. How can Claire sit there so calmly, rocking to and fro in time with the music, sipping her chocolate so delicately. Can't she see? I WANT YOUR HUSBAND. I WANT HIM TO TAKE ME AND MAKE LOVE TO ME UNTIL I'M WHIMPERING AND HELPLESS AND SATISFIED.

"Would you like to use the bathroom first, Vivienne?"

"What? Oh. Yes, thank you." Vivienne blesses the dark as she realises how hard and how viciously she has been staring at Claire.

"Are you sure you have everything you need upstairs?" says Claire. Vivienne stares. Is she trying to be funny? "Yes thanks, Claire. Well, goodnight then ... 'Night Alex."

He doesn't get up. " 'Night, Vivvy. Sleep well. We don't get up early on Sundays so you can have a good lie-in tomorrow."

Vivienne hovers by the door for a second and then leaves them alone in the firelight, feeling like a child sent to bed early and missing all sorts of imaginary excitement downstairs with the grownups. She had pictured Alex escorting her to her room, telling her if he touched her now he would have to have her immediately, but that he would come as soon as Claire was asleep.

Quickly she brushes her teeth, removes her make-up and rubs cream all over her body. Then she slides between the blue sheets and waits. After a long fifteen minutes she hears them come upstairs. The landing lights go out. Vivienne is breathless with anticipation. Please let Claire be tired, she prays. Let the old cow fall asleep quickly.

She strokes her breasts, warm and swollen with longing and rubs her hands up and down her anxious thighs. Oh, hurry up, Alex!

Ten

VIVIENNE WAKES TO find Alex drawing the blue hessian curtains on a dull early-November morning. He has brought her some tea.

She smiles, remembering her pent-up passion of the previous night. It all seems different now watching Alex in his red towelling robe and scruffy leather slippers. She is pleased to see he is wearing pyjamas, something he never does when he spends a rare night with her. He hitches them up to perch on the bed and for the first time she notices the prominent blue veins under the dark hairs on his legs.

He says: "It's marvellous having you here, Vivvy. Thanks for being so nice to Claire; she was very nervous about you coming and how it would all go off."

Claire, nervous? "I thought you said it was her idea."

"It was, but she was still worried about how we would all get on." Alex strokes her hair, chasing a long strand that leads beneath the covers to her breast. "She likes you, you know. She thinks you have a lot of potential."

Vivienne stiffens. His hand on her breast is irritating but she daren't tell him to stop. Bloody man. Why couldn't he have taken advantage of her last night when she was feeling randy?

"When did she tell you that?"

"After you'd gone to bed last night. God, Vivvy, you do look beautiful in the mornings?"

Vivienne nearly bites his hand. If he doesn't stop squeezing her tit like that she *will* bite him. How dare they sit downstairs together, cosily discussing her potential! What the fucking hell was that supposed to mean, anyway?

"What do you mean, darling, potential?"

"Ask Claire, angel, she's much better at explaining these things than me. It's all to do with basic development of personality and that sort of thing." Alex speaks like a child reciting a poem he's been forced to memorise. "Claire's quite hot on people learning to stretch themselves mentally to their full capacity. That's why she gets annoyed with me when I don't get on with my book."

"Oh I see." Vivienne does see but is reluctant to admit it. "Back to the self-discipline lecture we had last night, then?"

"No, don't knock her, Vivvy. The thing about Claire is that basically she's right. Her standards are high, both for herself and for other people. But what she's done is to sort out the value of things; she is quite clear in her own mind what is right and wrong and will never go along with the tide of popular feeling, or give false weight, false value to anything just for the sake of an easy life." He stands up. "Well never mind all that now. Sunday morning is hardly the time to get all earnest about life. As you get to know Claire better you'll understand more of what I'm getting at. I'm popping out to get the papers now. Is there anything I can get you?"

Hesitantly, she asks for some cigarettes, though her mouth tastes of sawdust from smoking too many yesterday. I can't possibly listen to Claire's views on self-discipline, she thinks wryly, unless I have a fag in my hand.

It is half past eleven when she arrives downstairs, noticing on her way that Claire's strange painting of the horses has been moved from the sitting room to the bottom of the stairs. Vivienne wonders why Claire has chosen this particular morning to move it.

Her hostess is in the kitchen, wearing her huge apron and efficiently rubbing seasoned flour on to a large piece of beef. Claire says good morning, and did you sleep well. Vivienne is suddenly aware that Claire seldom smiles when you expect her to: most people automatically smile when they say good morning, but Claire's look is one of mere polite enquiry.

"Would you like some breakfast? I was just going to make a big pot of coffee and you could have scrambled eggs, or bacon and sausage, whatever you like."

Vivienne decides on just toast, and volunteers to make the coffee, feeling gawky and helpless beside Claire's small busy frame. With her added height, she thinks, she should be able to make Claire look insignificant, but somehow it doesn't work out like that.

"No, no," says Claire. "All I have to do is switch on the percolator. Park yourself on a stool and enjoy doing nothing, my dear. Alexander will be back with the papers in a minute."

"Are you sure there's nothing I can do to help? Peel potatoes, perhaps?" Oh mother dear, you would be proud of me.

"It's very kind, but you know, Sunday lunch really cooks itself. The meat, potatoes, and Yorkshire do themselves in the oven and I'm cheating with frozen sprouts. I can't understand why so many women try to create such a mystique out of cooking a Sunday roast." She slams the oven door shut. "There, that's done. Do you like cooking, Vivienne?"

"I've never had the chance to do very much. My mother always made such a fuss about the whole thing, ending up with a shiny face, a million pans to wash up and platefuls of brown food all tasting of Bisto."

Claire doesn't laugh. "I know exactly what you mean. You didn't do any cooking while you were in France?"

"No, my Aunt Rose had a very ferocious cook who always chased us away if we got anywhere near the kitchen. Edouard and I used to spy on him through the window sometimes, and he would chase us out of the house, shouting and swearing. I think he enjoyed it really. Kept his waistline down."

"Edouard?" Claire's French accent is hard and precise, and again not a glimmer of a smile.

"A sort of cousin, my uncle's son by his first marriage," says Vivienne.

Claire says nothing and pours the coffee. But Vivienne feels forced to continue, like an interviewee who rushes to fill what she feels is an awkward silence, not realising she has been tricked into saying more than she intended.

"He's a few years older than me," she gabbles, "and I think he found me a little young." She doesn't mention that apart from their game with the mad cook, Edouard completely ignored her.

Vivienne waits for Claire to follow this up but instead she says,

"I shall be in the West End next week for some early Christmas shopping. Would you like to meet me for lunch?"

Vivienne, surprised, has to agree. She isn't sure she wants to spend her entire lunch hour alone with Claire but it seems impossible to refuse. "Where shall we meet?"

Claire suggests the main entrance of Wallis and Steadman, so they can have lunch in the store restaurant.

"Fine," agrees Vivienne, hoping Claire will be paying. "I have a friend who runs the Miss London department there," she says importantly.

"Have you?" Claire starts to sort the potatoes. Their tough, grey-brown skins remind Vivienne of the elephants she and Alex watched at the zoo in the summer. "Yes, Stella the girl in the flat next to me. She—" Vivienne tails away, remembering.

"Yes," says Claire, peeling steadily. "I think I met her. Shall we meet at one o'clock then?"

To Vivienne's relief Alex appears with the papers. He's had to go all the way up to the pub to get Vivienne's cigarettes. Sorry he's been so long.

"Would you like some coffee or are you a bit past that now?" asks Claire amiably.

"Well..."

"You could finish up the Veuve du Vernay then. I should grab the newspapers you want, Vivienne, because when Alexander gets hold of them they end up in the most awful mess."

"Lying bitch. By the way, I met Scotty in the pub. He's my agent," he tells Vivienne. "He was rushing off, of course, in a lather in case dear Ishbel should smell the demon drink on his breath. Anyway, we're invited round for a drink as usual on Christmas Eve."

"Oh Lord. I suppose that's a hint for us to start organising our own party. We always have one on Boxing Day," Claire explains to Vivienne.

"The trouble is," says Alexander, "they are always such a roaring success we can never get out of holding the next one. People start reminding us in June. Why we chose Boxing Day in the first place I can't imagine; it's the worst day to have a party. You feel terrible after all the boozing you've done over the previous week, all your bonhomie has run out and the shops aren't open if you've forgotten anything. Claire, do you remember that time..."

Vivienne shifts uneasily on her stool like a little girl on best behaviour at the tea table, forced to listen to the adult's conversation while itching to get down and run about. Her face feels as if it's covered with dried egg white in the effort to keep smiling and interested.

After lunch they sprawl in the comfortable sitting room, discussing items from the papers. Vivienne is surprised at Claire's breadth of knowledge: she appears to have something valid to say on any topic that arises.

Driving back to Chelsea later alone with Alex she asks him about it.

"Yes, she's like that," Alex says. "She tries very hard to be interested in everything she comes into contact with: to extract the best out of it and discard the rest. It's partly the way she was brought up, of course. Her father was a publisher, a very well-informed man and a very strict one. Claire admired him tremendously. I think I told you, his only weakness was for toffees."

"Very bad for your teeth."

"Oh, he didn't have any. He sometimes used to forget and leave his false set on the breadboard overnight. Claire used to practically die of shame if I saw them."

"What about her mother?" Vivienne asks quickly, not wanting to think of Alex and Claire young and in love.

"She was a Scot and died when Claire was born. Claire doesn't like to talk about it. For a long time she felt guilty at being alive at all and worked very hard to win her father's approval, learning everything he set her to learn, trying to be exactly the sort of person he demanded she should be. He sent her to her mother's old boarding school in Edinburgh and she did quite well there."

Quite well, thinks Vivienne. Head Girl and a scholarship. "It's odd, then, that she didn't marry someone like her father."

"Claire had never met anyone like me. All the people she'd

been introduced to *were* like her father ... serious and full of purpose."

"Why did she marry you then?" Vivienne persists.

"Oh various reasons. I think she was thrown off her guard, and once she'd recovered and had a good steady look at me, her brave Scots reforming zeal came to the surface. She's still at it, as you know."

"Don't you mind?"

"I'm used to it, I suppose. I admire Claire because in this world of instant sensation with everyone doing their own thing and to hell with everyone else, it's very refreshing to know someone with standards and values that they are prepared to stick to come what may. I mean, kids today grow up knowing they can have a fuck at fourteen, a car at eighteen, a mortgage at twenty-two, a divorce at twenty-seven ... it's all so easy. Too easy. They don't have to work for anything and they're in danger of ending up like the girl in the song, saying petulantly, 'Is that all there is?' "

Which is more or less what Claire was saying last night, Vivienne thinks as they arrive at the flat. Alex escorts her upstairs and they make love in the chilly room after he has given her 10p for the gas meter. They don't make love very easily as she knows he would prefer not to be too long away, and also she wants to be alone.

Eleven

"'LURE HIM INTO *the bathroom, pour out two glasses of champagne and discover the thrill of making love in the bath'.*" Stella throws the magazine on the floor. "*'Ten Ways to Entice Your Man'.* God, what a load of rubbish. Actually, it's very dangerous to fuck in the bath."

"Why?" Vivienne helps herself to more of Stella's Tia Maria and dips a piece of cotton wool into the dish of hair bleach she is using to retouch Stella's roots.

"Because it's possible to get an air bubble trapped inside you which could explode and splatter you in tiny unromantic bits all over the ceiling. Bob told me. Of course, Bob is so fat there's hardly room for the soap when he's in a bath, let alone me."

Vivienne laughs and takes a cigarette from the silver cigarette box on Stella's coffee table. She doesn't feel guilty about drinking her friend's booze and smoking her cigarettes, as Stella has just explained that they are all donated by Bob. Hidden away from Bob in a hat box on top of the wardrobe is a further cache of American cigarettes acquired from a New York boyfriend on one of his twice-yearly visits.

Stella's room is more of a museum for her trophies. The bookshelf holds a dozen assorted paperbacks and a magnum champagne bottle (in memory of the millionaire ex-boyfriend). On top of the portable colour television set (from the American) is a huge brandy glass (Bob) containing a collection of bookmatches from every smart restaurant and nightclub in London. Art Nouveau posters filched from work are pinned to the walls and the chest of drawers by the bed (a moving-in present from her mother) is graced by a cluster of expensive French perfumes sold by international airlines. The bedcover is an exotic African print, splashed with purple and green.

"Don't tell me you actually bought that yourself?" asks Vivienne.

"No, a West Indian lady I used to know gave it to me. She was three times my size and insisted on giving me cakes because she thought I needed fattening up. I kept telling her I was overweight already but she just used to laugh hysterically and tell me fat in leg is good in bed. We had some good laughs together, she and I. Not like the bloody mob I saw coming home on the train today—two Africans with an English guy. The younger African was like a child, full of wonder for the world, very naïve and enthusiastic, talking loudly about something, getting very excited and waving his hands around. The English guy was listening to all this very intently, being Very Encouraging and terribly conscious that here he was on a train, in public, with two Africans for heaven's sake. Quite pleasant chaps really, and of course one feels one has to do one's bit doncha know. What got me was the expression on the other African's face. He was obviously far more intelligent than the other two and he didn't say anything, but just stared at the English guy with a look of bored contempt. Then they got off at their station and went their separate ways, the English guy doing a lot of cheerios and good to see yous and obvious handwaving. Honestly Vivvy, I felt quite sick."

Vivienne puts the top on the bottle of bleach and wipes her hands on her jeans, saying nothing but thinking suddenly of

Claire. She would, Vivienne is sure, behave in exactly the same way as that Englishman with Africans or anyone else she felt was her social inferior.

Stella stretches out on her bed and offers more Tia Maria.

"I'd better not," Vivienne says reluctantly, "I'm going to the dentist tomorrow and I don't want to knock the poor man out with a whiff of my breath. He's incredibly good looking, too."

"You've got no chance, Vivvy. How can you hope to impress a guy when you're lying there dribbling, with what feels like half a bicycle in your mouth, giving him a perfect view up your nose?"

Vivienne, choking, says she'll have to make do with Alex then; she's taking the afternoon off work and he's coming round. However her conversations with Stella start, they always get back to Alex and Claire.

"Oh God," Stella groans. "Why on earth don't you find yourself a new man? It's pointless mooning around like this over a married bloke. You should play the field a bit while you've got the chance."

"I love him Stella."

"You mean you love what he does to you in bed."

"I don't want to sleep around."

"Having more than one lover isn't sleeping around, it's common sense. If you have just one bloke you're asking to be taken for granted, particularly if he's married and has to spend a decent amount of time with wifey. But if you have several blokes you call the tune. You won't be lonely or broody because you just won't have the time. And what will you do when Alex gets tired of you and runs away home to wifey?"

"It isn't like that. He loves me. Don't groan like that, he does love me. And Claire quite understands the situation, she accepts me because she loves Alex. A woman can't be all things to a man, you know."

"And one man can't be all things to a woman! You've just proved my point."

"I've proved nothing of the kind," says Vivienne irritably. "You're not trying to understand. Anyway, I'm having lunch with Claire at your rotten store on Thursday. Can I borrow a couple of quid in case she isn't paying?"

Alex arrives the following afternoon cheerfully brandishing a bottle of wine. For the next couple of hours they drink and make love, in the armchair, on the floor and finally, laughing, in bed. He tells her about his mother, a marvellous woman he says, who spent much of her married life in the heat of India and now finds it hard to adjust to a life of sedate English widowhood in Cheltenham.

"She wears pastel lilacs, lavenders and blues all the time and never, but never, goes out without a hat, even to hang out the washing. In India they all thought she was terribly eccentric and adored her, but of course in Cheltenham they very determinedly take no notice at all."

Vivienne thinks she sounds wonderfully colourful compared to her own drab mother. Then she feels disloyal, and vows to be especially considerate to her mother when she goes home this weekend.

"Let me tell you a joke," she says, refilling their glasses. "A West Indian friend of Stella told it to her. There was this woman who was having affairs with three men. This particular day her husband went off to work and as usual the doorbell rang and in came Eric, lover number one. They had just embraced in the hall when the doorbell rang again. 'My God, my husband!' she cried and told Eric to hide under the stairs. She opened the door and there stood Horace, lover number two. No sooner had they reached the bedroom than the doorbell rang again. 'My God, my husband!' she cried, and told Horace to hide in the bathroom. She opened the front door and a voice said, 'Hello deh,' and it was Sambo, lover number three. She took him into the kitchen and then the doorbell rang again. 'My God, my husband!' she cried and pushed Sambo into the larder. It *was* her husband, very suspicious. He rushed to the cupboard under the stairs and found Eric. 'You're my wife's lover!' he yelled. 'No, no,' said Eric, pointing at the meters. 'I'm just the gas man.' So the husband rushed upstairs and discovered Horace in the bathroom. 'You're my wife's lover!' 'No, no,' said Horace, 'I'm just the plumber come to mend the tap.' Furious, the husband tore downstairs and discovered Sambo cowering in the larder. '*You're* my wife's lover!' he screamed. 'No, sah, no I ain't,' said Sambo. 'I's just the golly off the top of the jam!'"

As if on cue, Vivienne's door bell rings.

Claire! Oh God. Vivienne freezes as Alex shoots to his feet and, still naked, hidden behind the curtain, peers out of the window to the street below.

"Well it's not my wife," he says, clearly relieved. "There's a big Citroën parked down there and a middle-aged couple with a young man. The two males have reddish-blonde hair."

"Oh no!" Vivienne wails, snatching on her dress. No time for refinements like knickers and tights. "Alex, it's my aunt and uncle from France, with Edouard."

"Who's Edouard?"

"My half cousin; my uncle's first wife was French. Then he married my mother's sister. They're on their way to visit my parents and said they might call in on the way ... I completely forgot."

The doorbell sounds again, three insistent rings, and the elder of the two redheads steps back, craning his neck to look up at the window. Alex quickly dodges away. Vivienne scoops up his clothes and bundles them into his arms, saying frantically;

"Darling, please disappear into the bathroom and then you can get down the stairs and out once I've brought them safely in here."

"But why can't you pretend—"

"Alex, *please!*"

He laughs and obediently pads off to the bathroom on the landing, while Vivienne dashes about, straightening the bedcover, throwing wine and glasses into her wardrobe. Then she plunges downstairs and wrenches open the door.

"Vivienne my dear!" cries her uncle. "We had almost given you up!"

"I'm terribly sorry, I was in the bathroom and didn't hear the bell. Do come in everyone, it is nice to see you. Hello Aunt Rose," as her aunt pecks the air near Vivienne's ear, "and Edouard. I didn't know *you* were coming?"

They follow her upstairs. Edouard, tall and thin, his long hair flopping over silver rimmed spectacles, explains that he is between jobs so thought he may as well hitch a lift with his parents.

"Shall I take you to see the changing of the guard and all that rubbish?" asks Vivienne. Edouard smiles and says he'd rather see some strip clubs.

"Edouard!" Aunt Rose and her sister, Vivienne's mother, have much in common. "Well! So this is where you live, Vivienne," she says, wincing delicately.

"Yes Aunt Rose. It's not very marvellous, but London is expensive you know. Shall I take your coat?" Vivienne hangs up the shapeless dung-coloured garment, marvelling that for twenty years her aunt has staunchly refused to be influenced by any suggestion of French fashion flair and chic.

"Thank you, dear. I wonder," Aunt Rose leans forward conspiratorially, "if I could visit the little girl's room? We've been such a long time in the car."

Vivienne's stomach lurches. "What?" she says guiltily. "Oh, er, yes of course. I'll, er ... could you just hang on a sec, Aunt, I, er, I left some undies dripping in there." Surely Alex will be dressed and gone by now. Vivienne crosses the landing and taps softly on the bathroom door.

"Are you still there?" she hisses.

"Het i luddy poos," hisses back Alex.

"What?"

"I *pooooos!*"

"I can't hear you but for heaven's sake hurry up. My aunt is practically wetting herself."

Alex opens the door a fraction. "My *boots,* you bloody fool! Under the bed!" He slams the door shut.

Vivienne rushes into the kitchen and then joins the others in her room, saying brightly, "Shan't be a sec, Aunt, and meanwhile I've put the kettle on for a nice cup of English tea. Tell me, what do you think of my latest acquisition?" She points out a small piece of framed tapestry work given to her by Claire last weekend and now hanging at one end of the fireplace. As her visitors turn to look, Vivienne quickly whisks Alex's boots out from under the bed and into the carrier bag she brought from the kitchen. She feels quite stunned at her own brilliance, until she notices her aunt and uncle staring hard, not at the tapestry but at some other objects on the mantelpiece. A vibrant orange tie, some loose change, a pair of cuff-links and a man's watch.

Vivienne tries to speak but her mouth seems to be full of glue and for no reason she suddenly remembers she hasn't any knickers on. Smiling idiotically, she palms the objects into her carrier bag and backs out of the room, feeling like a third-rate burglar. She throws the bag into the bathroom and runs back into the kitchen. A heavily breathing Aunt Rose arrives ten seconds later, demanding to know what is Going On.

"Where does that door lead to, Vivienne?"

"It belongs to a girl called Stella I share the kitchen with who has the flat next door."

"Why are you sounding so peculiar?"

"I've been to the dentist, Aunt. The injection hasn't worn off yet."

"I see." Aunt Rose looks as if she is about to say something else but changes her mind and, houndlike, stalks out on to the landing.

"And which is the bathroom? May I use it now?"

The bathroom door opens and Alex emerges, mercifully clothed, holding the orange tie in one hand and his boots in the other.

Oh God, please let me die, prays Vivienne. Now. Immediately.

"I think you should introduce us," says Aunt Rose crisply.

"Oh yes, of course," Vivienne falters. "Er, Alexander Mallender, my aunt, Mrs, er, Madame Lejeune."

The temperature round Aunt Rose plummets to sub zero but Alex does not waver. "How do you do, Madame," he says, with his most charming successful-novelist smile. Vivienne waits for him to shake hands and drop his boots but he just says, moving smoothly towards the stairs: "I'm delighted to have met you and must apologise for having to dash off like this. I do hope you enjoy your tea. Good afternoon." Before they have time to recover, the front door has slammed.

Gloomily, Vivienne goes to make the tea. The reaction of the two men, she can see, is surprised amusement, while Aunt

Rose must be sitting on the loo hugging herself with glee as she plans to hot-foot it down to Sussex and enlighten Vivienne's mother.

Twelve

"AUNT CLAIRE, WHEN did you first realise you'd grown old?" Belinda had once asked, before being bundled out of the room by the horrified Joyce.

Claire remembers the incident now as she sits staring at her face in the pink and mauve rest room at Wallis and Steadman. You first realise you've grown old, she decides, when one day you look at yourself and think how tired you look, your skin crumpled and dull, your eyes ringed and worn as if from too many sleepless nights; and then you realise it isn't tiredness at all. You are always going to look like this, as if your face badly needs ironing. And it will get worse.

It is worse today, as she shifts uncomfortably in the padded pink chair and checks through her shopping, chiding herself for not having made a proper list at home. But it had, she thinks, been the curse that had disorganised her. She loathes the red sticky messy business of it all, the cotton wool saddled between her swollen legs and the pain that makes it agony to walk.

"Other women don't make such a stupid fuss," Alexander said, conned by advertisements of glowing, hatefully liberated girls, running, jumping and diving into sky blue swimming pools. "Other women use tampons and take special tablets," said Alexander, the only man Claire knows who is *not* a hypochondriac and does not turn ashen at the sight of blood. Claire retorted tartly that his extraordinary ability to ignore pain was probably due to the permanent anaesthetising effect of all the alcohol in his blood.

The special tablets have no effect on Claire, and she has tried the tampons. Once she crouched for two hours on the freezing stone floor of the Prefects Bathroom reading and rereading the luridly illustrated instruction sheet, convinced that her own insides couldn't possibly look like that, and even if she did get the thing in, it would be swallowed up in her womb and the school doctor would have to be told and the Headmistress and, horrors, her father. Finally, in a nervous sweat, she forced the tampon—which in her mind had by now assumed the proportions of a table leg—into her dry, unwilling body, and waddled self-consciously off to play hockey. At half time, unable to bear the searing pain any longer she fled to the changing room and to Joyce, a worldly girl who always spent hockey lessons lying down recovering from strange spells of dizziness. She watched Claire yanking frantically at the white communication cord and then announced laconically: "You are daft, Claire, no wonder it hurts. You've left the cardboard tube inside you as well! Don't you know *anything*?"

It was a fair comment. Claire's father did not remarry and left his daughter's sex instruction in the hands of his housekeeper, Claire's Edinburgh boarding school, and God.

The housekeeper was a middle-aged spinster who kept romantic paperbacks interleaved with her underwear and told the young Claire that all she had to do was be a good girl and wait for Mr Right. He would surely come along one day. Claire sneaked a look at some of the novels and gleaned that Mr Right was most likely to be named Stephen or Mark, or Angus if he was Scottish. From the endings of the books she learnt that he would take her in his arms and as she melted under his kiss they would turn to watch the sunset and face a brighter, more hopeful tomorrow ... together. Claire, thirsting for more accurate information, had high hopes of her school biology lessons but the teacher stalled at the diagram of the male rabbit's genitals. It was rumoured that her predecessor had daringly drawn on the board a diagram of a man's genitals and ordered the class to copy it down, remarking, "this is not for your examination, girrls, but you will find it useful for fu-turre raiferrence." The school governors had not invited her to return the following term. God, represented in practical terms by Claire's Scripture mistress, was even more unhelpful, giving the girls lessons in purity and instructing visiting workmen, during a sweltering summer, not to take their shirts off in front of the girls, and the girls not to lounge around or, especially, *lie down* in the grounds as it would excite the workmen.

Eventually, after Claire had made enough public *faux pas,* her father was goaded into action and during one school holiday she found lying on her bed a pamphlet, *Telling Your Daughter, Part* 2. She never discovered what happened to Part 1, but with the help of Part 2, Joyce, and jokes she didn't fully understand about pokers in oak trees she pieced it all together and didn't much like what she saw. Impossible to believe her adored father had done those things to her poor mother!

Claire met Alexander when she was teaching in a dull northern town where he was chief reporter on the local newspaper. Several unsatisfactory affairs had almost completely diminished her interest in sex, so the passion Alexander aroused in her surprised them both. They married in her home town of Bristol, Alexander accompanied by his mother in lilac velvet, his father querulous in a wheelchair, a few of his collection of brothers and a mass of drunken friends. She had Joyce and her father. Her mother's relatives, with hard

Scots vengeance, refused to come when they learnt it was not to be a Church wedding. When, later, they heard about the reason for the marriage they sat together in the austere front parlours of their dark Edinburgh homes and shook their heads. "Poor Margaret," they chanted, elevating Claire's mother to something like saint status, "she should never have married that bustling little Englishman ... it's bad blood indeed."

Claire knows her husband is still deeply ashamed of all they did to try and get rid of the baby. She dare not tell her father, they had no money for an abortion and Alexander would not let her face a back-street affair. So one evening they had drunk themselves silly and she had lain crying on her bed while he punched her stomach, over and over again until she was screaming and he was sobbing and they knew it wasn't going to work.

Two years after the wedding her father died, leaving her the Bristol publishing house to control and the house in Highgate. They moved to London, and while Alexander got a job in Fleet Street, Claire busied herself setting up a London office and appointing people to run the Bristol business for her. Then Robin was drowned, and there was the drink and then Switzerland, clean and pure, and feeling better, feeling whole again. It was good for a while after that, even when Alexander was made redundant. He wrote *Street* and seemed to enjoy setting up his own PR company. There was the occasional girl, each one marked by the change in the scent on his clothes, but nothing for Claire to worry about.

Now there was this girl. This one was different. This one she had to take out to lunch and be pleasant to. At the time, the invitation had seemed such a good idea, to find out more about her and establish for both of them Claire's firm control over the situation. But now her stomach hurts, her legs ache, her head throbs. She thinks longingly of bed and a hot water bottle; the last thing she wants to do is entertain her husband's mistress to lunch.

Mistress, she reflects, is putting it rather strongly. The word conjures up images of witty glamorous women, fashionably if not tastefully dressed, sure of themselves and the love of the men they have borrowed.

Vivienne, standing waiting inside the big main doors of the scented store, looks young, faintly sulky and very wet. She is trying, unsuccessfully, to force a dripping red fold-up umbrella into a large canvas handbag.

Vivienne is furious. She made a hash of a difficult piece of translation this morning and her boss insisted on discussing it all with her, line by boring line. Just when she wanted to get away early for lunch, too. Her mother phoned twice, and was finally very rude to the switchboard girl, making it clear she knew Vivienne *was* there as she had rung the flat four times. Vivienne is sickly aware that the confrontation when her mother finally catches up with her will be classic. She wishes she had the simple courage to tell her mother to bugger off and let her run her life, particularly her sex life, her own way.

Then, of course, it had to be raining. Her tights are splashed and this stupid, folding umbrella is behaving like a rebellious deckchair, determined to make a fool of her. She feels totally out of place in this elegant store, surrounded by expensive-smelling fur-coated women with tiny crocodile handbags dangling on fine gold chains from their leather-gloved wrists.

How on earth do they get everything *in* those silly bags, she wonders. Claire, she notices, is more practically dressed in a blue wool trouser suit and black velvet peaked cap.

"Where's all your shopping?" Vivienne asks as they walk towards the lift.

"Oh, I took it all to the gift wrap counter, and then it will be delivered. I'm afraid I refuse to act as pack horse just because Christmas is coming."

Claire looks paler than usual but her eyes, Vivienne notes, are as vibrant as always, boring into you, adding extra weight to everything she says.

"If it gets out of control the best thing to do is jump up and down and hope you're up when it crashes," Vivienne says, embarrassed by the enforced intimacy of the lift.

"Really?" Claire, her mind on Christmas presents, sounds bewildered.

Hell, thinks Vivienne, she isn't what you might call the most relaxing person in the world to be with. And whatever are we going to talk about? Girlish trivia about clothes and make-up? Hardly Claire's style, and anyway, Claire doesn't wear much make-up. Remembering her new pink-toned eye shadow and matching lipstick Vivienne feels superior, and marginally more confident.

"I think it would be a good idea if we had the set lunch, Vivienne, if you haven't too much time," Claire says, after the heavily-corseted manageress has bossed them to a table.

"It's all right, I can push it to two-thirty today instead of two, so there's not too much of a rush." God, that bloody translation to be redone, and mother bullying the switchboard girl again ... don't think about it. Enjoy your lunch; the money you borrowed from Stella will cover it. Now for heaven's sake think of something sociable to say to Claire.

Vivienne smiles, suddenly remembering a play she saw where the wife has lunch with her husband's mistress and discovers that they both, for various reasons, hate him so much they join forces and plot his death.

"I got Alexander some beautiful silk shirts," Claire says, wondering why Vivienne is grinning like that.

"Oh yes. Have you nearly finished your shopping?"

"I'm getting on, the worst is done anyway. Some other afternoon I shall enjoy myself pottering round choosing books for people."

"Trouble is," says Vivienne, heavily polite, "there are always so many one wants to buy for oneself."

"Yes, quite."

Simultaneously they both think: oh God, I suppose I shall have to buy something for *her*.

"What will you do for Christmas, Vivienne? Join your family at home?"

"I don't know. Yes, I suppose so." Unreasonably, Vivienne realises she has almost been expecting to spend Christmas with Alex. "Things are difficult at home at the moment because they keep on and on at me to marry the boy next door." Vivienne makes a face and then, feeling childish, wishes she hadn't.

"And of course you don't feel ready to," says Claire, dredging up the maturely sympathetic voice she has used on so many occasions in the past to unmarried prospective mothers.

"Of course I don't." God, what a stupid thing to ask. How could anyone involved with Alex even contemplate marrying anyone else, let alone Doug.

Claire is pleased with the way the conversation is going. "Well, it's foolish to rush into marriage. And I expect in London it is quite easy for an attractive girl like you to have lots of boyfriends, isn't it?"

Vivienne stares hard at her empty soup plate. She means, how many men have you slept with? "It depends," she says carefully, aware of Claire waiting to snatch up her words and bear them off for ruthless analysis. "It depends on what you want. You meet lots of men who just want to get you into ... who just want you for one thing, you know, but if you want to have a proper relationship it's much harder."

"Yes I can quite understand," Claire says, ladling mouse-coloured tartar sauce on to her plate. "It's completely against your principles, then, to experiment sexually with different men?" She was going to add "and women" but Vivienne's outraged face stops her.

"Of course it is."

"Why?"

"Because I don't sleep around, that's why." I'll hit her in a minute, thinks Vivienne. Instead, she bites back: "Did you sleep around before you met Alex?"

"Yes, but I didn't call it sleeping around. I simply reasoned that I was young, unattached and at the same time I knew practically nothing about sex. The only way to learn was, obviously, by doing it." Claire watches this sink in.

"Alex is teaching me all I want to know, thanks." Hell, the woman isn't human. There isn't a flicker of anger, jealousy, *anything* on her face. She looks as if we're discussing whether to watch Panorama or the horror movie.

Claire is unmoved, because the jealousy she feels for her husband is not sexual, but, remembering the passion Alexander once stirred in her, she can quite understand the intensity of Vivienne's feelings. She goes on: "But inevitably, Vivienne, you learn something new from each person you know. I don't mean just sexually of course. You are an intelligent girl, obviously interested in developing your mind, being open to new ideas and stimulated by contact with other people. Well why not do the same thing with your body and develop that to its full potential? Experiment, in every direction you can, while you're young and without too many responsibilities." Claire eats her last potato. Oh dear, the girl obviously wishes that fish she's stabbing were me. I'd better talk about something else.

Vivienne is remembering the time her mother came to tea: "It's me I'm interested in mum. I want to find out who I am and what I can do. I want to stretch a bit, find out what my limits are ..."

As the green ice cream arrives Claire breaks the silence and invites Vivienne over to Highgate on Sunday.

"I'm supposed to be going home, but I'm not sure how long I'll be welcome for, frankly." Vivienne smiles half conspiratorially wondering if Claire knows about the fiasco with Aunt Rose and Alex.

"Well if you get fed up come for Sunday lunch. We're having people to dinner on Saturday so Sunday will just be leftovers disguised as cottage pie I'm afraid."

Claire settles the bill, waving aside Vivienne's tentative grope for her purse. They finish their sweet and leave the restaurant, each feeling depressed and anxious to be rid of the other.

"It's still raining!" exclaims Vivienne at the front door. "I hate the tube when it's like this, don't you? All steamy and dank like a bathroom full of dripping clothes. Still, at least you'll miss the rush hour." And you haven't got to go and slog in an office for another three hours.

For once, Claire isn't listening. The pain that before lunch had nibbled is now taking huge bites out of her stomach. "It'll be murder trying to get a taxi," she says, peering into the gloom of wet afternoon traffic. Ignoring her Scottish conscience's outraged screams of extravagance she hands the enquiring doorman 50p. Obediently, magically, he produces a taxi. "Thank God," says Claire. Home, bed, warmth, sleeping tablet. She turns to Vivienne who is hovering balefully in the doorway, fiddling with her umbrella.

"Can I give you a lift?"

Thirteen

IT IS STILL raining on Friday evening as Vivienne joins commuters and the tribe of other weekending girls at Victoria Station. November. Nine months ago she was limply making her way across the station to meet Alex for their weekend in Brighton, almost fainting at the thought of all that was before them.

"Look at all those girls," Alex had laughed then. "You see them every weekend at Victoria, standing round clutching huge bunches of flowers like forlorn bridesmaids at the fag end of a wedding. They dutifully take the flowers home to mum, and on Sunday night they spill into the station again, carrying more foliage, this time from mum's garden."

Artfully, Vivienne prises herself into the only remaining six inches of seat on the packed train. People mutter and squeeze up to make room. She is only just in time. As the train moves off, she wonders if, somewhere on the station, a young girl with damp knickers and thumping heart is walking to meet her lover. It had been such a lovely weekend in Brighton, so special and perfect. Why on earth had she let Alex involve her with Claire like this? It had been so much easier when she didn't know Claire, when his wife was just some vague, drab figure lurking off stage. It had all been such fun before. Now she is all tied up with Claire and her talk of "potential," and Alex isn't hers any more because whatever they do, wherever they are, she keeps seeing Claire's grave face looming over them. And Claire isn't fun. All the time, Vivienne has the impression she's being judged, and found wanting. She makes Alex seem different, too, less like a lover, not so exciting.

The train lurches and stops, it seems forever, at a signal. Vivienne stares listlessly out into the night, watching the elongated tadpoles of rain swim down the grimy window. If the train is late she will miss her connecting bus and have to walk the mile home. Wearily, she lights a cigarette, not really enjoying it amidst the crush of wet mackintoshes, the smell of sodden wool. She had dodged talking to her mother yesterday by sending a postcard confirming her arrival home tonight as arranged. The postcard showed Buckingham Palace; her mother would like that. Vivienne's mother is the only person she knows who stands up to attention when they play the national anthem on television.

Vivienne always has mixed feelings about going home. Inevitably, there are rows, arguments, recriminations, accompanied by tears and slammed doors. But at the same time, home is her refuge from the hurts and disappointments of the world outside. It means warmth and safety, a fridge full of food, the comfort of the known against the unknown. There have been some weekends when Vivienne has boarded the train back to London and huddled in a corner in tears, cowed by the prospect of returning to her cold room, the struggle to make her money last, the feelings of loneliness and uncertainty. She has longed for someone, anyone, to be waiting at Victoria to meet her and daydreamed that perhaps, magically, Alex would be there, smiling and waving on the other side of the barrier. But of course, he never was.

The train is late. Vivienne humps down her case, puts up her umbrella and walks briskly out of the suburban Sussex station, resigned to a long walk in the rain.

"Hey! Vivvy!" Surprised, she sees the big Citroën ease

to a halt beside her. Edouard opens the door. "I waited for three London trains; if you weren't on this one I was going off to sulk in the pub." He smiles and pushes the long red hair off his face.

"Oh Edouard, this is nice of you." As always when people are unexpectedly kind, Vivienne feels near to tears.

"It's all right." He speaks soothingly. "I thought we might have a quick drink together. Actually I was glad to get out of the house. There's a terrible atmosphere."

"Oh. I can guess what about."

Edouard offers her a cigarette and drives off down the dimly-lit main street of the town.

"Well, your mother tried to phone you at your flat last night but each time she said she got the same girl with various assumed foreign accents insisting you weren't there. Your mother thinks it was you."

Vivienne laughs and chokes on the cigarette. "Goodness, I'd forgotten how foul these French things are. No, it wasn't me, it was Stella."

"Well, I thought I'd come and warn you."

"Thanks. Look, there's a pub just there on the right."

Stella had shared a bottle of champagne with Vivienne last night to celebrate the buying trip to New York her store is sending her on next month. She had chattered on excitedly, until Vivienne had protested:

"Now do stop yakking about New York, will you, and tell me what I can say to calm my mother down tomorrow."

Stella gargled with her champagne: "Tell her to mind her own bloody business."

"Mind your own bloody business!"

Mrs Tyler grips the steam iron a little harder with her small plump hand and grimly pursues a wayward crease in her husband's shirt. For as long as Vivienne can remember, all discussions classified by her mother as "difficult" have taken place with Mrs Tyler barricaded behind her ironing board, the perfection of the ironing increasing in direct proportion to the level of her embarrassment. Vivienne is gloomily confident that today her mother is poised to smash all previous records. She is slumped in an armchair just to the right of her mother so they can avoid looking straight at one another.

"I think," says Mrs Tyler, glaring at the shirt with round, boot-button brown eyes, "I think my daughter's virginity *is* my business. Your father and I did our best to bring you up properly, Vivienne."

That's right, drag poor old dad into it. He's missing his Saturday afternoon sport on the telly because you packed him and the others off for a "little drive" so you could have a go at me.

"... good home, you didn't need to go and live in that nasty flat. I knew something bad would happen to you. But we trusted you. We thought we'd brought you up to be decent, to have some respect for yourself. When you left here you were ... you were intact..."

I wasn't. I'd been fucking Doug, here in this room, on the carpet.

"... first thing you do when you leave is to go running off with a married man. I can't tell you how ashamed I felt when your Aunt Rose told me. And he'd been at your flat in the *afternoon!*"

"I love Alex, mum." Hell, I should never have admitted he was married.

"How can you possibly love a married man? That's adultery, not love. I suppose you'll be telling me next you're to be cited in a divorce case?"

"There's no question of his getting divorced."

"And what about his wife? What has she got to say about all this? Let me tell you, when she finds out what's been going on, there most certainly will be divorce proceedings. No decent woman would stand for her husband philandering round with young girls."

"It's not girls and it's not philandering." Vivienne pulls a thick strand of hair over her shoulder and starts to plait it.

"*I* certainly wouldn't have put up with your father playing around." Mrs Tyler bangs the iron triumphantly on to its stand and picks up a pile of handkerchiefs. "A man who's worth anything has some respect for his wife. This Alec—"

"A*lex*, mum."

"Well, whatever his name is, he's nothing but a worthless ... playboy!"

God, she's been sneaking looks at dad's *News of the World* again. She'll be calling Alex a Monster and Sex Maniac next.

"And Aunt Rose thought he looked thoroughly shifty."

"Yes, well, she didn't exactly see him at his best ..."

"Creeping out of the bathroom like that. And in the *afternoon!*"

"Oh, for heaven's sake mum, there's nothing terrible about making love in the afternoon. There's no law that says you have to do it on Saturday nights with the light out." Exasperated, Vivienne lights another cigarette, watching her mother's face turn crimson as she punishes a lace hanky.

"It's most disappointing, Vivienne. I was so looking forward to your wedding day and your white dress, feeling so proud watching your father give you away. I wanted you to be pure and untouched for your husband. Well it's all spoilt now isn't it? You won't be able to get married in white now, you know, not second-hand goods like you!"

"Stop talking in clichés, mum. Even the worst women's magazines don't spell out that sort of guff nowadays. Apart from the fact that I'm not interested in getting married, men now don't expect you to be a virgin."

Mrs Tyler pushes her newly-permed hair back from her forehead. She is feeling very hot. "I suppose you intend to live in sin then?" she challenges.

"I might live with a man, yes. I don't see the need for marriage."

Mrs Tyler collects herself, and grimaces. What she is trying to do is assume a wise, motherly expression like the pictures she's seen of Evelyn Home, or the Queen Mother. She takes a deep breath, assured now of familiar ground.

"Marriage, Vivienne," she surges, "marriage cements your love. And don't sneer. I'm your mother and I know. Marriage is an institution blessed by God ... Vivienne don't turn your head away like that when I'm talking to you."

Vivienne is staring moodily at the net curtains criss-crossing the window. Knicker pink, she thinks. How could anyone actually *choose* knicker-pink net curtains?

"As your mother, Vivienne, as the person who brought you into the world and brought you up and gave you the best of everything I could possibly afford, I don't like to think of you being used just for *sex*." Little drops of spittle shoot on to the steam iron and hiss applause.

"I'm not being used. I love him and he loves me and sex is just a part of it. We have a very good relationship."

"Relationship! You don't know what you're talking about. How can a child of your age talk of having a relationship with a man, a married man, twelve years older than yourself? It's disgusting and you both ought to be ashamed of your-selves. And what am I to tell all our friends here when they ask how you are, and are you engaged yet? A proper fool

I'm going to look, aren't I?" Mrs Tyler holds on to the ironing board as if she's afraid it will run away. "And what am I supposed to do when you get pregnant? I don't suppose you've thought of that, have you? Well don't think you can turn up here and—"

"I won't get pregnant, I'm on the Pill."

"You went to Dr Jackson and got the *Pill*?" Mrs Tyler is outraged.

"No, of course not. You know how that receptionist bird of his gossips. It would have been all over town. No, I went to a family-planning clinic in London."

"I see. How very modern."

With relief Vivienne notices that her mother has only a silk petticoat left to iron.

"And what about his wife?" Mrs Tyler bursts out. "She's the one I feel sorry for. Have you thought how you're breaking up a marriage? What's she going to feel when she finds out her husband has been cheating on her?"

Vivienne closes her eyes for a second and thinks of last weekend with Claire and Alex. She makes an effort, speaking slowly and clearly as she would to a backward ten-year-old.

"His wife. Knows all about it. She understands. We get on. Very well. Tomorrow. I am going to their house. For lunch."

Her mother's eyes bulge. "There? For Sunday dinner?"

O Sacred Institution. "Not dinner, mum. Just lunch. Cottage pie or something."

"They have cottage pie for Sunday dinner?" squeaks Mrs Tyler, genuinely confused. "Well, they sound very strange people to me, and I wash my hands of the whole affair. I'm bitterly disappointed, that's all, especially with your Aunt and Uncle here. You've let me down very badly, Vivienne, and your poor father." She slams the ironing board flat.

"I'm over eighteen, mum, and quite capable of leading my own life." Vivienne empties the full ashtray and lights another cigarette.

"And all this smoking. I suppose that's something else *he* encourages you to do?"

"Alex doesn't smoke."

"Mmm. So. You'll be leaving tomorrow morning then. And what time will madam be requiring her breakfast? You do still eat a normal bacon-and-egg meal, I suppose, and not fish and chips or cream cakes?"

"I shan't want anything, thanks, because I'm going back to town tonight. Edouard said he'd drive me as he's got to go in anyway."

"I'm surprised he has anything to do with you," is all Mrs Tyler can think of as a parting shot as she surges importantly away with the clothes horse.

Edouard, Vivienne realises, is dying to have lots to do with her. He has been watching her all day, his blue eyes amused and interested behind his glasses as she moved around the the house, provocative in her short flared skirt. Pleased, she had put on as much of a display for him as she could get away with without Aunt Rose noticing. Four years older than Vivienne, Edouard had regarded her as a silly little girl when she stayed with his family in France but now, for the first time, Vivienne is experiencing the power of success. Edouard knows Alex wants her, so now he wants her too. She decides she must have been looking particularly well fucked when he saw her that Wednesday afternoon at the flat.

Vivienne enjoys the drive back through Sussex in the Citroën. It is so pleasant to curl up in the big warm car, cut off from the cold world outside and listen to Edouard's cassettes of Sacha Distel. She feels faintly dangerous, knowing

Edouard is burning to touch her, that he is following every slight movement of her thigh where her cape falls open. She basks in his attention, his curiosity and her secret knowledge that she has bathed at home with special care, lathering her mother's scented soap on to her body and then admiring herself for a long time in the big bathroom mirror. She has put on her very best lacy black knickers and left off her bra. Her breasts now, against the blue sweater, feel heavy and urgent.

"You've grown up, Vivvy," Edouard says. "I remember you as a gangly, rather prim adolescent and now here you are having a torrid affair with a married man and looking very ..."

"Very what?" Indulgently, Vivienne stretches out her legs.

"Very ... womanly."

Satisfied, she draws hard on her cigarette. "Unfortunately, to my mother I'm still a child. I could be sixty-five and so long as I wasn't married she'd still think of me as a naughty little girl."

"What is all this with you and this guy then? Is he getting divorced?"

"No, of course not," Vivienne drawls. "We are just having a very interesting affair with no strings attached. I get on very well with Claire, his wife, and she quite understands the situation." God, all I seem to have done this week is parrot on about my lover's wife understanding him.

"That sounds very civilised."

"Yes, it is. As you're half French and work in Paris I would expect you to understand. But Aunt Rose, your father and my parents are all so bloody provincial, you really can't expect them to grasp the situation." Vivienne feels heady, as if she's just drunk a bottle of wine.

"Shall we stop for a drink?" she suggests.

He doesn't look at her. "Sure. You'd better direct me or I'll get hopelessly lost."

She takes him to a small, chintzy pub full of copper warming pans and the local Arran-sweatered Rugby heroes thrilling themselves with naughty songs in the corner by the bar. Edouard is delighted. He tells her about the new job he'll be starting when he goes back to Paris, as Chief Accountant in a new international cosmetics company. Vivienne half listens, lapping up his obvious admiration along with a stream of large Scotches, chain smoking and becoming increasingly very talkative. She feels incredibly witty and amusing. As the big brass bell rings for last orders, she is telling Edouard about this world of instant sensation.

"The thing is, Edouard, kids nowadays grow up expecting a fuck at fourteen, a car at eighteen, a mortgage—" He is looking at her intently but he isn't listening. She picks up her drink, sits back and waits.

"I want to go to bed with you Vivienne."

"Where?" What lovely long wrists he has.

"Anywhere you like. I'm supposed to be staying with some friend of my parents but they won't make a fuss if I don't turn up."

Vivienne thinks of her flat, not cleaned for a fortnight and looking like the wreckage after an air raid. Anyway, she doesn't fancy her smelly old divan tonight. Tonight she feels glamorous, ready for something more exotic than a bedsit.

All in a rush she says, "IwouldliketogototheHilton."

"Fine," Edouard smiles. Vivienne is amazed that it could be all this easy.

He says, "I should have known you wouldn't be happy in the back seat of a car. Do you think they'll give us a room this late at night? It'll be after midnight by the time we get there."

"Well I'm sure I can rely on you to arrange something satisfactory." Vivienne is staggered to hear herself talking like this. Bye, bye little girl in damp knickers, she thinks, as Edouard holds open the heavy pub door. The cold November air makes her head spin so she is glad to reach the car. Edouard starts the engine and impulsively turns to kiss her: she thinks immediately of Alex, who taught her to kiss.

"When I first met you, you used your mouth like a little rubber sucker," he had said.

Edouard loses his way in the winding Sussex lanes on the drive back, so it is after one thirty when they reach Park Lane.

"I think if you go round the side a little man will leap out and offer to park the car," Vivienne instructs. Thinks: thank you Stella. God, Vivvy, you *are* pissed.

The revolving front doors of the hotel find an answering chord in Vivienne's head as she stands just inside watching Edouard approach the reception desk. She has never been here before and feels disappointed. The newspaper kiosk and flower shop are closed, and the lobby isn't thronged with smart, jet-setting people as she had imagined. There aren't even any obvious prostitutes, as Stella had once described, picking up rich Americans, settling terms and disappearing upstairs all in a matter of minutes. Instead, there are only a few middle-aged couples waiting for the lift, the women in bunchy long dresses, the men hunched into bumpy dinner suits.

Three uniformed young men with brooms appear and carefully sweep round Vivienne. She wonders what they think of her. But they show no curiosity and she realises they have seen it all before. Suddenly the lights in the lobby seem bright and hard, beginning to hurt her eyes. Distantly, as if in a dream, she watches the receptionist reach behind him and take a key off the rack. He looks across at her but his face, too, registers no interest. In two seconds, Vivienne sobers.

I can't.

You must. Edouard has booked the room now.

I can't. It's sordid and nasty.

Rubbish. This is the Hilton, not a smutty back-street hotel.

I've been in a smutty back-street hotel with Alex and I didn't feel dirty then.

You can't back out now. Edouard would think you were a complete fool; he's used to more sophisticated women. Anyway, he's just signed the register. What's he supposed to do with a double room? It's not cheap you know.

I feel cheap. That receptionist, those boys sweeping up, they all know.

Don't be so childish and amateur-night.

I can't.

Quickly she turns and leaves the hotel, past an unsurprised doorman, and runs. She runs through the underpass connecting Park Lane with Knightsbridge, and then on down the cobbled backstreets that lead to Chelsea, lined with their pretty mews houses. She feels exhilarated, as if she could run forever, and pretends she is being chased by a highwayman.

When she arrives home, panting and laughing, she finds Edouard already there, leaning against the Citroën, smoking.

"Oh." She looks at him uncertainly.

"Would you like a cigarette?"

"Yes please, I've run out." He doesn't look angry, anyway. She hopes he isn't going to make her feel foolish.

He lights a Gauloise and hands it to her. It is a cold night, but she is warm from her running and all the alcohol. They sit together on the wide front steps of the house.

"Look, I'm very sorry. But I couldn't, you know ..."

"It's all right, I understand."

"You do?"

"Of course. I simply couldn't understand where you'd got to, that's all. At first I assumed you'd gone to the Ladies, but after I'd hung round for a bit one of the cleaning boys came up and told me you'd left. So I gathered what had happened and came back here."

"What about the room?"

Edouard laughs. "Well I had to go back to the receptionist and explain that in fact I didn't want the room any more because, I said, my wife is one of those incredible people who are always going into hotels and then deciding at the last minute they don't want to stay there after all. I really couldn't think of any other explanation on the spur of the moment. The man just looked at me, very bored, and said in leaden tones he quite understood, Sir, and I gave him the key and he gave me my money and that was that."

"Would you like some coffee?"

"Well, it is a little chilly out here."

The next day, Sunday, Vivienne wakes at seven o'clock with a fur-encrusted tongue and a memory of making coffee followed by nothing.

"You passed out," mutters Edouard from underneath the eiderdown in the armchair.

"What are you doing over there?" she says sleepily. "Come to bed and keep me warm." She removes the flowers from the glass jar on the bedside table and gulps down the water. "It's all right, Edouard, it's fresh water. About the only thing in this flat that is. Can you try and wake me up at eleven? I have to go out to lunch."

As he slips into the bed beside her, she thinks drowsily of Alex. Well, what the hell. I feel sexy and Edouard is here. I'll see Alex today but we won't be able to make love, and then I'll have to face Monday and rotten work feeling frustrated and snappy. Edouard is here, now, that's the main thing.

Fourteen

On Sunday afternoon Claire walks by the river at Kew. She has delivered some old clothes to friends in the Red Cross here and is wondering how long it will take Alexander to overcome his surprise at her going out, decide he has time to make love to Vivienne before she comes back, crush down any noble feelings or stabs of conscience and then go on and get it all over with. When she told him this morning she had to come over to Kew, Alexander was understandably confused but made no attempt to dissuade her. As usual with things she didn't really want to do, she announced it quickly and firmly before she had time to reflect and change her mind.

She looks at her watch. Three o'clock. She can't go back yet. Absent-mindedly she starts to shred an old tissue buried deep in the pocket of her wool coat. A young silver birch shivers daintily in the wind, outlined against the greeny-grey water and the softer grey of the sunless November sky. Two rowing crews race by, oars slicing through the water, the harsh cries of the coxes breaking the silence of the afternoon. The sound of their voices makes her feel lonely and she wishes she'd thought of bringing some bread for the ducks; they would at least be a sort of company. She remembers asking Vivienne once what she usually did at weekends and it amounted to wandering about pretending to have a purpose and feeling dismally alone. Like this. A young couple in love stroll past, and Claire envies their linked arms, their total absorption in one another.

Ten past three. Oh God, what am I doing? She wants desperately to run back to the car and drive quickly home.

No. *I* decided to invite the girl to the house in the first place and it's ridiculous to have her and Alexander mentally undressing one another the whole time, resenting my presence.

However she realises now it is one thing to acknowledge that intellectually and quite another to accept it emotionally.

I mustn't get engulfed in self pity or pathetic notions that I've been pushed out of my own home. But all the same, one would have thought the sex thing between them would have been on the wane by now. I will stay out till half past four, she decides; that's lighting-up time. Claire hates driving, particularly in the dark. Half an hour to drive back, that's an hour and a quarter to kill. She knows she could go and have a cup of tea somewhere, or drop in and beg one from friends, but she doesn't feel inclined to polite conversation. She wants to wallow in this grey day as she wallowed in alcohol when Robin died.

Robin. Poor little boy. You weren't wanted in the first place, and then I was so sure you were going to be a girl I could call Margaret after my mother, and dress up in pretty clothes. You were such an awful disappointment, red and wrinkled and slimy from my body. I felt so guilty at not being able to love you. A perfect mother they all called me; wonderful, devoted, kind, loving, understanding. They didn't know how much I hated the demands you made on me, the washing, the feeding, the crying, making me so *tired*. You knew I didn't love you, of course. It's probably why you were so late learning to talk. You used to sit on the floor, crying on and on, watching me watching you, knowing that sometimes I was longing to bash your head to pieces against the wall.

I didn't think motherhood would be like that, you see. No

one told me. Once I'd got used to the idea of having you, I thought it would be a fulfilling, rewarding experience. I thought you would enrich me as a person, make me the mature woman I always longed to be. But how could you, you tiny, dependent, messy little thing? How could you possibly know, or care, what I wanted from you?

I wasn't entirely selfish though. I thought as you got older I could teach you things. We would learn to read together, paint, listen to music and you could have a little kitten or puppy to look after. I was so looking forward to the wonder on your face. But by the time you were four we knew, secretly, didn't we, that we loathed one another, so it was Alexander you always ran to and laughed with and showed things to. You even looked like him.

Which made it worse, of course, on the beach that day, when I fell asleep and woke up to find you drowned, and my first reaction was one of relief. You were my son and I was glad you were dead. Glad to be free of the responsibility for the reproach in those young blue eyes.

They all thought I turned to drink out of remorse because I felt responsible for your death. They were kind to me, sending carefully worded letters in big writing on one side of the notepaper. But it was your whole wretched life I felt guilty about, wanted to blot from my mind. So when I came back from Switzerland and hung up the painting I'd done there, Alexander thought it was to serve as a permanent warning against drink. He tells people how brave I am, moving it about the house so I never become accustomed to it in one place, an everlasting reminder of my wicked ways.

In fact Claire uses the painting as she uses the Pill: to stop herself from having another child. Like all women, she occasionally feels dangerously "nesty" and then the painting is moved to her bedroom, the first thing she sees in the morning, the last at night.

She glances again at her watch. Twenty to four. Claire reaches the end of the tow-path and turns back. It is ironical, she thinks, this failure as a mother to my son when I am such an excellent emotional mother to my husband. I suppose I expected Alexander to be like my father. Adult, benign, someone who would always know the answers to everything, whose judgement one could respect and on whom one could rely absolutely. I remember my father like that, but I expect he was really a self-indulgent child, like most men. Alexander remembers him eating toffees all the time, but I don't recall that.

Men think it's just sentiment that women cry at weddings, but I believe it's sorrow for what no one has dared tell the bride. She thinks she's going to be a wife, but really she'll just be taking over from his mother. And if mother isn't the typical, matronly type, it's even worse, for the man will yearn for someone to give him comfort, pet him and make him the centre of attraction. He will suck at her breasts and lay his head with relief on her stomach. One day he will come home, helpless with laughter, with a story of how his girlfriend's frosty aunt caught him, shoes in hand, creeping out of the bathroom, and the wife will be expected to smile indulgently, sharing the joke.

"What's Alex's mother like?" Vivienne had asked, and Claire had replied conventionally, saying she was extremely vivacious and energetic for her age. What she wanted to say was that Mrs Mallender is a disorganised scatterbrain who after years in India has grown used to relying totally on other people to cope with the boring chores of life like shopping, cooking and housework. Her four sons adore her, regarding her as the quintessence of femininity with her drifting pastel dresses, picture hats; even, Claire groans, her lavender-scented lace hankies. "Mother, you're impossible," say her sons admiringly when the phone is cut off because she spent the money on new silk curtains. With Claire she is patronising, insisting, to Claire's fury, on calling her Elizabeth, the name of one of Alexander's ex-girlfriends of whom Mrs Mallender had approved because she was so colourless she provided no competition. But Alexander had married Claire, attracted by her practical ordered mind, excited by the passion he was able to arouse in this coolly intelligent woman.

A clock strikes four as some children dash in front of Claire and run, shouting, into one of the brightly-lit houses overlooking the river, slamming the door behind them. She walks on, feeling alone. It is odd, this loneliness, when usually she does not object to her own company. Married to someone like Alexander you grew to accept it. Early in her marriage Claire faced the fact that her husband was always going to have other women around and she could either go along with this or eat herself up with jealousy and run the risk of losing him.

"Take a lover and make him jealous," Joyce had urged.

She had tried it once, when Robin was a year old and she felt as if she were turning into a walking wet nappy. Howard was an old flame whose attentions she found flattering with Alexander out night after night, ostensibly "working" at Press parties. It was a relief to escape from baby talk and be treated as a civilised human being again, going to concerts and theatres or just enjoying some adult conversation laced with mild flirtation. Howard, a florid failed actor in his early forties, put on plays in the West End and entertained her with endless backstage anecdotes and rather bad mimicry of the casts. Alexander never queried her explanations about seeing Joyce, or doing something for the Red Cross and besides, she was always home and in bed before him. Well, home anyway. Alexander had probably been in bed somewhere in London since the middle of the afternoon.

One evening Howard drove her out of town to see a play on its pre-London run. Afterwards, they got involved in a party and it was only when he took five attempts to reverse out of the theatre parking bay that she realised how drunk he was. He wanted her to spend the night with him. She refused, foolishly adding that he was drunk and driving too fast which, naturally, only goaded him into driving more furiously.

Afterwards she remembered looking at the speedometer as they raced down the road towards the roundabout. It registered seventy-five. He must be able to *see* the roundabout, she thought, and glanced at the clock again. Still seventy-five. God, he's so drunk he can't see it! It was too late to speak, scream, even feel very afraid. Too late, as the car hurtled into the mound and Claire slithered down in her seat, Howard finally braked. The impact was milder than she expected and she sent a prayer of thanks to whoever it was on the local Rural District Council who voted for flower beds instead of concrete on roundabouts.

"I'm terribly sorry, Claire. I didn't see it," Howard said, thickly and unnecessarily. "I think I've bruised my ribs, but otherwise I seem to be all right. No bones broken. God, I feel awful, though."

"I'm not hurt, actually, Howard. But thanks for asking," said Claire, still shaken. He ignored her and half fell out of the car on to a bed of wallflowers. A minute later he announced that they were stuck, and would she mind helping him push.

"Look, I'm five foot three, eight stone and drunk. What good can I do?"

"Claire, darling, if I don't get this bloody car off here the bloody police will arrive and I'll get booked for being drunk in charge and, no doubt, wilful damage to council property, viz these fuck-awful wallflowers. Now will you get off your backside and help."

After five minutes' energetic heaving they had moved the car four inches and Howard was so exhausted he couldn't even swear coherently. Claire leaned wearily against the bonnet, wondering what on earth she was doing stuck on this God-forsaken roundabout, thirty miles from home at midnight with a creature like Howard. A few cars approached, but with typically British indifference sped on.

Then, unable to believe her eyes, she saw two figures in dressing gowns emerge from a nearby house. They walked up to the car, positioned themselves at the rear and pushed, assisted by a dazed Howard and Claire. Sulkily the car rolled on to the road and the two figures turned and headed back to the house. No one spoke and Claire's cries of thanks were ignored. Howard had already forgotten them because he discovered that the car was taking revenge for its removal from its idyll among the wallflowers: it wouldn't start.

"Now what do we do?" said Claire.

"You look as charming and appealing as possible, darling, because the police have just arrived."

Claire peered out of the window. "I've got news for you. It's not the police, it's the Army."

"It's both. They're military police. Oh Christ."

As it happened, the Army couldn't have been more helpful. They could arrange to have the car towed down the road to their HQ where some of their boys could fix it tomorrow. Meanwhile, did the gentleman have any friends in the area he could contact for assistance? Luckily, Howard did. Good, well he could phone them from HQ. If he and his wife wouldn't mind climbing into the truck? No trouble at all, Sir, we're getting out of this bloody lot next week so it's no skin off our nose ... makes a nice change from rounding up AWOL privates.

At HQ, Howard made his phone call. He was beginning to enjoy himself: "Hello Gilbert? It's Howard ... Howard Fleming. Yes. Yes I know it's gone midnight but I'm in a sort of police station near you. No, I haven't exactly been arrested but I'm in a spot of bother ..."

After what seemed to Claire a mile of long-winded, over-dramatised explanation he came back to announce that Gilbert would lend them his wife's car to travel home in. Howard then concentrated on chatting up the Army.

"I heard this story about a Private who was chosen to appear in those recruiting films, you know, all about the wonderful man's life and rugged challenge, join the professionals and all that, for which the Army very decently gave him quite a good fee. Thanks very much, said the Private and promptly used the cash to buy himself out. Is it true, do you think?"

Claire was beginning to feel sick, thinking how she was going to explain her very late arrival to Alexander, and wondering what his reaction would be. Thank God her baby sitter always stayed all night.

At last two cars scrunched to a halt outside. It was Gilbert and wife, both looking sleepy and both in dressing gowns and slippers. Later, Claire was sure everyone, including herself, Howard and the Army, had all been wearing dressing gowns that night.

After explanations and thanks had been disposed of, a sobered Claire and Howard drove off towards London. At

Claire's request, he dropped her at the end of her road. Somewhere a clock struck two as she groped in her bag for the key.

It wasn't there.

Her stomach somersaulted. It had to be there. But she knew it wasn't. She remembered now, it was with her car keys on the dressing table. Angrily, she glared at the door, willing it to open; she thought wildly of breaking a window. None of them would have been left open as the baby sitter was meticulous about closing all front windows before she went to bed. Well, she would have to ring the bell and pray the baby sitter heard before Alexander did. Making him jealous was one thing, but a brawl on the doorstep at two in the morning ...

Alexander opened the door, his eyes red-rimmed and watery. When he saw who it was he turned round and went unsteadily back to bed and was unconscious by the time Claire joined him. It was the one time she was thankful for his heavy drinking. The next day he nursed a hangover and obviously had no recollection of much that had happened the night before. He certainly asked no questions.

But it killed in Claire the desire for any more adventures. If she was going to have any affairs, she decided, she would be open about them and if Alexander was going to have any serious romances she would encourage him to be open too. Besides, she thinks, approaching Kew Bridge again, I don't want any more drama in my marriage. We've had quite enough already. I want my life and Alexander's to flow along like this river, peacefully, with high and low tides but no tidal waves. And I won't have my river polluted by garbage like Vivienne. She must be broken down and filtered off into bigger waters. It's all very well when you are Vivienne's age; you crave excitement then. I can understand that, but I do wish the girl could have selected someone other than my husband to provide it.

The light is fading now and Claire must hurry to reach home before dark. She passes a brilliantly-coloured poster for tomato soup and feels suddenly hungry.

"I wonder if they'll have my tea ready?"

That evening Vivienne lounges on the settee listening to Claire and Alex bickering amiably over the invitation list for their Boxing Day party. Claire has changed into a clinging long cream jersey dress and is sitting in the rocking chair writing down names on a big foolscap pad in her old-fashioned copper-plate hand. Alex has drawn up a chair beside her and is leafing through a tattered address book looking, Vivienne thinks resentfully, totally content.

Inevitably, she and Edouard had not got up at eleven and she had been late arriving here for lunch; then instead of the quiet afternoon browsing through the papers she had been looking forward to, Claire had cleared off to some charity do and Alex had insisted on fucking her over the kitchen table. It had seemed to go on for ever and her stomach still hurts from where the edge of the table had dug into it. He would want to do something a bit mad, she thinks, the one time I didn't feel like it, especially when I'd been with Edouard. Still, it wasn't bad going, two men in five hours, and both quite different. Edouard was impressively gentle, stroking and caressing her until she melted under him. Alex had been acting out a fantasy and was delighted with himself.

"Marvellous to think of my wife doing good at the Red Cross while I do you across the table," he had said, gripping her behind and thrusting into her. Afterwards he had taken her upstairs and bathed her, very tenderly, telling her how much he loved her, until she sat naked in his arms on the damp bathroom floor and wept.

"I'm sorry Alex. I didn't mean ... it's just that I didn't know we were going to ... that Claire was going out and I hadn't expected ..."

He dabbed at her eyes with the fluffy towel. "No, I know, angel. I think it's an incredible thing for her to do, really. I have an idea she did it deliberately, so we could make love."

"Oh come on. I know she does a lot of charity work but this is ridiculous."

"Don't be bitchy, Vivvy. Claire never does things by halves, remember, and having accepted you into our lives she would also accept that we make love when you come here. And of course we will be away next week visiting my mother—"

"You're going away?"

"Christ, didn't I tell you? Oh, I'm sorry. We always go and see her for a week before Christmas."

"When will you be back?"

"A week Monday, I think. Claire knows all the arrangements, we'll ask her."

"I see." Vivienne stood up and pulled on her sweater. "And you really think she gave us some time together because you're going away?"

"For heaven's sake, Vivvy, put your pants on or I shall have to have you again over the bath."

She quickly wriggled into her knickers. "Do you think that's why she went out?"

"What? Yes, I do." He held her to him and stroked her hair. "I think I'm a very lucky man having two wonderful women like this. I love you so much, angel, and I do appreciate that it isn't always easy for you. You won't ever stop loving me will you Vivvy?"

"I couldn't if I tried," she said.

Now she looks across at him and Claire, resenting their absorption in this party. She feels excluded, as no one has suggested that she should be invited, and they are laughing and talking about people she has never heard of. She finds it hard to accept that Alex and Claire had once lived a life in which she had no part, and doesn't like to see them now discussing something that is obviously not intended to concern her. They are the most important people in her world; when she is not with either of them she is thinking about them and because they are so essential to her, Vivienne has imagined they think of her in the same way. It comes as a shock now to see that they can plan a party and not consider including her.

She shifts round on the settee, envying Claire her composure. Vivienne is sure her own skirt is too short and her knickers have twisted up in her crotch. She squirms, trying to ease them, but finally gives up and lights a cigarette. Claire looks up.

"This must be very boring for Vivienne, Alexander, but I would like to get it settled before we go to your mother's."

"Sure. Would you like to watch television Vivvy? There's a good play just started." Not waiting for her reply, he reaches forward and turns on the set.

"Darling, there's some Suchard chocolate in the kitchen. Shall we treat ourselves?" Claire tucks her feet under her and lays down the pad on the marble-topped table. "My friends in Vevey got me a new cherry cup and sent some chocolate as well, so I think I'll indulge myself before the horrors of tomorrow. It's my fast day," she tells Vivienne. "Once a fortnight I have a day without food, just fruit juice. I think it does the body good once in a while and it's an

interesting exercise in self-discipline. You should try it,
Vivienne."

Alex laughs and hands round the chocolate. "Don't talk
to Vivvy about discipline, Claire. You'd die if you had to go
an hour without food or cigarettes, wouldn't you darling?"

The "darling" takes the sting out of it for Vivienne.

"How many do you smoke a day, Vivienne?" Claire asks.

"About twenty," Vivienne lies.

"And you don't worry about cancer?"

"I don't think about it. Besides, I enjoy smoking. I don't
want to give it up."

"Tell the truth," says Alex, "you couldn't if you tried."

Vivienne turns away and concentrates on the play, fingering some amber beads Claire insisted on giving her. Alex
and Claire exchange a quick glance and go back to their
party list.

Later, at the Tube, Vivienne tackles him about the party.
She had refused his offer of a lift home partly out of pique,
partly because she doesn't want him to make love to her
again tonight.

"Can't I come to your party?" she says brightly, knowing
she is being unreasonable. Alex looks uncomfortable.

"Darling I thought you'd be at home with your folks over
Christmas."

"I can come back for Boxing Day."

"Yes, but Vivvy, it might be a bit difficult ..."

"I thought you said Claire accepted me as part of your
lives? I thought you said she always carried things right
through?"

"Yes I know, it's all right with just us three, but with
all our friends..."

"What's more important to you, me or your friends? And
I wouldn't have thought anyone would have time to notice

me in a crowd of people. Please, Alex, I'm not going to see you for a week."

"Oh, all right."

"Promise?"

"I promise, you funny girl. Now run, or you'll miss your train."

Fifteen

VIVIENNE LIES ON Stella's bed chewing gum and watching her sort out clothes to take to New York. It was a real sock in the eye for all the other swanky buyers at the store, Stella says, when she was chosen for this trip. If she doesn't louse it up it will mean promotion and more lovely money.

"I thought Bob had enough lovely money for both of you," says Vivienne crabbily.

Stella empties a drawerful of sweaters on to the floor. "Look, why don't you go and get yourself some fags? This is your fifth day on the wagon and I'm only glad I won't be here to see your final agonised writhings."

"Sorry."

"All right. And as for Bob, well he's sweet but he won't be around for ever, will he? It's not as if I want to marry the guy."

"Why not?" Vivienne crams more gum into her mouth.

"Because I don't want to marry anyone, love. I had a shining example of what a rotten marriage does to you in my mother. I want my own job, my own money, my own flat and no one to tell me what to do. And I'm prepared to work for it. But while I'm at it I intend to beat the bastards at their own game, get right to the top of my particular tree and screw all the bunce I can out of them." She lays out two jersey suits on the floor. "Which do you like best?"

"The black one's more elegant, but the blue has a sexier neckline." Surprisingly, Stella packs the black. "I can't believe you're as hard as all that, Stella. Don't you believe in love?"

"Sure, being in love is nice, but it never lasts, does it? Inevitably you grow out of people and then someone gets their teeth kicked in, feels bitter and takes it out on the next person they have an affair with."

"I believe in love," Vivienne says.

"At the moment you haven't got much choice, have you?" says Stella tartly.

"It can have a good effect on you," Vivienne persists. "Alex was telling me Claire says he's become a much better person since he's known me."

"She means he's been feeling so guilty he's been treating *her* better," says Stella, stuffing rolled-up wads of knickers into her shoes. "And how can you sit there and talk about love having a good effect. Have you looked at yourself recently?" Stella's tone is abrasive but not unkind. "Your face is all to hell, dead white and scaley, your eyes are dull and puffy, and I bet you're not getting enough sleep because you're lying there smoking thinking of HIM."

"I've given up smoking," Vivienne sulks, fiddling with the amber beads.

"Yes, and why? To show *her* you've got the will power to do it. It's all very well her sitting in a centrally-heated house playing at disciplining mind and body; I see objects like her all the time in the store and I don't like them. When she tells you to give up smoking or have a little fast day, she doesn't know what it's like, does she, in a cold furnished flat after a day doing a job you don't really like. She probably eats so much she *needs* a day without grub occasionally to give her system a rest; it doesn't occur to her that most days all you have to eat is some eggs and cheese and that your ciggies are just about the only luxury you have. It's easy for her, isn't it, to dole out little presents of amber beads—they are very pretty, by the way—and send you off feeling inadequate because you can't compete on her terms."

"She doesn't. It isn't like that. And I'm sure she just gives me things to be kind, like you give me make-up or the odd sweater occasionally." Unconsciously imitating her mother, Vivienne skirts the trip wires leading to facts she won't admit. and concentrates instead on the trivia.

"Nonsense, Vivvy. I give you things because I've got masses of junk I don't need, and anyway I get clothes cheaply from the store. But I assure you, if you were knocking around with my husband all you'd get from me would be a six-inch nail driven into your head." She stands on a chair to heave down from the top of the wardrobe a large canvas hold-all; a shower of dust cascades down on to her blonde curls. "Ugh. I don't know, Vivvy, I simply think you have to live for now, and you're not living, you're only mooning about and vegetating."

Vivienne rolls on to her stomach and chews the fringe on Stella's African bedspread, desperate for a cigarette.

"Is that a hint I'm supposed to help instead of lolling about?" she asks, evading the issue again. "Anyway I'm not mooning about, I'm going out to a party with Edouard later on."

"Good," Stella says. "There's no point in looking as ill as you do for nothing. I was looking through some old diaries last night, and one period in April was absolutely crammed with lunch and dinner dates until after three weeks there was an entry in very shaky writing: Sunday: Gastric Flu, Monday: see doctor. I was ill for three weeks but it was worth it." She rummages in the bag and brings out a small package. "What Pills do you take?"

Vivienne tells her the name, and Stella throws the package across.

"Here you are, then. My doctor changed me on to a

different brand so these are no use to me."

Vivienne is delighted. She was dreading, she says, another visit to the clinic for her next six month's supply. The first time she went, not knowing what to expect, she was greeted by a gushy woman doctor who told her to "come in, come in and tell me all about it."

"All about what?"

"Your boyfriend, my dear. Are you engaged?"

"No."

"Well I expect you are *going* to be engaged very soon, aren't you?"

"No."

The doctor had leaned forward, allowing her sagging bosom to rest on the desk. "This is all quite confidential, you know. Your mother and father will never be told. I want you to feel free to discuss any problems with me."

"I don't have any problems, doctor. I just want the Pill."

"Do you have ... more than *one* boyfriend then?"

"No."

"Ah!" the doctor jerked upright. "So you are going steady! Good, good. And will we be hearing wedding bells soon?"

"No."

"You see, most of the girls we have in here are *engaged*. And they *all* feel free to talk to me, in confidence, about any little problems they may have bothering them. I'd like you to feel you could do the same."

"Well, I'm afraid I'm not engaged, I don't want to be engaged and I don't have any problems. Is that any bar to me having the Pill?"

The doctor sagged on to the desk again, defeated. "No. Just take off your tights and panties and go and wait next door."

"Imagine," Vivienne tells Stella, "sitting there draughtily

with a benchful of girls and knowing they've all got their tights and knickers rolled up in their handbags like you."

Stella says: "And I suppose the old bag took it out on you."

"You can say that again. She rummaged around as if she was looking for gold. I have to go back every six months to be checked over and each time I'm very conscious of being unsuitable."

At eight o'clock Vivienne says goodbye, send me a card, be a good girl to Stella who is leaving early tomorrow morning, and goes to get ready for the party. Not smoking has made her hungry, but she has nothing in the flat to eat except a dry piece of cheese and some strong peppermints she used to chew to take the tobacco smell off her breath. She swallows the cheese whole and prays there will be food, real food at the party. Before she leaves to meet Edouard she holds her nose and gulps down three tablespoons of cooking oil: it would be too embarrassing, she thinks, to get drunk and make a fool of myself in front of Edouard for the second time.

The party, which is being given by some student friends-of-friends of Edouard's, is on the top floor of a dejected house in Islington, the sort of place that used to be called "lodgings" or, more accurately, "rooms". Corduroyed young men and girls with long cotton-wool hair spill over the old busted leather armchairs. There is beer and acidic red wine but Vivienne is too late for the few packets of crisps provided by the anonymous host. They stay for a couple of hours, anyway, until the beer runs out and a young, eager-faced man leaning against the lavatory-green wall gesticulates with his paper cup full of wine and asks his band of female admirers: "But how do you *know* the table is really there? Because it is solid? But what does solid *mean*? Just because you can touch it, does that *prove* it is really there?" One of the girls sways in ecstasy.

"Grouplets," scorns Vivienne, her stomach rumbling.

Mercifully, Edouard takes her to eat, at an all-night Greek restaurant in Soho. They decide to stay up all night so Edouard can achieve his ambition to go to Covent Garden and have a drink at five-thirty in the morning. To kill time, they walk across Charing Cross bridge and sit on a wooden seat near the Festival Hall, overlooking the river. The air is damp and cold. Edouard folds his big leather coat round the shivering Vivienne and tells her he is going back to France in a few days to start his new job.

"Why don't you come too?" he asks.

Vivienne stares at him. She has been thinking of Alex who will be home on Monday, and how much she has missed him.

Edouard goes on: "We could get a flat; your French is good, you could get a job easily enough, probably with the firm I'm going to work for. And you aren't really happy at the moment, are you Vivvy?"

She doesn't deny it. "Edouard, of course I can't come to Paris. I love Alex, I thought you understood that."

"I understand that he's married and going to stay married and there's nothing in it for you. You're tense and miserable and I don't like to see you like this. I'd look after you, you know that don't you?"

"Oh Edouard!" Something in Vivienne collapses at the wonderful thought of being looked after. She feels tearful, as usual when she is trying not to appear unhappy and someone sees through to all the misery underneath. "I know loving Alex isn't making me terribly happy at the moment, but I'd be unhappier without him. And love isn't always a fun thing, is it? Sometimes it's a suffering thing too."

"It's always a suffering thing for young single girls knocking around with married men."

"I think you have to stick to what you believe in, and I believe that if you love someone then you stay with them, don't you, whatever happens. You don't just up and off when things get difficult."

"It may be difficult for you, Vivvy, but it seems to me he's got jam on it. A wife and a mistress, it's every man's dream. Don't tell me he's making any sacrifices? There's an old joke, you know, where someone says to a man: if your wife and your mistress were drowning, which one would you save? And the man says, my wife, because my mistress would understand."

Vivienne looks away and sighs. First Stella, now Edouard doing nothing but get at her all the time. Why won't anyone make an effort to appreciate what I'm doing? With a large meal and a huge amount of wine inside her Vivienne feels very Brave New World, ready to overcome all opposition to the way of life she thinks she has chosen.

"Where is this thing of yours going?" Edouard persists.

"It doesn't have to go anywhere," snaps Vivienne, who often wonders the same thing herself. "But Alex once said it might be possible for us to live together one day—"

"Oh, for God's sake!"

"Well why not if we all get on together? Don't be so bourgeois, Edouard. Claire isn't a conventional person and—"

"Has she suggested you live together?"

"No, we—"

"Exactly!"

"Stop interrupting me! You're just like ..." Alex, she was going to say. "You have to give these things time, Edouard."

"I think it's time you woke up and stopped kidding yourself." He draws her close and kisses her softly, his mouth warm in the cold night. "Think about coming to Paris, Vivvy. We can have fun there."

"I'll let you know," she says, feeling sorry for him for not understanding what love is, and what it means to her.

Sixteen

VIVIENNE IS EXCITED. She rarely receives letters, not even circulars and now, returning home late from Italian evening class, there are three waiting for her, postmarked Paris, New York and London W.11. Quickly she prepares a bowl of soup and settles herself on a cushion in front of the spluttering gas fire, preparing to enjoy herself.

She opens Edouard's letter first. As she anticipated, he is chatty and funny, telling her about his new colleagues at work and the large sunny flat he's found. *There's loads of room for you if you change your mind about coming to Paris.* She smiles, warmed by the heat of the fire, the hot soup inside her and the knowledge that miles away in a foreign country, a man is missing her.

Happily she picks up the airmail envelope from New York, surprised that Stella is able to type. She rips it open and takes out a piece of onion skin paper, marked *Personal.*

From the Desk of the Personnel Director
Wallis & Steadman (NY) Ltd.,
Fifth Avenue, New York, NY 100101

Monday 27 November

Dear Miss Tyler,
I deeply regret to have to inform you that Miss Stella Mary Caxton was killed in a car crash on the outskirts of this city last night. Our information from the police department is that the car collided with a fully-loaded petrol tanker causing

*Miss Caxton and her companion to be killed instantaneously.
The enclosed postcard, addressed to you, was found in her
handbag. We thought you would like to have it.*

The card is a picture of the Statue of Liberty. On the back
Stella had scrawled: *Hell, it's freezing here but they all move
so fast I'm in a sweat trying to keep up. See you soon! Luv, S.*

Vivienne waits for a reaction; tears, collapse into overwhelming grief. But nothing happens. Just a chilling, paralys-
ing numbness. She inches nearer the fire and glances at the
rest of the airmail letter. *Body being flown to England*—they
mean what's left of it ... *next of kin informed*—oh hell, I
shall have to write to her mother ... *accept our deepest sympathy ... tragic loss.* Conventional phrases, she thinks, but
what else do you expect them to say? Obviously no one in the
Personnel Department ever met Stella and anyway they must
send out half a dozen of these letters a year; they're probably
filed under Death, standard letter, condolence, female.

She laughs hysterically and then stops, appalled. In her
first contact with death she does not understand that laughter is a natural safety valve, shielding her, the living, from
the terror of something her mind cannot yet accept. Stella is
dead, Vivienne tells herself. Bright, buoyant, happy Stella
who loved to live has been smashed to pieces by a petrol
tanker. I am alive. She is dead. Why don't I *feel* anything?
She wonders who the "companion" was with Stella. The
mysterious New York boyfriend probably. Trust Stella.

Vivienne suddenly remembers Bob and the third letter. She
tears it open and reads:

My Dear Vivvy, I am most desperately sorry to tell you ...

The short, sad note arouses in her an overwhelming urge
to talk to someone about Stella. Quickly, she dials the number printed on Bob's letterhead, but there is no reply.

Who else is there that knows Stella? *Knew* Stella. Richard? No, she didn't want to talk to him. For the first time in months, she thinks of her father; he met Stella briefly when he first helped Vivienne move her things from home. Her father would listen, say the right things, make her feel something. She picks up the phone again and glances at her watch. Eight thirty. They'll have finished supper and be sitting watching television, Dad in the big rust-coloured cardigan Mum knitted him for Christmas.

"Oh, hello mum. Yes. No, I'm all right, I just wondered if I could have a word with dad? Oh has he? Will he be back late then? Yes I see. No, I just wanted to talk to him ... well because I've just had some dreadful news, you see. Stella has been killed in a car crash in New York ... *Stella*, mum, the girl in the flat next door. I've *told* you about her hundreds of times. Yes. No, there wasn't anything special I wanted to *tell* dad, I simply wanted to talk to him about it. No, he doesn't know her very well ... Once ... Yes ... Yes I remember when Auntie Ivy died. I know. Awful. Yes..." Vivienne sighs and gives up as her mother launches into Funerals I Have Known, which comes second in her repertoire, to Operations I Nearly Had. Frustrated, Vivienne hurriedly says goodbye and rings off. Blast her father. He's got no right to be out when she needs him.

I'll have a cigarette instead, she decides. Just one won't do any harm; there are bound to be some left in Stella's cigarette box. She takes the spare key from the ledge on top of the door, admitting to herself a morbid urge to look at Stella's room again.

Remembering the haste with which Stella had packed, Vivienne expected to find the room in total disarray, but looking round she sees a neatly-made bed, drawers and cupboards closed, shoes stacked tidily on a metal rack, everything in perfect order apart from a sprinkling of talcum powder on the grey carpet. Patiently, in massive shuttered silence, the room seems to be waiting for its impulsive owner to return and bring it to life again.

Stealthily, Vivienne takes a cigarette from the silver box, lights it with the heavy crystal table lighter and chokes. It is her first cigarette in more than two weeks, and she feels dizzy with smoke and the unbearable realisation that here are Stella's things, but she will never use them again. Someone— Mrs Caxton?—will have to come and sort through it all and the tangible evidence of twenty-six years of living, the bizarre treasures Stella was so proud of, will be given away or borne off in dusty cardboard boxes to be mused at, mourned over, and finally broken or forgotten.

What is it all for? Vivienne wonders. She takes the remaining cigarettes out of the box and returns, depressed, to her own room.

She wants desperately to phone Alex, but he had told her his agent was coming round to dinner. He'd been so bored at his mother's apparently, that he had started work again on his book; it was going well and he was excited about it.

Oh hell, I want to *talk* to somebody. I want to talk to Alex. Shit his bloody dinner party, she decides, I need him. Now. Shakily, she dials the Highgate number. Claire answers.

"Oh, hello Claire. How are you?" Vivienne enquires stupidly.

"Who is that?" Claire. Cool, distant.

"Me. Vivienne." She waits in vain for Claire to say something welcoming. "Er, I wondered if I could have a word with Alex?"

Claire sounds as if she is speaking from another planet: "Vivienne, it is a little difficult at the moment. You know Alexander made considerable progress with his novel while we were away and he and his agent are having a conference at the moment, discussing it all and setting final deadlines. It has taken so long to reach this point I would really much rather not interrupt them."

Vivienne swallows hard, fighting back hot, bitter tears of disappointment and defeat. Everything is going wrong. Everyone is out or gone away or dead.

"Hello, Vivienne?"

"Yes. I see." Vivienne whispers.

"Is anything wrong? Are you all right?" Claire sounds concerned.

"Oh Claire, it's awful. Stella's dead!" Vivienne blurts out, her sense of rejection starting to melt the numbness, making her feel something genuine at last—if only self pity. "She was killed in a car crash . . . I've only just heard." She begins to sob, wiping away the tears on the rough woollen sleeve of her dress.

"Oh my dear, I am so very sorry. Have you no one with you?" Vivienne cannot answer. "Look, Vivienne, I'm going to drive over to you now. Are you listening?"

Vivienne nods.

"Vivienne?"

"What about your dinner party?" Vivienne sniffs.

"That doesn't matter. They can get along perfectly well without me and I don't think you should be alone. Just go down *now* and unlock the front door for me will you? Then I can come straight up. I'll be there as soon as I can." She rings off.

Vivienne stumbles downstairs and puts the catch on the front door. Then she collapses on to her bed and starts to cry, her grief not for the friend she has lost but for herself and her own loneliness.

This is where Claire finds her half an hour afterwards. Tactfully, she says nothing, but touches the crumpled girl on the shoulder to let her know she is there, and then lets her cry on while she lights two red candles on the mantelpiece, turning out the harsh electric light. Eventually Vivienne sits up and wipes her puffy, wet face with the damp flannel Claire has fetched from the bathroom.

"I'm going to make myself some tea," Claire says, "but I thought you might prefer something stronger so I brought this." She places a half-bottle of brandy on the bedside table.

"Thank you," says Vivienne dully. "The kitchen ... I'll show you—"

"It's all right, I'll find everything. Just pour yourself a drink and take it easy. You've had a dreadful shock, I know."

The sympathetic words make the tears well up again and Vivienne hastily pours a drink, gulping it down, forgetting that she usually dislikes brandy. It helps. She drinks some more and lights a cigarette. Noticing the letter from New York and Stella's card still lying on the floor she picks them up and sadly reads them again as Claire pulls the armchair up to the hearth and pours her tea. Vivienne sits on the floor, her arms round her knees, warming the brandy in front of the fire.

"She was so *alive*," says Vivienne hopelessly, ashamed now of her fraudulent, selfish tears.

"Tell me about her."

It is what Vivienne needs. She talks for an hour and Claire watches the raw, desolate look gradually leave the girl's face.

"I've never known anyone who died before," Vivienne says incoherently after her fifth brandy. "It's strange how you desperately want to talk about them, isn't it? I always used to laugh at people who made a big deal thing out of funerals but now I feel I want to do something very positive, like going out and ordering a huge wreath, just something to show in a small way how I feel. Do you know what I mean?"

"Yes I know," says Claire, her face luminous in the candle-light. "Funerals are really for the living not the dead: they help those who are left behind to come to terms with death. The worst thing in any situation is the feeling that there is nothing you can do. At a funeral you are doing something, just by making the effort to be there; and all the religious ceremony and ritual give people something to do and hang on to, stop them feeling quite so useless."

They sit in silence for a few minutes, staring into the trans-lucent blue and pink flames of the gas fire. Vivienne, warm now and protected, feels a tremendous drunken rapport with this understanding older woman. I needed someone and she came, Vivienne thinks, in a heady rush of alcoholic senti-mentality. Feeling the barriers are down, now Claire has seen her at her wretched worst, Vivienne has the urge to share secrets, wanting Claire in her turn to confide in her so she too can show sympathy and understanding.

"Is ... is this how you felt when your son died?" Vivienne ventures shyly, her eyes still on the fire, not daring to look at Claire's face.

"No, it was different," Claire replies, playing with the sash on her long cream dress. "Because Robin was drowned and I felt responsible." She speaks crisply, like a cookery teacher comparing recipes for shortbread. Vivienne feels rebuked.

"I'm sorry. I shouldn't have mentioned it."

Claire hesitates, on the verge of saying something else, but the phone rings, and the moment is lost.

It is Alex, worried about them both.

"Tell Claire to bring you back with her for the weekend."

"Alex, I don't know if I ought to stay here in case—"

"Don't argue, Vivvy. You're in no state to stay in that gloomy flat by yourself. Look, put Claire on, I'll speak to her."

It takes some time to reach Ambassador Drive because

Claire drives slowly, nervous of the traffic in the dark. When they arrive, Vivienne is sent straight to bed in the little blue room while Alex brings hot chocolate, which she doesn't really want on top of the brandy. He sits on the edge of the bed and talks gently to her.

"I'm sorry I couldn't come myself, angel. I felt very bad about it."

"Don't worry, Alex, Claire was terribly kind. She seemed to know all the right things to do and say. And then I had to go and ask her about Robin dying. I simply didn't think." She looks at him anxiously.

"Never mind, it was a long time ago."

"I can imagine how she must have felt. Do you go and visit his grave?"

"My mother does. She takes flowers, keeps the grave looking what she calls respectable. She says she likes to sit and think there for ten minutes, remembering her grandson, but I feel, and Claire agrees, that we would rather remember him in our own way, rather than indulge in a ritualised ten minute think-in once a fortnight."

Vivienne sips her chocolate. "What do you mean, in your own way? What do you do?"

"We don't exactly *do* anything in particular, but there are always things that remind us. Every time I see a five-year-old boy, or a ginger cat—he had a passion for ginger cats—I think of Robin. All sorts of daft little things remind us. And Claire keeps that picture she painted as her own personal reminder." Alex takes her cup away and kisses her tenderly on the brow. "Come on now, get your head down. You've had one hell of a day, poor love."

"I don't know if I'll be able to sleep," she says, not wanting him to go.

He says from the door: "Yes you will, angel. Claire crushed

one of her sleeping pills into your chocolate. You'll sleep till lunch time tomorrow, and it will do you good. Goodnight."

Not knowing whether to feel angry or grateful, Vivienne slides down under the covers and waits for oblivion, thinking guiltily that she had meant to thank Claire for all her kindness, but had forgot.

Claire brings Vivienne lunch on a tray. Alexander was up at eight, she says, working on his novel, and has suggested that this afternoon they should all go for a walk in the park.

They walk fast, huddled together against the cold, Alex with an arm through each of theirs, Claire clutching a bag of bread for the ducks. They start throwing the bread into the icy water of the pond, but when the swans arrive to chase the ducks away Claire takes some bread and leads them off further up the muddy bank, leaving Alex and Vivienne alone with the squabbling ducks.

Alex looks morose, his face drawn into fine tight lines, and Vivienne tries to think of something cheerful to say, but can't. Gazing out across the pond, he suddenly starts to recite:

> "When I am old, no doubt
>   the cruel Fates will let you find me
>   in the park, feeding the ducks.
>   I will look at you and you at me
>   and we'll be horrified;
>   what's worse, we won't be able
>   to do anything about us.
>
> "You see (a duck sinks under a barrage of Hovis)
>   men die younger than grandmas,
>   mainly because they're exhausted

with living in the same world
as the women they wanted but couldn't have
and the women they didn't want but have got.

"So, when you see me there,
with my newspaper full of stale doughnuts,
don't jump naked out of the bushes
or call an undertaker,
just sit quietly next to me on the bench
and say you're sorry for being old."

Viciously he hurls the last piece of bread at a duck's head. It misses. Confused, Vivienne says: "Did you write that?"

"No. It's in a book of poems I've got at home."

"It's sad and funny."

"And very true."

Claire comes back and sees their faces. Alexander miserable and trapped, Vivienne as usual taking her mood from him, miserable and bewildered. Annoyed, wondering what they have been saying to one another, she hurries them on towards the playing field where a Saturday afternoon football match has just started. There is a team in blue, balding, middle-aged and self-consciously keen, against a side in yellow who all seem drunk. Their supporters, also drunk, lurch along the sidelines yelling slurred encouragement or derision according to which side has possession of the muddy ball.

"Christ, look at the poor old fella, he's just dropped his bleedin' pension book in the penalty area! Come on George, *run*, man ... *run* you lazy bastard! Jeez, whassa madder with him? He moves like he's just shit his shorts..."

They watch until the blues score the first goal, to the wild accompaniment of jeers and a torrent of four-lettered abuse from the sidelines before walking home over Parliament Hill

Fields. Alex, more cheerful now, loudly reminisces about the time he scored the winning goal in a vital match against a rival school. His face is alive with enthusiasm and Claire, suddenly loving him very much, smiles across him at Vivienne as if to say: oh these men and their memories of adolescent victories; if we women recalled our glories on the hockey field we'd be laughed out of sight for being childish and trivial.

But Vivienne is looking away, for once not listening to Alex. She wishes he would stop going on about boring football and remember instead the summer night when they walked along this very path and, wild with wine, threw off their clothes to make love under a tree, playing giggly statues when anyone came past. A little grey kitten had come running up to join the fun, purring happily against Vivienne's thighs as she lay naked in the grass.

Now, watching the red winter sun melting like butter behind the trees she wonders unhappily what is going to become of them all.

In the evening they go to see a film, a comedy which Alex and Vivienne greatly enjoy, although she notices that Claire doesn't laugh much. But Claire never laughs much anyway; Vivienne realises she has never heard Claire let go and enjoy a real belly laugh. Later, as they sit listening to Scarlatti, Vivienne wonders if Claire will spike her bedtime drink again, but the music makes her feel melancholy, so she doesn't make a joke of it. Not wanting to be sent to bed again by Claire, she gets up quickly and says goodnight.

Through the day she has been kept active, deliberately, she suspects; but now, lying in bed, it is impossible to drive away thoughts of Stella. What was it like, driving along, chatting and flirting with an old boyfriend in a new country ... and then what? The great looming mass of the petrol tanker, the car swerving, tyres squealing ... How long would there be between seeing the tanker and realising you were going to hit it and then hitting it and knowing in a split second your body was going to be smashed and crushed and hurt and ... STOP IT, STOP IT! Stop thinking like this. Vivienne is sweating, rivers of wet running between her breasts. She can't help it. She can't understand how she can be so upset at the death of someone who was basically, a brittle, surface person; there were plenty more dedicated, worthy people around, doing good, kind, unselfish things. Stella was like tinsel compared to them. But with Stella the loss is harder to bear because to Vivienne she was one of those rare spirits who really *enjoyed* life and as such was the antithesis of the sensible, responsible, Head-Girl-Hilary model impressed on Vivienne as the ideal in her childhood. It seems totally unjust that the Hilarys of the world should go on existing, while Stella has lost out. She thinks of Stella sitting cross-legged in her room having her roots retouched, Stella dancing crazily in that expensive restaurant, Stella who cheerfully gave her money, clothes, make-up and well-intentioned advice, a girl desperate for life, fizzing with a man in a car, bubbling with an excitement that suddenly freezes to horror. A scream, a crash, her body smashed and bloody, her face a mangled mess, her eyes...

Vivienne only realises she is screaming when Alex picks her up and carries her in his arms like a child out of the room. Through her sobs she is distantly conscious of being laid down gently in a different bed, Alex's arms around her and his voice running on and on, soothing, calming. Then, as he cradles her and talks to her (although she will never be able to remember what it was he said) she becomes aware of different hands stroking her hair, another body, Claire's, lying next to her, warm and comforting. Slowly, lulled by their caresses, she finally trembles into an exhausted sleep.

*   *   *

She wakes on Sunday morning in her own bed in the blue bedroom. Alone. Her watch has stopped (she forgot to wind it last night) but from the gloomy, greyish-yellow light seeping in through the curtains she guesses it must be about eight o'clock. She slips out of bed and pads across the carpeted landing to the bathroom, blessing the central heating. She thinks of her own chilly bathroom, always coldly damp, with Stella's pink bath salts and false eyelashes lying forlorn on the windowsill. They'll be coming to clear up her things. Vivienne reminds herself to get into Stella's room first and remove all those illicit packs of American cigarettes hidden away on top of the wardrobe, relieved that she can now think clearly about it all without being engulfed in misery.

Downstairs she can hear the erratic tap-tappity-tap of Alex's typewriter, but there is no sign nor sound that Claire is up. She hesitates on the landing but decides not to go down: Alex told her he worked best in the morning and she doesn't want to annoy him. Instead, she drifts back to bed, feeling vaguely ashamed because she wants to make love and Stella is dead.

The second time she wakes up she smells coffee, pulls on her dressing gown and hurries downstairs. Claire and Alex sit at the kitchen table, the cherry coffee pot in front of them, the papers still neatly folded and unread pushed to one side. They look at her with concern as she hesitates by the door like a child who steals down in the night for hot milk and blunders in on her parents anxiously discussing her school report. They give her coffee, ask how she slept and how she is feeling while she wonders uneasily what they have been saying about her. As they drink their coffee Alex talks about his book and then reads them the more eccentric items from the *News of the World*—The Screws, he laughingly calls it— while Claire sits quietly threading peanuts for the birds. Her hands are rarely still, Vivienne thinks, wondering if Claire will clear off again for the afternoon and leave her alone with Alex.

After lunch as they sit comfortably together watching the old film on television, Alex suggests that Vivienne stay over with them tonight instead of going back to the flat. Vivienne agrees, looking across for Claire's approval, but she is sitting upright in her rocking chair watching the television, her face impassive.

Afterwards, Vivienne remembers that afternoon and evening as a time when she felt totally and gratefully at peace. A rare and welcome experience. With the curtains drawn and the lamps lit, she is warm, safe and loved. Oddly, she feels she has come home. I belong here, she thinks, watching Claire lay out crumpets and chocolate cake for tea. This is more my home than the flat or my parents' house is. And Alex and Claire are kind to her, making her laugh, involving her, making her feel wanted. Alex gets out his old press-cuttings book from his days as a provincial reporter, full of stories in what he calls the "All is quiet tonight in riot-torn Hull" style. Later they drink glasses of brandy and ginger while Claire shows Vivienne a new way to do her face, using the barest make-up to maximum effect, so Vivienne begins to glow again, her big grey eyes luminous with pleasure. For her it is a gift of a time, as if they have given her a parcel which she opens, expecting nothing extraordinary, and finds instead a selection of wonderful things, all carefully chosen with her happiness in mind.

Hugging this new-found joy to herself, she goes up to bed wishing, as always, that Alex could come with her. She hears Claire and Alex come up. The landing light is switched off. Then, to her delight, the door opens softly and Alex comes in. Pleased, she pulls him down on to her.

"You are a sod, Alex. I've wanted you all day."

He sits her up and kisses her, tasting of brandy-laced tooth-paste.

"This bed's too small," he says.

"We've managed all right on it before!"

"Come with me to my bed."

"Don't be an idiot, darling. Your wife is in your bed."

"I know. I want you to come too."

Vivienne feels clammy. "Alex, what the hell are you talking about?"

"I simply want to take you into my bed and make love to you, that's all."

"With your wife looking on, I suppose, and cheering?"

"Claire doesn't mind. It was her idea."

"Oh *God*!"

"What's the matter? She told me to bring you in last night when you were upset ... and this morning we talked about it and agreed it was silly for us all to be together during the day and then split up at bedtime."

"Oh. Well, thanks for telling me."

"Look, just come with me and lie with us for a little while. We don't have to do anything if you don't want to. But I'm going to look pretty silly if I have to go back to Claire now and tell her you won't come."

Vivienne sighs, rubbing her face against his shoulder. Why does he always want to complicate everything?

"Please, Vivvy. I love you so very much. Please do this for me ... with me." He lifts her hair and muzzles the back of her neck.

Vivienne groans.

"All right," says Vivienne, who has never been able to refuse him anything.

Seventeen

THE WHITE ROOM with the apricot ceiling is lit by a single soft light on Claire's side of the big bed. She is sitting up wearing a white silk nightie, meticulously rubbing cream into her hands; the nightie is low cut, and Vivienne can see slight blue veins etched on Claire's small breasts. At least mine are bigger Vivienne reassures herself as Claire, looking faintly victimised, smiles at them both and moves over to make room.

Alex takes off his pyjama top while Vivienne slowly unties the belt on her dressing gown, making the simple action last as long as possible, conscious that she has nothing on underneath and resenting that in a moment they will make her feel awkwardly naked.

Alex says: "I'm just going to fetch us something to drink, Vivvy. Do you want anything, Claire?"

"No, thank you." Claire is still smoothing in hand cream, calmly watching Vivienne's slow-motion performance with the dressing gown. Finally Vivienne jerkily turns her back, lets the robe fall and slithers hastily into bed, lying rigid with the sheet pulled up to her chin. After a few minutes Claire puts the bottle of hand cream on the bedside table and picks up a bristle hairbrush.

Vivienne stares at her, terrified, but Claire merely says: "You've got such lovely long hair, Vivienne. May I brush it for you?"

"If you like."

"Sit up a little, then."

Vivienne pulls herself up on to one elbow, her back to Claire, thankful that her hair is clean but praying there are no ugly spots on her shoulders. Claire strokes the hair, slowly, drawing the brush through the full length of each strand before letting it fall to tickle Vivienne's shoulders. Vivienne begins to relax. It is a long time since anyone brushed her hair; she had forgotten how pleasant it is. Now Claire angles the brush at the back of the girl's neck, raising the hair up, till Vivienne's spine stars to prickle and her nipples stiffen under cover of the sheet.

Alex returns and sits on the bed next to Vivienne. As she opens her eyes to take the glass of wine he offers, the sheet falls away from her breasts and she sees Alex looking at them, heavy and ripe, hard with waiting. Claire has stopped brushing her hair now and is lightly sweeping the brush down her back. Vivienne sips her drink and closes her eyes, almost purring with nervous excitement as Alex's hand moves down past her throat, softly encircling her breasts. He removes her glass and pushes her gently down on to the pillow, still stroking. Thoroughly aroused, she gives herself up to the black unknown, pretending this is all a dream where she has no will, no control over events, but has simply to let these sensational things happen until she wakes up.

Far, far away she hears them talking about her breasts.

"They're beautiful," she is amazed to hear Claire say, "larger than mine, but the nipples are smaller and pinker. Isn't that strange?"

"Take your nightie off so Vivienne can see."

Her eyes clamped shut, Vivienne feels the movement beside her, hears the soft rustle of silk.

"Look, Vivienne, how different you are."

Unwillingly, Vivienne stares for half a second at Claire's breasts, then turns away.

"Claire does special exercises every morning to keep them firm, and puts cream on to keep the skin nice and soft." Alex reaches out and holds Claire's left breast, his hand completely covering it. "Feel how soft it is," he says to Vivienne.

It is the last thing she wants to do.

"Go on," urges Claire, gently.

Reluctantly, Vivienne stretches out a limp hand. It is a strange, almost obscene experience touching another woman intimately for the first time, feeling smooth hairless skin instead of the more familiar rough hardness of a man. Claire's skin, Vivienne realises curiously, is particularly silky, almost slippery in texture.

"Lie down now," Alex commands, "and we'll put some of Claire's cream on you."

Closing her eyes, Vivienne hears a faint click as the light is turned out. Something cold is poured on her breasts; hands are smoothing the scented lotion into her skin. Claire's hands, she realises, fascinated, as Alex, naked, slips into the bed beside her. He does not touch her but Claire gasps and Vivienne guesses he is doing something to her. She is glad of the dark —she doesn't want to see Alex touch Claire.

Gradually, the pressure of the hands on her breasts increases, rougher now, kneading, scratching, pushing them up, pinching them together. Then the hands stop and there is more cream suddenly on her stomach, while Alex takes one of her breasts in his mouth, sucking and biting it as his hands close round her thighs. Vivienne begins to burn with the agonising contrast between the pain he is inflicting and the delicious stabs of pleasure round her loins: Claire has found her clitoris and is inching slowly, oh so tantalisingly slowly round it with her finger, until Vivienne involuntarily arches her back and cries out. Swiftly then, Alex moves astride her, inside her and Claire, oh God, Claire is kissing her hair, neck, face, until her body drowns in a great hot sea of sensation that suddenly explodes, throwing her up, carrying her along on a huge fast wave that finally crashes and ebbs away, leaving her wet, shuddering and exhausted.

Drained, but totally satisfied, Vivienne lies and floats for a while, relishing the calm joy spreading to every part of her body, even to her toes and fingertips. Stretching luxuriously, as women do when they are pleased with their lovemaking, her eyes become accustomed to the dark and the two bulky shapes beside her that have begun to make love. Curiously, she notices how incredibly gentle Alex is with Claire, as they move rhythmically, familiarly together. Jealously, Vivienne turns away from the two twisting silhouettes, feeling left out but at the same time wanting to ignore them. But she is not to be left alone, for Alex pulls her over and caresses both women together. Then he enters Claire, at the same time bringing Vivienne's head down, holding it on the small hard breasts, giving the girl no choice but to kiss them. Fiercely, Vivienne sinks her teeth into the large tough nipple, viciously hanging on until Claire writhes to a climax and pushes her away.

Tired now, and longing for sleep, Vivienne rolls over to the far side of the bed. But Alex has not finished. He sits up, drains his Scotch and reaches out again for Vivienne.

"Turn over."

Oh no, Alex, not *now* for heaven's sake, please, not with Claire watching! As a compromise she moves on to her side, but he seizes her behind, shoving her roughly up on to her knees. Resigned, she can feel the drops of sweat dripping from his brow on to her back as she waits, still moist and sticky from the last time. Then he tears into her, thrusting harder and harder, on and on, gripping and bruising the flesh round her thighs until at last, grunting and roaring, he comes, collapsing on top of her and she tastes blood on her lip where she's bit it to stop from crying out.

After a while Alex says, "That was bloody marvellous." Claire says, "Yes, it was good." Vivienne lies with her eyes closed, saying nothing. There is a long silence, until at last she hears Claire say, "I think, perhaps, it is time now for Vivienne to go back to her own bed."

Alex grunts, but does not move.

Dazed, and a little disappointed, Vivienne gets up, puts on her dressing gown and silently stumbles back to her room.

Alex phones Vivienne at work the next day to tell her, he says, how much he loves her. Vivienne's stomach somersaults, as always when she hears his voice.

"Sorry we missed you this morning," he goes on. "We felt so concerned for you over the weekend. Claire wanted to make sure you felt included in everything."

"Yes. Well. I see what you mean about her not doing anything by halves."

He laughs. "Didn't you enjoy it?"

"Yes, of course." Had she? She isn't sure. Her initial reaction of shock passed quickly, leaving her only with the certainty that the event is far too special ever to be discussed outside the three of them. "I was rather surprised, that's all." She draws a big black sunflower on her blotter.

"You're not depressed any more though, are you? You'll be all right by yourself tonight at the flat?"

"Yes thanks. I'm launderetting." She thinks wearily of the pile of dirty clothes sitting at the bottom of her wardrobe.

"Tomorrow I have to go to some Press do in the evening, but Claire wondered if you'd like to go to the pictures with her. There's some new arty French film on at Academy Two she thinks you might both enjoy."

Vivienne isn't so sure, but agrees, reminding him that she has Wednesday afternoon off work for Stella's funeral, hoping he will offer to take her out to dinner afterwards. But he tells her Claire has arranged a dinner party for that evening. "You can always ring up if you feel low."

The church ceremony is short, which is merciful because Stella's father, a big red-faced man in a brown suit, has started to cry. His wife, ignoring the large loudly-blubbing man at her side, stares straight ahead, her eyes two dry tired currants collapsed in the crust of her defeated face. The other twenty or so people there, embarrassed, sing *Abide With Me* extra loudly to cover the noise of the sobs and the violent trumpetings of Mr Caxton into his ineffectual slippery silk handkerchief.

As Claire said, Vivienne remembers, we are grateful for something positive to do.

They file silently out into the freezing December afternoon and group themselves round the freshly-dug grave. Two men in grey overcoats are already there, a little apart from everyone else, standing like soldiers at stiff ease on parade. "Representatives from Wallis & Steadman," whispers Bob. Vivienne, in a rush of affection for the scented store, is sorry for the two men who have had to come and stand in this harsh wind, pretending sympathy for a girl they've probably never met. They remind her of newsreel shots showing teenage cadets paying mindless tribute at the Grave of the Unknown Soldier, their expressions, dutifully blank, contrasting with the searing memories mirrored in the faces of the war veterans alongside them.

Vivienne looks away, across at the Vicar who is chanting, very fast: "Man that is born of a woman hath but a short time to live, and is full of misery." Oh, very cheerful, thank you very much. And what on earth has it got to do with Stella? She didn't live very long, true, but she was never miserable.

"... commit her body to the ground; earth to earth, ashes to ashes, dust to dust..." The dull clunk of earth on the flower-laden coffin as Stella's father buries his face again in the soggy silk handkerchief. Vivienne standing immediately behind him, is aware of a strong smell of whisky.

"Almighty God ... we give thee hearty thanks, for that it hath pleased thee to deliver this our sister out of the miseries of this sinful world; beseeching thee..." Hell, here we go again. Stella wouldn't have approved of this at all. "... shortly to accomplish the number of thine elect, and to hasten thy kingdom; that we, with all those that are departed in the true faith of thy holy Name, may have our perfect consummation and bliss..." The fool. He seems to be committing verbal hara-kiri while inflicting a death wish on us, like asking for us all to be wiped out by the plague so we can get to heaven quicker. Anyway, I thought this was supposed to be a formal send-off for *Stella*, not a frantic grovelling to the effect that OK, God, we've done our bit by her and with any luck she's safely across to the other side. Now the important item on the agenda. *Us* (well, me really of course but I have to pretend to include all these other morons as well.) "... raise us from the death of sin into the life of righteousness; that, when we shall depart this life, we may rest in him, as our hope is this our sister doth..." What I'm trying to say, is that all this guff about the dear departed has made me nervous about the old credit rating and I'd just like to make it clear that I've always believed in you really, God, in spite of all those foolish jokes I've told about you. "... and that at the general Resurrection in the last day, we may be found acceptable in thy sight." Dear God, nice God, you will make me good so I can go to heaven too, won't you? Thank you, thank you and Amen.

It is over. They walk away. Everyone is going back to Mrs Caxton's for sherry except the men in grey from Wallis & Steadman and Mr Caxton who is already driving off, alone.

As Vivienne looks back to the new grave she sees two men with shovels emerge from the nearby trees. One is carrying an umbrella. He kneels down, and with the curved end begins to hoist up the wreaths from the top of the coffin.

Eighteen

THE KING'S ROAD, ten days later, seems to be full of bad-tempered people all going the opposite way to Vivienne and all carrying Christmas trees. Like anxious extras in *Macbeth*, she thinks, ducking under a passing branch, who have lost their way to Dunsinane.

With a week to go, Vivienne has just finished her Christmas shopping and is now doing frantic sums which all come out the same way: yesterday was pay-day and she now has exactly £1.51p to last until Friday. Aware suddenly that her knickers are damp, she remembers the date, links it to her nagging head and, groaning, dodges through the five o'clock traffic jam to the cut-price chemist. Tampax and aspirin, that leaves £1.35. Lucky I've given up fags because there definitely isn't enough left even for ten.

On the other hand, if I walk home from work a couple of times ... just one occasionally won't hurt ... I'll make them last. Despising her weakness, she stops at the tobacconist's.

It is quiet at the flat without Stella banging about next door. Don't think about that, Vivienne orders herself briskly. Stella is gone and you are alive. ALIVE! she shouts at herself in the mirror. That means don't mope, don't feel lonely, don't get upset because you're short of money, don't feel resentful because you can't see more of Alex. Just be glad you're not dead with gravediggers fishing flowers off your coffin. Whatever do they *do* with those wreaths? Take them home to their wives, or stick laurel round and sell them to the trendy

Chelsea set for their festive Christmas front doors?

She turns on the radio, and harpsichord music fills the kitchen, rising and falling like a shower of tiny golden needles.

The recipe for the quiche lorraine is in her new French cookery book which she finds eventually under the unmade bed, its glossy pages smeared with two dusty apple cores. It is an annoying book, full of recipes that fire her with enthusiasm to get on and cook something *now*, until she turns over the page and reads "add the beans which you have soaked overnight" or "pour all the ingredients into your liquidiser..." Not exactly helpful for someone who hasn't even got a bloody whisk, Vivienne thinks. She decides to have one cigarette with her tea and aspirins while the frozen pastry thaws.

Vivienne is sure that one day something magical will happen and she will find herself in a large rambling house in the country, with a big pine kitchen where she will make fruit pies using real, not frozen, pastry. There will be a sweet-smelling herb garden outside the kitchen door, and perhaps a few chickens. She will bake her own bread and in the summer squeeze dozens of oranges and lemons into a large glass jug for them to drink when they have made love. Them. The man is shadowy ... not Alex. (Alex comes into the other daydream where she lives with him and Claire in the Highgate house.) She and the man won't have much money but it won't matter. They will spend their days making love, eating and talking about the baby they are going to make together. They will work out when her most fertile time of the month is and then, in the never-to-be-forgotten passion of that night, she will conceive their child.

There the dream ends. Vivienne finishes her tea, extinguishes her cigarette in the dregs and laughs at her own fantasies.

In fact in seven years' time she will be living in a large house with a man who isn't Alex. At first they won't have much money and it *will* matter; they will have terrible rows about it, smashing furniture and themselves in their rage. She will bake her own bread sometimes because it is cheaper, but will forget all about wanting to make fruit pies: yoghurt for dessert is easier. There will be no chickens, just cows in the field next door escaping into her garden and trampling over the lettuces. She will have her herb garden and will lay out her newly-washed underwear over the lavender bush to make it smell sweet. But because of the interesting rambling nature of the house she will have twenty-four stairs to climb to the kitchen and twenty-four back with the next load of washing. Every washday she will do the journey fifteen times. At half past four a little girl with the face of the man's first wife will come home from school, sit on Vivienne's knee and tell her every single thing that happened to her that day, and Vivienne will love the child, because she is like a young animal, in need of love and care. The man too, she will love, gratefully at first, then with pity and finally with the cool assurance of one who has learnt to understand and accept her role in the lives of others.

But when friends write to say how brave they think she is, she will refuse to understand what they mean.

"I'm pissed," Alex announces unnecessarily, dropping his coat on the floor and stretching out on Vivienne's bed.

"Never mind," she says, picking up the coat. She *does* mind. She's spent an exhausting afternoon shopping, prepared a meal and smoked four guilty cigarettes waiting for him to come. Now instead of cheering her up he's lolling on her bed telling her what a terrible day *he's* had. If I don't make a fuss, she reasons, he'll think I'm a doormat and won't respect me. I must make a stand.

Unused to criticising him, it takes all her courage to blurt out, "You're very late."

It is quite the wrong moment. He looks at her, his eyes bloodshot. "Look, don't start."

"I'm not starting, I—"

"I've had a tough time with those bloody goons at the office today and this morning I had a flaming row with Claire. That's quite enough aggro for one day without you pitching in as well." He drinks his wine and pours himself some more, ignoring her empty glass. She wishes he would stop interrupting her; but she is secretly pleased about the row and asks what it was about.

"I don't know. Some domestic thing. Anyway, she's gone off to see her friend Joyce tonight."

Vivienne gets up quickly and fetches the food, not wanting to hear about Claire or her friends. Sometimes it seems as if they talk about nothing else but Claire; if they are not physically with her she's there in spirit, being discussed, wafting grave responsibility and good sense about the place.

Alex has said he is hungry but eats little.

"I thought you liked quiche lorraine," says Vivienne, disappointed. "You always eat it when Claire does it."

He tells her he doesn't want her always to cook the same things as Claire; he likes a change. She thinks it would be pleasant if he took her out for a meal occasionally. It seems ages since they ate out without Claire. But he had suggested this evening in. "You cook something and I'll bring a bottle. It'll be just like old times," he had said, and Vivienne had panicked. Surely they weren't looking back with nostalgia already? Not yet, please, not yet.

The phone rings and she snatches it up. If this is *her* ...

"Hello? Yes it is ... Who? ... Oh, Richard, yes, yes of

course I remember ... I know, it was a dreadful shock; the funeral was over a week ago ... yes ... no ... I can't actually, well, no ... it's a bit difficult at the moment ... yes ... yes ... all right. Bye."

Vivienne smiles nervously at Alex.

"Who's Richard?"

"I went out to dinner with him once, in a four with Stella and Bob. I told you about it."

"Just dinner?"

"Just dinner."

Alex watches her light a cigarette. "He didn't try anything at all then? You shook hands at the door and said—"

"For God's sake, Alex, he came in for coffee and—"

"Oh? He came in for coffee?"

"Yes, well I thought ... it just seemed polite." Annoyed at her own confusion, Vivienne shouts, "Well why shouldn't I invite him in for coffee? You came in for coffee the first night I met you and nothing happened."

"I had every intention that something should happen, but you were so woebegone and bunged up with flu I decided to act the nice guy to pave the way for the next time. And it worked, too, didn't it?"

Vivienne glares, hating him.

He smiles coldly and goes on, "But you were telling me about Richard. You both drank your cups of instant and then what happened?"

"Nothing."

"Look at me." He twists her head round. "What happened?"

"Oh, he had a bit of a go and I threw him out."

"And you haven't seen him since?"

"No."

"But just now on the phone he asked you out and when he

realised you had someone here he said he'd phone back. Right?" Alex is still gripping her face.

No answer. Vivienne is inflamed with hate for him.

"Are you going?"

"No. And let go of me, you're hurting."

He does not let go. "Have you been fucked by anyone else since you've known me?"

"No." Edouard doesn't count.

"Are you sure?"

"*Yes*. Let *go* Alex!"

He releases her and, instantly apologetic, pulls her on top of him. She says she can't, her period...

"Oh shit." Angrily he pushes her away. Then he stretches out his hand. "I'm sorry, Vivvy. I'm being extremely boorish tonight. Actually it's very modern of you to call it your period. With Claire it's always the curse."

Claire again. "My mother always refers to it as 'your lady pains'," Vivienne smiles. Alex laughs and looks at her warmly for the first time that evening. The sense of strain begins to leave her.

Drunkenly, he says: "You know, Vivvy, you do look lovely when you're angry. Your face just now, all pink and glowing with rage; whether I know you for one year or twenty I'll never forget that look."

Disturbed, she runs away to the kitchen. "Never forget... *forget!*" Surely they will always love each other? They *must*. Whatever happens, she thinks, I will always love Alex, even if he's pissed and argumentative like tonight, I'll still keep trying because isn't that what love is all about?

She takes in the tea and finds Alex still lying leadenly on her bed, now fast asleep. Vivienne bangs down the tea tray and slaps his face. "You've got to try too! You can't leave it all to me!" she shouts furiously. Alex does not stir. Impulsively, her loving intentions evaporating, Vivienne decides to phone Claire.

"Your husband," she rehearses crisply, "having loused up my entire evening, has now blacked out on my bed. As it is now eleven o'clock and I want to get some sleep, I should be very glad if you would come and remove your property from my flat."

Marvellous. I'll do it, I'll phone her up, she thinks, knowing she won't. Of course I can't. It's not her fault and she has been so generous to me. I should feel sorry for her really. With relief she realises that Claire won't be back from Joyce's yet anyway.

Alex, now taking up the entire bed, has begun to snore. Resisting the urge to jam her alarm clock into his gaping mouth, Vivienne snatches the pillow and two blankets from under him. He doesn't move and at this moment she wishes he would die. Sulkily, she stabs at the light switch, lies down on the rug in front of the fireplace, and tries to sleep.

Joyce is fair, fat and thirty-six with a face like a toffee apple: from a distance it looks glossy and smooth, but a closer view reveals dozens of fine lines cracking the shiny ruddy surface. As a child she lived in Teheran, attending the elite American school there until one day, shortly after her thirteenth birthday, when she was sitting at home by the swimming-pool painting her nails scarlet to match the bikini she nearly wasn't wearing, one of her father's colleagues caught sight of her from inside the house. Entranced, he started to walk towards her and crashed straight through the plate-glass sliding doors. Her father hurriedly contacted the respected Gabbitas Thring organisation for the name of a good strict boarding school and the following month Joyce joined Claire at the school in Edinburgh where the contents of her suitcase—crammed with illicit Iranian vodka and caviar—ensured her immediate popularity.

At seventeen, while Claire and the rest of her class were worrying over A-Levels, Joyce played truant for lessons of a spicier sort with a nationally-known male singer on tour in Scotland. Her outraged father talked long distance from Iran to an equally outraged headmistress in Edinburgh on whose advice Joyce was packed off to a Brussels convent school, two days before the story broke in the *News of the World*, leaked by the singer's wife who then happily collected a large payment from the newspaper, a divorce and substantial alimony. The patience of the long-suffering Belgian nuns lasted six months before they washed their hands of their charge and put her, unprotesting, on a plane back to Edinburgh. Joyce left the plane at London and by the time her bewildered father caught up with her three months later, she was pregnant. The surprising culprit, a fragile young clarinettist who played traditional jazz on the suburban pub circuit, offered little resistance when Joyce's by now exhausted father bulldozed them towards a Register Office. Joyce was happy with the clarinettist and their baby daughter Belinda for two years until one night he left them as usual to play with the group, and never came back. Her father hired the same detective agency he had used to trace Joyce in London and finally the reluctant husband was unearthed, living peacefully with his boyfriend in Bromley.

A quiet divorce was arranged, while Joyce's father consulted his wife, two psychiatrists, his male colleagues and the problem columnist on a woman's magazine on what to do with his daughter. They all said, in different ways, that what she needed was a more secure home background and a good secretarial course to fall back on.

For the first time in his life Joyce's father went against

professional advice and obeyed his intuition. Shrewdly, he
sent his daughter on a round-the-world cruise from which she
returned wearing a tan and a seven-diamond engagement
ring, a present from one Maxwell Roberts, a pleasant,
paunchy, Canadian building contractor intent on making a
take-over bid for Battersea. He also insisted on calling everyone, including his future father-in-law, "hunne". Battersea
hadn't been quite what Joyce's father had had in mind, but
Joyce seemed content enough and his detective agency
privately assured him that their comprehensive investigations
revealed no homosexual history in Maxwell Roberts.

Now Joyce, having efficiently chased her three younger
children off to bed, is serving coffee and cinnamon cake to
Claire. Maxwell is out at a Rotary Club meeting, while
Belinda, now a nubile seventeen, is upstairs revising for ex-
aminations.

"She wants to be a Queen Alexandra nurse," Joyce says, "so
she can see the world in what she calls a *worthwhile* manner. I think this is meant to be a dig at me. She's very dis-
approving of my past and the way I used to racket around,
though goodness knows, I'm respectable enough now. Parent
Teacher Association, a loyal Rotary wife, on the Beat Pollu-
tion in Battersea committee ... I even volunteered to take
over as local Brown Owl only for some reason they found
someone else. What more does Belinda want?"

"Oh, children are always embarrassed if there is any sug-
gestion that at one time mum chased men instead of under-
stains, or hidden nasties round the bend," says Claire. "They
admire a racy grandmother, but mums have to be respectable and safe, like they are on the telly."

Joyce says, "Well, Belinda is determined to thwart the racy
grandmother bit too. I am informed that it is 'anti-social to

clutter up our already over-populated world with more children mummy'. Here, Rossy, have some more cinnamon cake."

"It is delicious."

"Belinda made a big batch of it for her end-of-term party at school. I do sometimes wish she'd be a trifle more light-hearted about life, although I must say she's much more practical than I was at that age."

"I'm staggered she has time to bake cakes. At seventeen I was always overwhelmed with work for exams."

"Yes, well I must say I dipped out of that," Joyce laughs. "I remember you as such a cool, remote person at school, before I got to know you when you got that tampax stuck up your whatsit. If only all those juniors with crushes on you could have seen their adored Head Girl then! They just about fainted if you so much as looked at them."

Claire smiles, thinking how relaxing it is being with someone who has known you since schooldays; there is no need to explain or amplify because so much is understood between them, born out of an intimate knowledge of each other's backgrounds and all the things that have happened to influence them over the years. With their differing personalities it is on the surface a strange friendship, Claire supposes, but there are strong bonds between the two women, apart from the length of time they have known one another. As adolescents living away from their families they both acquired an early independence of spirit which they have never lost; and of course they both had to get married because they were pregnant. And for Claire, Joyce is important in that she is the only person with whom she feels totally at ease and is completely honest. Even with her husband Claire is aware of the need to keep a small secret part of herself detached and locked away from his mental assaults on her strength of mind. She regards it as her refuge, a place she can withdraw to in peace during the times when Alexander is expecting too much of her. But from Joyce there are no secrets, no dark shadowy corners, and Claire enjoys the luxury of talking freely, not having to vet quickly her conversation as she does with everyone else, knowing that with Joyce anything she says will simply be accepted with tolerance, interest or sympathy.

The freedom Claire is experiencing shows in her language, for the only time she uses slang is with Joyce; and, schoolgirlishly, when they are alone they still call one another by the names they were known by then, Gardner and Ross. Now, seated in Gardner's drawing room, comfortable rather than elegant, they are talking about Claire's (or Ross's) Boxing Day party.

"Of course we're coming, and thanks for inviting Belinda this year. She says she doesn't usually like the kind of parties my friends give but she is gracing yours with her presence because she regards you as a very *worthwhile* person for not littering up the world with children and doing a wonderful job coping so well with such a difficult husband. By difficult I think she means sexy."

Claire drains her coffee and asks for a cigarette. "I don't know why I always feel like smoking when I'm with you." She lights the cigarette Joyce passes her, and continues: "Of course, Belinda is more accurate than she realises. At least I hope it's more than she realises. At the moment I am doing a wonderful job coping with my difficult husband and his sexy young mistress."

Joyce looks thoughtful, and unsurprised.

"Well, Ross, I mean Alex has always been the type to play around a bit, hasn't he? You've never worried about it before."

"This one is different. She isn't an empty-headed dolly bird, she's intelligent, sensitive and desperately in love with

Alexander. You know how *intense* girls in their early twenties are about love. They want the Big Experience, the Grand Passion."

"But that sort of thing usually fizzles out pretty quickly."

"This has been going on for nearly a year now," says Claire.

"For heaven's sake, Rossy! Why the hell haven't you talked to me about it before?" Joyce's fine-lined face crinkles up like over-used tin foil.

"I thought it would all blow over, like the others. Alexander finally spilled the beans when we came back from that ghastly holiday in France, but I knew ages before that of course..." With relief, she tells Joyce everything that has happened.

"You did what? Ross, are you mad? Don't tell me you *fancy* the bloody girl?" For once, Joyce is shaken.

"No, it isn't that. I knew Alexander would like it. It is every man's dream, after all, wife and mistress rolling about together in bed, and although he hadn't come right out and said so, it was obvious that he'd fantasised about it. Besides, you know I always believe in bringing things out into the open. They are much less frightening that way."

Joyce is curious. "Did you enjoy it?"

Claire considers. "No," she says at last, "I don't think enjoy is the right word, but I didn't mind as much as I thought I was going to. And of course it was very fraught, with Alexander intent on giving the performance of the year. But I think under different circumstances, with a different girl, it might be quite good. After all, most of us, if we are honest, do have physical feelings towards people of the same sex that we are taught by convention to repress. It's only a continuation of, for example, those girls at school having a crush on me."

Joyce shivers. "You frighten me sometimes, Ross, you really

do. And I suppose Alex regards all this as an enormous expression of your undying devotion to him?"

Claire smiles.

Joyce sighs. "Yes. I thought so. I don't know, bloody gang bangs in respectable Highgate. And *I* was the one who got plastered all over the *News of the World*, just for having a measly affair with a singer. He wasn't even very good at it, I've since discovered. Even my homo clarinettist put up a better show."

"Well, if you accept that men can love men, surely you can accept that women can feel attracted to one another too, without being raving Lesbians?"

"Are you attracted to fat old me, then?" Joyce jokes apprehensively.

"The thing about overweight women is that they nearly always have beautiful shoulders, like yours," says Claire. "When you wear a dress that shows them off I always feel I want to touch you. I wouldn't, because I know you would be surprised and upset but the feeling is there all the same."

Joyce laughs. "How amazing to think of the three of you sitting watching the telly together and you quietly sizing the girl up, deciding you want to stroke her tits! Really, you should be sitting there being wittily beastly to one another."

Claire says: "That only happens to people *on* the television, not the ones watching it. Actually we don't watch much now, with Alexander concentrating on his book, but at one time there seemed to be a gamut of eternal triangle plays on television which Alexander and I used to watch by ourselves all the way through without looking at one another or exchanging a single word. It was most uncomfortable. You forget about the scriptwriter, able to spend an hour thinking up each barbed line. In reality of course it is better to be incredibly charming to one another. Scoring points only puts you in the wrong. That's if you care, of course. I sometimes think if I didn't care it would be so much easier. I could relax, then, and enjoy firing all my little poisoned darts."

"Do you like the girl?" Joyce asks.

"No. But she thinks I do, and so does Alexander. I think he fondly pictures us sitting cosily together on the settee swopping recipes for his favourite puddings."

"What you're doing, then, is letting things ride and hoping this girl will get tired of you masterminding her sex life?"

"Joyce, how crude you are!"

"You mean, how right."

It is half past eleven and as Claire prepares to leave, Belinda suddenly appears and offers to drive her home. Blonde, like her mother, but taller and slimmer, she has been standing outside the door listening, fascinated, to the last half of the conversation. Understandably intrigued, she realises that maddeningly she has missed hearing one vital fact about Uncle Alex's mistress. Her name.

Nineteen

"I suppose you're going off to see your fancy man?" says Mrs Tyler.

It is the evening of Christmas Day. Mrs Tyler and her daughter started bickering last night when Vivienne had announced she would not be accompanying her parents to the midnight carol service. "It would be hypocritical. I don't believe in any of it." After an inconclusive exchange on the virtues of Christianity and Vivienne's greatly reduced chances of entering Heaven, it became apparent that what Mrs Tyler really feared from her daughter's non-appearance at church was not the wrath of God but, more important, her own loss of face in the eyes of her neighbours, all of whom were sure to be surrounded by a dutiful entourage of offspring. So finally, to please her mother, Vivienne agreed to go.

She now wishes she hadn't. "He's not a fancy man," she retorts. Mrs Tyler prepares to unbottle all the resentment she's been storing up since Vivienne's last visit, but unexpectedly her husband intervenes.

"Now, Mother. It is Christmas Day. Let's just be glad we are all together. It's probably not a bad idea for Vivienne to go back to London tomorrow, what with Douglas having his engagement party in the evening. Save a lot of embarrassment all round."

"Yes, you missed the boat good and proper there, didn't you my girl. Didn't take him long to find someone else, did it?"

"Second best, mother." She realises that her mother can sense her faint feeling of betrayal that Douglas could go off and get engaged to someone else so quickly. Although she is sure she does not want to marry him, she will always think of Douglas as her own special property, who, albeit out on indefinite loan, may be reclaimed at a moment's notice.

Mrs Tyler goes on: "Well, you've lost your chance now. They are to be married in June. A *white* wedding, of course."

"Oh, of course."

"Maureen's a very pretty girl."

"She's not. She's got a face like a squeezed lemon."

Mr Tyler laughs. "She has that. Now, Vivvy, crack me a brazil nut and shut up, there's a good girl."

The Tylers' Christmas Day has remained the same, ever since Vivienne can remember. The family rise late and self-consciously wish each other all the permutations of "Merry Christmas, mum." "Merry Christmas, Vivienne." "Merry Christmas, dad." "That's right, Merry Christmas, dear. Merry Christmas, Mother." "Thank you Stanley. Merry Christmas." A singularly idiotic greeting, Vivienne thinks. Why not "Merry New Year" and "Merry Birthday" too?

Drinks with the people next door is followed by lunch, the turkey carved by Mr Tyler smiling determinedly under his special Christmas paper hat which will afterwards be folded up by Mrs Tyler and put away until next year. Then Vivienne and her father wash up; *no* presents to be opened until all the washing up is done, Mrs Tyler always says firmly, as if suspecting that her husband is jigging with excitement, ready to lead a raiding party on the pile of presents. They lie piled under the silver Christmas tree (less mess) which stands in the window, festooned with fairy lights and topped by a sulky-looking angel. Other people in the street may have bigger, real trees but Mrs Tyler always ensures that hers has the most lights. This is known as "making a good show". After the presents and the Queen's Speech, Mrs Tyler insists on the others going out for a brisk walk round the park, to work off their heavy meal and make room for their tea; they stay out for an hour exactly by the clock, meeting other families who have also been sent out and are aimlessly wandering round in the cold, showing off new scarves, gloves, bicycles and dolls' prams.

Back from their walk, they slump in front of the television for the evening, automatically starting to consume nuts, chocolates and tangerines that they don't really want. At six o'clock Mrs Tyler, heralded by an imaginary roll of drums, wheels in fruit, cream and The Cake, a hard-iced affair decorated with red plastic Father Christmasses. It is eaten stoically by Mrs Tyler who, having made it, has to support it; courageously by Mr Tyler who knows it will give him indigestion; and not at all by Vivienne who crumbles it up and tries to hide it under a rubbery lump of marzipan.

Vivienne's Christmas card to her parents has pride of place alone on top of the television. The others are strewn along the mantelpiece, the sideboard or hung on strips of sticky tape from the picture rail. A cunning idea, Mrs Tyler thinks. She has her own cards printed. "A Merry Christmas and a Prosperous New Year from Mr and Mrs Stanley Tyler," they read, in ornate black script. She enjoys sending the cards, about two hundred of them, sometimes crossing out Mr and Mrs Stanley Tyler and writing in, *Love from Lillian and Stanley*. Never Lil and Stan, of course. After Christmas the cards are collected up and given to the local hospital along with all the old copies of her women's magazines, minus the knitting patterns which she has torn out. Mrs Tyler, a conscientious knitter, gave her husband his usual pullover for

Christmas, over which he exclaimed with delight, pretending he hadn't seen it in unfinished stages every evening for the past month. For Vivienne they bought a leather jewellery box into which will go the string of pearls they gave her when she passed her eleven-plus examination, the sapphire brooch inherited from her Auntie Ivy and the gold watch, her twenty-first birthday present. Mrs Tyler was determined to do her daughter proud on her twenty-first. They hired a band and a hall and invited a hundred and fifty people to a dinner dance. The young singer (actually he was forty with dyed blond hair) held Vivienne's hand and sang "Twenty-One Today" while Vivienne, embarrassed beyond words, looked the other way and everyone was given a glass of champagne to drink her health.

By half past ten Mrs Tyler, on her third port and lemon, has reached the stage in My Girlhood Christmas where she looks nostalgically at the fruit bowl and says the smell of oranges always reminds her of Christmas because that was the only time in the year her family ever had them. One year her sister Rose got up early and tied the oranges to the holly bush in the little back yard ... it had looked so pretty and her poor mother had cried. Vivienne has heard this story ten times before but is still amazed that icy Aunt Rose could ever have displayed such imagination. She notices the smudge of red on her mother's little finger that Mrs Tyler has used to smooth in her lipstick; if the smell of oranges means Christmas to Mrs Tyler, that tiny smudge of red will always mean mother, and security, to Vivienne.

Mr Tyler is matching his wife glass for glass with Drambuie. It is the fourth Christmas this same bottle has made an appearance and at midnight it will be locked away in the mahogany sideboard until his birthday in August. He is waiting for his wife to stop talking or leave the room for a moment so he can tell about his Christmas in North Africa during the war.

Vivienne is not drinking. She is thinking of the party to-morrow, planning how she will bathe, do her hair and put on the new aubergine-coloured dress she bought with her Christmas bonus money. It is cut lower than anything she has owned before and she is burning to wear it.

She imagines arriving at the house in Ambassador Drive; the road full of cars, with lights, music and laughter coming from the house. Alex there to greet her at the door, kissing her forehead, telling her she looks beautiful. "I feel so proud of you. Come and meet some people." Putting his arm protectively round her shoulders as he guides her into the party. Claire will be there surrounded by people, looking incredibly elegant, and she will look across at them, smile, and come over with a drink for Vivienne. There will be a warm closeness about the three of them, a secret shared. "Who is that girl?" people will ask. "There's something about her." For once she won't be paralysed with fear at the thought of having to talk to strangers. She will chat to people easily, confidently and they will wonder about her as she looks up and catches Claire's eye across the room, or Alex comes and lightly kisses the back of her neck. As it gets late, Alex will whisper, "You are staying, aren't you?" so when everyone has gone they will sit, the three of them, drinking coffee and saying how well it all went, and who on earth was that terrible girl with Christopher... Then they will go upstairs to bed. Claire will brush her hair again and Alex will make very gentle love to them both before they fall asleep entwined together. It will all be wonderful.

Twenty

"SURELY JOYCE ROBERTS isn't wearing false eyelashes?"

"Darling, where? Which one is she?"

"The buxom blonde behind the cleavage, talking to dear Claire by the window. I'm sure they *are* false, you know. God, at her age and with those lines under her eyes, every time she blinks it puts you in mind of the national grid."

"Yes, I see what you mean. Frightful. And I wouldn't so much say lines as *ditches*, dear."

"Quite. Don't you know about Joyce? Oh my dear, let me tell you, it's fascinating. You see, her *first* husband..."

"Is *she* here yet?" Joyce is asking Claire.

"Yes, she's hidden herself away in the kitchen to butter bridge rolls for me. She *arrived* at seven o'clock."

"Oh for heaven's sake."

"I know. I was only just out of my bath, and had to rush around inventing little jobs for her to do. Anyway, never mind about her now. Where have Belinda and Maxwell got to? I haven't said hello to them yet."

They gaze round the crowded room, Joyce with the relaxed smile of a welcome guest who has nothing to do but enjoy herself, Claire with the practised, slightly anxious eye of the hostess, noting empty glasses, overflowing ashtrays and frantic eye-rollings from people wanting to be rescued. One such is Belinda.

"I can't see Maxwell," Claire says, "but poor Belinda is

stuck in the corner with Ishbel, the wife of Alexander's agent. Actually although she's dull she's terribly *worthwhile* so in theory Belinda should be getting along famously with her."

Joyce drains her Martini. "You mean that pipecleaner in the red taffeta dress? Yes, well Belinda looks about ready to push her face in. I know the signs."

"Oh dear. I'll go and join them then."

"Thanks. I think I'll get myself another drink and saunter into the kitchen to see how Cinderella is getting on."

"Now you just behave yourself, Joyce."

"My dear Claire, I shall be the very soul of discretion."

"Who's that gorgeous young blonde talking to my wife, Alex?"

"She's my god-daughter and out of your league, I'm afraid Scotty. Belinda is interested in A Levels, nursing and good causes, of which I come high on the list, according to Claire. Evidently Belinda thinks I'm sexy, alcoholic and, I'm delighted to say, in need of reform."

"She can come and reform me any day," says Scotty, staring doggily at Belinda's undulating behind as she shifts, bored, from foot to foot. Ishbel, seeing her husband ogling, lifts her thin white arm in greeting and Scotty responds weakly, his smile not even reaching the triple bags under his eyes.

Alex says: "Sorry Scotty. Sober, middle-aged literary agents don't qualify for Belinda's youthful crusading zeal. You have to have a touch of the debauched about you or she's not interested. Have another drink instead."

Scotty hesitates. "I'd better take it easy, Alex. Ishbel's already making breathalising signals."

"Oh go on, man, enjoy yourself, it's bloody Boxing Day. What was it, gin?"

"Oh well, thanks. By the way, will you still be keeping to the February deadline for the new book?"

"Yes I should think so, Scotty. It's going very well at the moment."

"Good, because I'm probably going to be able to do a deal with one of the book clubs..."

"Oh *there* you are, Maxwell! Are you supposed to be Buttons or one of the Ugly Sisters?"

"What are you talking about hunne? May I introduce Miss, er, Miss ... What did you say your name was, hunne?"

"Vivienne."

"Sure. Well, Vivienne, this is my wife Joyce."

"Hello Vivienne. I must congratulate you. The only book I've ever seen Maxwell read is a ready-reckoner to work out his profits. What have you got there that he finds so absorbing?"

"It's a collection of Aubrey Beardsley prints. Claire gave it to me for Christmas."

"Oh how nice. Culture in the kitchen. Max, it's very naughty of you to distract Vivienne when I know she's supposed to be busy buttering rolls for Claire."

"They're finished, on the dresser, and Max wasn't distracting me at all. Claire didn't really need the rolls—you know how well organised she is about everything. She was just giving me something to do because I arrived too early."

"Well, can I fetch you ladies another drink?"

"Thank you dear. I think you should put the book away now, Vivienne, and come and join the party. You can't skulk in here all night."

"Yes, all right, in a minute. I must just go to the bathroom first, if you'll excuse me."

Claire appears.

"What have you done with her?"

"Nothing, Claire, honestly. I found her in here reading the dirty book you gave her, with Max leaning over her shoulder practically falling down the front of her dress. She has now run away to pee."

"Oh God. Joyce, what did you *say*?"

Vivienne is sitting on the bathroom floor, the long auber-gine dress spread like a rich stain around her as she moodily flicks cigarette ash down the lavatory pan, working up cour-age to go downstairs. She will have to move soon because people are banging on the door threatening drastic action if she doesn't hurry up and let them get in. Nervously, she combs her hair for the fourth time and studies her face to see if any spots have erupted since she last looked, two min-utes ago. At last, unable to delay any longer, she pushes her way through the indignant queue outside the door and walks slowly down the stairs, taking deep breaths in an attempt to calm herself.

Had she felt less agitated she would have been impressed by the glittering scene in the big main room, where huge sprays of silver and green leaves provide a perfect background for the guests, whose splendid glowing velvets, rich silks and vibrant-patterned cottons splash before the eyes into a bril-liant moving patchwork of jewel colours.

But Vivienne's reaction to all this splendour, as she hovers by the door, is merely one of relief that in her long dress she is at least wearing the right thing. How mortifying if all the other women had been wearing short dresses! Trying not to look anxious she studies the blur of confident, laughing faces, trying to pick out someone familiar to talk to. Claire is easy to spot as she listens attentively to a mournful man in the corner, outstanding in her dress of velvet, dyed a myriad of bright stained-glass colours. There's Alex chatting to a thin woman in red, and Joyce making faces at her husband across the room. Joyce suddenly looks towards the door and Vivienne hastily turns away, attaching herself to a small female group where a witchy girl in a pink ostrich boa is saying confidentially:

". . . and I couldn't think what on earth to do so I just went ahead and *swallowed* it! Well, I couldn't very well spit it out, could I?"

"What did it taste like?" breathes a girl with white candy-floss hair.

"Sort of . . . sweetish really."

"You're looking very charming tonight, Ishbel. That shade of red really suits you."

"Oh, thank you Alex. I made it myself, you know, and thought maybe it was a wee bit too short?"

"It looks wonderful. I don't know how you find the time with Scotty and the children and all the gardening you do, too. How is the garden? It really looked marvellous last time I saw it."

"Well, there's not much to do at this time of year, of course, but next summer Scotty has promised he'll build me a wee patio. I've seen some very attractive pinky-coloured stone to match the brickwork on the house, and I've heard you can get big open-weave bricks to go round the edge, you know what I mean?" Ishbel is the kind of irritatingly earnest person who ends every statement with a question, like a waspish schoolteacher making sure her unwilling class has fully grasped all the regular verbs before she starts them on what she knows will be an uphill struggle with the irregular ones.

"You see, Alex, the snag with a patio is that if you're not

careful to lay the stones the correct way, the rain won't drain away properly. Do you see that?"

"Oh yes. Quite," Alex agrees, his eyes glazed.

"I was mentioning this to a young girl here earlier tonight. Belinda, that was her name. A pretty young thing, if a wee bit *forward*, you know, and she was telling me that on their patio at home—"

"Really? Well, that's fabulous Ishbel, I'm sure we'll see you gracing the pages of *Homes and Gardens* yet. Look, would you excuse me a moment? There's someone over there who looks lost." Alex has seen Vivienne by the door. He makes his way across and Vivienne greets him with relief. The witchy girl is now entertaining her friends with a detailed account of the bizarre things her boyfriend can do to himself with a daffodil.

"Thought I'd come and rescue you; you looked ready to bolt," Alex is saying. "Now come over here and I'll give you a nice big drink. This isn't a St Bernard, it's Scotty my agent, and this is Maxwell Roberts who keeps pulling down Battersea and building it up again for huge profits. This is Vivienne Tyler."

Vivienne is conscious that Alex has omitted to give her an identifying label and the other two men are looking at her curiously, wondering where she fits in.

"We've met already haven't we hunne?" smiles Maxwell, uneasily aware of Joyce looming up behind him like a vast, scented whale.

"And what do you do for a living, Vivienne?" asks Scotty, with what he hopes is craggy old-world charm.

They all turn and look at her, smiling, waiting, while her throat slowly fills up with cement.

"I'm a French translator," she croaks at last.

"*Really?*" enthuses Joyce before anyone else can say

anything. "That must be *very* interesting! Have you lived in France at all?"

Vivienne senses the attention of the men ebbing away as Alex says, "That reminds me, Max, have you heard about the time when Pierre Trudeau ..."

"... you'll be able to tell me something I've always wanted to know," Joyce is saying loudly to Vivienne. "Is it *true* that all French prostitutes shave their pubic hair?"

"Joyce, do go and dance with Alexander," Claire interrupts swiftly. "It might encourage everyone else, especially that pale young man with Belinda who seems to regard my mantel-piece as an ashtray."

Pretending not to notice his wife signalling from the other side of the room, Scotty asks Vivienne to dance, leaving Claire to bear off Maxwell to do his turn of duty with the stranded Ishbel.

Some new people arrive, noisily determined to make an entrance, and are seized on excitedly by a girl in a tinselly dress:

"*Dar*lings, I haven't seen you for *a*ges! Where have you *been*?"

"Oh, Morocco, actually."

"No! How *marvellous*. What was it like?"

"Well, hot, you know."

"Oh. Yes. Well *gosh*, I should jolly well think so. We were going to go there ourselves, but we ended up in Tunis."

"Really? How super. What was that like?"

"Actually, you know ... jolly hot."

Scotty is also hot, grey pebbles of sweat beginning to form on his ridged forehead with the effort of dancing while trying to hold his stomach in.

"So how do you come to know Alex?" he asks Vivienne, breathlessly.

"I'm just a friend."

"Ah. Yes, I see." Eagerly, he guides her out of Ishbel's laser beam gaze and draws her close, enjoying the feel of her breasts in the low-cut dress squeezed tightly up against his chest.

Gasping, not wanting to be rude to this clammy mess who is Alex's agent, Vivienne looks desperately round for help; but Claire is talking to a tall girl in glasses while Alex is dancing and playing the fool with that awful Joyce woman.

Scotty catches her glance.

"You want to watch old Alex, you know," he warns, with the frank disloyalty males display behind the backs of men who are supposed to be their friends. "The girls he plays around with usually end up getting hurt, and I'd hate to see that happen to someone as lovely as you."

"I can look after myself."

"I hope so."

Finally, Vivienne escapes and buries herself in a crowd gathered round a supper table piled with food. Hungrily, she heaps her plate with garlic chicken and salad, listening idly to the conversation flowing round her.

"I was just passing the beauty counter, not even looking at anything in particular, when suddenly the assistant—one of those superior gold-lidded goddess types—leaned forward and shrieked: 'But my dear ... *whatever* are you going to do about your appalling open *pores*?' Well. *Everyone* all around stopped *dead* and stared goggle-eyed, obviously expecting to see some pitted creature with massive gaping *craters* in her face, and I mean, I was so em*barr*assed. I never even knew I *had* open pores..."

Smiling, Vivienne moves round the table, picks up some

celery and tunes in to two flaccid men dressed in matching brown-velvet smoking jackets.

"My dear, do stop lip-reading and pay some attention to me."

"Sorry. Claire has just got to the point where she tells her husband's secretary, who lives in a basement in Earls Court, that they like this house not because it's worth £30,000, or stands in a terribly chic road in one of the most fashionable parts of town, no, none of that, they like it because it has *character*!"

"Mmm. Do have some chicken, it's delicious. Tell me, is this the secretary Alex is having a thing with?"

"No, you're about a year out of date, that was the last one, Melanie. Pretty girl, married now I think. I must say, I admired Alex's cool with that one. Apparently Claire went away for a couple of days to Bristol to do her Lady Muck bit at her publishing house I suppose, and Alex had it all set up for Melanie to come round here on the Saturday evening, when lo, late Saturday afternoon, in walks dear Claire back a day early. Well, Melanie wasn't on the phone, and Alex couldn't go out himself to warn her because he'd sprained his ankle and couldn't drive the car. So what does he do? He sends Claire round to Melanie's place with some urgent message about getting to the office very early on Monday because he had some important letters to get off before the morning conference."

"Who the hell told you all this?"

"Melanie of course. Could you pass the potato salad? Thanks. She said she nearly had a fit when she opened the door and found Claire there, and Claire herself obviously found the whole thing very strange."

"I should think so. Mind you, I think most of the stories about our Alex are exaggerated. Sure, he has the odd fling but it's never serious. He would never do anything to smash his marriage."

"You mean Claire would never let him do anything to smash *her* marriage."

"Tell me, does she ever ..."

"Never the faintest whiff, dear boy. But if she had a hundred lovers there wouldn't be much Alex could do about it without making himself look extremely foolish. This is her house, remember, and she has money of her own. Here, have some more quiche, it's the last piece."

"No, please, you have it. I was sure, though, I heard some rumour about their marriage being on the rocks, with Alex getting very serious about a new sexy young piece. I think it was Geoffrey who saw them a few months ago doing the moonlight and roses bit in a restaurant in Chelsea."

"Oh *that*. Yes of course, everyone knew and for ages poor Claire tried to ignore the whole thing, but in the end she had to move in and frighten the filly away. They have been seen, one understands, dining *à trois*, so one can imagine ..."

Stunned, Vivienne watches them drift away. It's not like that! she wants to scream. You don't understand! Full of hurt she pushes her way through the crowd and rushes upstairs to her little blue room, amazed that two anonymous people whom she has never seen before and will never meet again could come into her life and without knowing what they are doing, or caring, stab her in the stomach and twist the hard cold blade of truth before disappearing forever into their own world again.

"So your husband is in property, Mrs Roberts? That's wonderful because I'm desperate for a new house. My present one is so *small*, you wouldn't believe. Now a house like this would be ideal," says a satchel-mouthed woman to Joyce.

"But this house isn't very big," says Joyce, "and there's no garden."

"It hasn't even got a patio," chimes in Ishbel with a rustle of red taffeta. "Do you have a patio?"

"Yes of course. It's just that the rooms are so *small*."

"My house is tiny too, but I'm having a patio—"

"No one has a house that's smaller than mine. It really is the smallest house I've ever seen in my life."

"Well why don't you knock two rooms into one?" suggests Joyce, trying to edge away.

"But we *have*, and they're still min*ute*."

"Mummy," says Belinda, joining the little group, "who was that girl in the purple dress Mr Scott was slobbering over just now?"

"Oh, er, that was a friend of Alex's—that was someone called Vivienne, dear," says Joyce, flustered. "And this is *Mrs* Scott."

Hearing the door open, Vivienne hastily sits up and stares at the blonde girl who has just come in.

"You must be Vivienne."

"Yes."

"I'm Belinda. I saw the way you were looking at Uncle Alex. I want to talk to you."

"Alex! Alex, I must talk to you!" Vivienne's face is contorted by wild terror. Quickly Alex guides her away from the intrigued eyes of the girl in the tinselly dress to a quiet corner of the hall. "Now what's all this about?" he says.

"You've been telling everyone about us! I overheard two men in velvet coats saying all sorts of things about you, and they knew about me, and then just now a girl called Belinda came and said she knew all we'd been doing and it was dis-

gusting and I was a marriage-breaker and Claire hated me
and—"

"Knew all what we'd been doing?" Alex says, confused.

"You and me and Claire. You *know*. Everyone knows.
You've been having a good old snigger behind my back, pretending we all had such a special relationship and—"

"Christ, Vivvy, I don't know how this got about but I
promise you I haven't—"

"You bloody well have. It must have been you. Claire
would never have told anyone. And I *trusted* you."

"Look, we can't talk about this now. I'm supposed to be the
genial host at this bunfight. Frankly I don't care what anyone
else thinks, but—"

"I care. Where's my cape, I'm going home."

"Upstairs in my room. I'll get it for you. But Vivvy, listen—"

"I'll get it myself. You go away and giggle with your gossipy
friends. Tell them your sexy young filly just reared and kicked
you in the teeth."

Vivienne slams upstairs, lights a cigarette and hunts for
her cape in the mound of coats piled on Claire's bed. She feels
like smashing up everything in the room but finally contents
herself with grinding her cigarette out on the carpet.
"Childish," she reproaches herself, leaving the room.

The landing is in darkness, but she can dimly make out a
couple embracing at the top of the stairs. It is Alex and
Belinda.

Disdainfully, Vivienne sweeps past, her head high, praying
she won't trip on the long dress going downstairs. Behind her
she hears Belinda's smothered laugh. Alex swears.

"Vivvy!"

"Richard! What are you doing here?"

"Oh, I came with some people. What are *you* doing here?"

"I know the hosts." I *knew* the hosts.

"You're not going, are you?"

"I am, yes. Why don't you come with me?" Vivienne smiles up at Richard, hoping Alex is looking.

Richard stares back, calculating the odds. It is midnight and most of the birds at the party will have been snapped up, and even if there is a bit of spare, it might not be willing to come across. On the other hand, here is pretty Vivvy with the big boobs, asking to be taken home and looking ready to throw it around. He'd like another crack at that.

"You're on," he says.

"Where's Vivienne got to, Alexander?" asks Claire an hour later.

"Oh, she overheard someone saying something about her, and rushed off, saying she was going home. I thought she'd gone, and then she saw me having a cuddle with Belinda, got huffy and cleared off with a skinny character being worn by a pink shirt."

"Oh dear. Surely she's not taking a party flirtation seriously?"

"Oh, she was all in a state, something to do with other people, including Belinda, knowing all about us. I spoke to Belinda who denies talking to Vivienne at all, so of course I let it drop there before the girl got curious. Then I tried to catch Vivvy to tell her not to be so sensitive but she ignored me. I suppose she's trying to teach me a lesson by going off with someone else, but frankly I don't think I've got the energy to get worked up about it."

"She'll calm down."

"Yes, I think she'll have to."

"What have you done with Belinda?"

"Given her back to the pale young man with glasses. Every time I tried to kiss her she squirmed around and said, 'Isn't

Claire marvellous.' So I got the message."

"Well as a penance you can go and talk to Ishbel. She's all alone again."

"Oh God, she'll grow roots if she stands there much longer ... Ishbel my lovely, come and dance with me ..."

Twenty-one

"Vivvy I do wish you would tell your boyfriends I don't function properly before ten in the morning," pleads the exhausted voice of the office switchboard girl. "There's a Mr Richard Bennett on the line sounding so full of purpose that I fully expect him to come striding down the wire and jump out at my ear. It's extremely tiring."

Vivienne sees her point as Richard bellows urgently: "Vivienne! This is very important. Have you made up your quarrel with your friend Alex yet?"

Vivienne gathers herself together. "Yes, I suppose so. We saw the New Year in at Trafalgar Square last night. I'd always wanted to do that you know, and—"

"Did you go to bed with him?"

Vivienne smiles. So that's it. Poor dear Richard is jealous. "Yes I did," she says gently, preparing to explain, kindly, that she is very fond of Richard and it is perfectly possible to have a satisfactory relationship with two men at once. But Richard is shouting again. "Sorry, Richard, I didn't quite catch that. You spent New Year's Eve *where*? ... What special clinic?"

Richard sounds aggrieved. "The special clinic at my local hospital. I've got a fucking dose." Vivienne still does not respond. "Are you thick or something? VD, Vivvy, clap, Saigon Rose, the thing you catch more easily than measles nowadays. Savvy? Well the hospital said I should let you know so you can go and have a check-up."

"Me? But I haven't got..." Slowly the full outrage of his

words breaks over her. "You fucking bastard. You filthy stinking—"

"Now hang on, Vivvy. I don't want to sound ungallant, but you gave this to *me*."

"I bloody didn't!" Vivienne squeaks. "I've never had anything like that in my life and I've only been sleeping with Alex recently and I know he's clean. So it must have been you. Definitely."

"Well look. The important thing is that I've told you. It would have been much easier not to, and just disappeared out of your life, you know. Now all you have to do is ring up your nearest hospital, ask if they have a special clinic and make an appointment for today. Will you promise me to do that?"

"Why do they call it a special clinic?" asks Vivienne bitterly. "Why don't they come right out and call it a VD Department for people who've had dirty sex?"

"They try to save you embarrassment," says Richard, with restraint. "The other thing is, you will have to tell your friend Alex."

"My God. I *can't*." Vivienne realises that for some reason they are both speaking in loud stage-whispers.

"You must," breathes Richard. "It's only fair. If you have got it, you might have passed it on to him and you must tell him before he gives it to his wife."

Vivienne rings off and hurtles into the Ladies, cursing herself for ignoring all the articles and publicity about VD. But VD is something other people get, girls who sleep around with someone different every night, not nice girls like her. It isn't fair. The one time she sleeps with someone else, this has to happen. How was she to know Richard was poxed up? He looked clean enough. It's degrading, horrible. She peers into her knickers, remembering something she once read about a

discharge. But she always has a slight discharge. Is there more
of it than usual? Yes ... no ... impossible to say. Oh God,
how awful it all is, like having a minge full of maggots, it
makes you cringe away from yourself. She can't possibly tell
Alex, it's too humiliating. She must tell Alex or he will give
it to Claire. Hell. What on earth would her mother say if she
knew? The idea makes Vivienne laugh and, slightly more
cheerful, she goes to phone the hospital.

By 6.30 Vivienne is terrified again, having spent the entire
day working herself into a panic, rushing off every half hour
to inspect her knickers for any fresh developments. She walks
with downcast eyes into Outpatients, illogically convinced
that every single person in and around this hospital must
know what she's there for.

As there are no direction signs, she is forced to enquire at
Reception.

"Could you tell me where the VD Clinic is?" she asks
clearly, addressing the middle button on the receptionist's
white coat. No point in beating about the bush, she thinks.
VD is VD and that's that.

"The Special Clinic is round the corner to your left,"
whispers the coat.

Chastened, she turns the corner and recognises them at
once. All men, wouldn't you know, and all totally absorbed
staring at the stone floor, the ceiling, the green-painted walls,
newspapers and a notice board containing a list of fixtures for
the hospital hockey team. The men ignore her as, heart
pounding, she joins the end of the queue and shuffles nervously with it towards a doctor asking questions and filling in
forms at a desk. No one else speaks and it is not until Vivienne
reaches the doctor that a nurse rushes forward and accuses her
of being in the wrong line: the Women's Department is
through the pink door on the left, she says, hustling Vivienne

away like a small girl caught snooping in the boy's lavatory. Hesitantly Vivienne pushes open the anonymous pink door, noting indignantly the absence of any sign or label to distinguish it from all the other mysteriously blank pink doors in the corridor.

Inside, she finds herself in a room eight feet square containing eleven chairs and ten girls, all with faces as white and worried as her own. Vivienne sits down and smiles timidly round but the girls, wary and anxious, avoid each other's eyes.

A red-haired nurse rustles in.

"Now. Have you all got numbers?"

Vivienne stands up. "No, I haven't. My name is Tyler, I have an appointment—"

"No, no, no," the nurse snaps, "we don't have names here, we have numbers. Have you got a number?"

"No, I'm afraid I haven't," says Vivienne.

"Well come with me and I'll give you a card and a number. Have you been before? No. Well here's your card with your number on it, 421. Bring the card with you each time you come. Now pop into that room there for your examination."

In the room she is greeted reassuringly by a pretty young nurse who tells her to remove her tights and pants and then helps her into what looks like a dentist's chair, set on a high plinth. The doctor appears, introduces himself as Dr Townsend and tells her not to worry because this isn't going to take long. Now he is going to lift her legs into these stirrups here, that's right, so he can get at her more easily, and he is just going to take three simple smears. There, that's the first one, yes it does hurt, that's why he likes to get it over with first. The other two are much easier, if she will just relax ... Good. Vivienne can get down now and go and sit in the waiting room while the slides are analysed.

Relieved, Vivienne dresses and watches the pretty nurse carefully label the three small germ-laden pieces of glass. Her germs. Richard's germs. God, how sickening it all is. The fresh, antiseptic aura of the nurse makes Vivienne feel soiled, so she hurries back to join her companions in the little waiting room.

The pink door opens, and the receptionist peers in. "Is there a Miss French here?" she asks.

"Yes, that's me," says a fat girl next to Vivienne.

The red-haired nurse bursts in, eyes popping. "No, no, *no*," she screams, "we don't have names here, we have *numbers*. No one, but no one has a *name*. Is that clear?"

"Sorry," says the receptionist, and retreats.

"Sorry," says the fat girl, ashamed because she's Miss French.

It breaks the ice. "The doctor is a sweetie," announces an angelic-looking girl with long thin plaits. "He's going to give me a double penicillin jab so I don't have to come back again next week."

"I think I'd rather open the box," jokes someone else.

The walls are thin and next door in the men's section they can hear the doctor questioning a patient, a foreigner it appears, with little command of English.

"When did you last have intercourse?" asks the doctor.
Silence.

"When ... Did ... You ... Last ... Have ... In-ter-*course*?"
Silence.

"Sex. When did you last have SEX?"

The word booms round the room. Vivienne shudders, and the girls fall quiet again, the silence broken occasionally by the red-haired nurse calling numbers for the girls to come and receive their verdicts from the doctor. Some of them, clearly old-timers, have brought knitting or books to read,

while others sit fidgeting and surreptitiously studying one another. Vivienne is surprised that they all look so normal;
naïvely she had expected blatant prostitutes with dyed hair,
or girls with oozing scabs, obviously riddled with syph. But
these girls are really just like her. Young, ordinary and trying
very hard not to look afraid.

The voice next door drones wearily on.

"How many girls have you had SEX with?... HOW MANY?
... One, two, three?... Two? You must give me their
NAMES."

Oh dear, surely you don't have to tell them that. Now she
will have to tell Alex. But how? "By the way, Alex, I've got
VD." "Alex, this is all quite ridiculously boring, but the fact
is..." "Alex, have you by any chance ever had gonorrhoea?"

"Number 421 come and have your blood test, please." The
bossy red-haired nurse is in charge of this. "Roll up your
sleeve. No, higher than that. No, that's not enough, you'll
have to take your dress off then." She sighs deeply, resenting
the unfair hand of fate that has placed her, so plain and un-
gainly, in a Venereal Department, instead of making her slim
and attractive, with men who desired her, like this pretty
grey-eyed girl she has to give a blood test to. Accurately, she
jabs the needle into Vivienne's arm. "Right, dress and go and
sit down again."

Half an hour goes by.

"When did you last have intercourse?" inquires the voice
next door for the eleventh time.

"421 to the doctor, please."

Her legs like half-set jelly, Vivienne follows the nurse to the
consulting room, as if prepared for her execution.

But Dr Townsend is overwhelmingly kind. He takes her
coat, hangs it up, settles her comfortably in a chair, chats
briefly about the weather. Now just a few routine questions,

he says. Nothing to worry about. He asks who sent her here and she tells him about Richard.

Have I got VD? she shouts silently.

"And when did you last have intercourse?"

"Last night." Oh God, I wish I hadn't, I wish I'd never ever had it in my life. "No, not with Richard, with someone else." Relief, he doesn't ask for a name.

"I see. Now you've had a blood test?"

"Yes." Have I got VD? She can see her file on the table in front of him. *Not to be Handled by the Patient* it says, along with her number and, gracious, her name written in red biro.

The doctor smiles. They won't have the results of the blood test for a few days but, he says, her main problem at the moment is a touch of Thrush. He will give her some pessaries to clear that up and will she come back and see him at this time next week. All right? He scribbles out a prescription.

"Yes, but have I got VD?"

The doctor looks surprised, as if the question is totally irrelevant, like, have I got sweaty feet?

"You have a slight infection," he says soothingly, "but it is nothing serious. You'll be taking Tetracyclin tablets for that. I've put them on the prescription." He stands up and starts to make go-away movements.

"What do you mean, a slight infection?" Vivienne persists.

"What I say," he says calmly, urging her into her coat. "You have not got syphilis or gonorrhoea. Well, we won't know for sure until we see the results of the blood test, but I'm pretty sure you haven't. All you've got is a mild infection which, because it is sexually transmitted, comes under the broad general heading of a venereal disease."

"Are you sure?" says Vivienne, aggressive in her relief.

"Well who's the doctor round here?" Then he takes pity on her and says kindly. "Look. Three times a week I come in here and face a roomful of wan girls like yourself and I should be very surprised if out of all the girls I see today there are two genuine cases of gonorrhoea or syphilis amongst them. Most of them will have what you've got, and like you they will take their pretty red Tetracyclin tablets and in a month's time they will be clear. But of course, you must come back and see me once a week until you are clear, so I can check on your progress. All right?"

Vivienne hesitates by the door. "Yes, fine. And should I, er, do I have to refrain from..."

"I should keep off it for the present. You'll have to put the pessaries in at night and they are rather messy so it will be a good excuse to keep the brute at arm's length." He smiles professionally, two seconds worth of crinkled eyes and twenty teeth, and ushers her out.

God, she thinks, another one who believes you only do it at night manacled screaming to the bed by the Big Bad Wolf.

Later that night, when Alex has gone, Vivienne shivers out of her clothes and pours a kettleful of boiling water into her tepid bath: the colder it is outside the more the geyser goes into decline, roaring like a strangled dragon and incapable of producing water hotter than lukewarm. Once in the gritty bath, Vivienne lies back with one toe wedged comfortably up the tap as she lights a cigarette, amazed at her own calm state of mind after the traumatic events of the evening.

She had met Alex at her local and, over four large sherries, stuttered out her story rehearsed innumerable times on the way to the pub.

To her relief Alex had taken it all philosophically, even laughing as he said, "Well, you know what they say Vivvy: *Don't Give a Dose to the One You Love the Most*. It doesn't sound terribly serious, love; it's not as if you've got raging syph and anyway it's the sort of thing that happens to everyone in a mild way at one time or another."

That part of it was fine, she thinks, like being a child again, all keyed up for a telling-off and getting a jam tart instead. It would probably have ended there if only she'd had the sense to shut up when Alex had commented, "It might teach you, though, next time you get in a drunken huff at a party, to be more careful whom you choose to sweep off to bed with." Stupidly, she'd retorted: "Richard says I must have got it from you."

Bang. That had done it. Exit man of the world Mallender, enter Saint Alexander, somewhat out of practice and propped up by staunch helpmeets Purity, Chastity and Innocence.

"You most certainly did not get it from me! I suppose the next thing you're going to tell me is that I got it from Claire? Well let me remind you that *she's* not the one round here who's been sleeping around."

That had stung.

"Not that it matters now, particularly," Alex went on icily, "but have you been fucked by anyone else apart from Richard?"

Vivienne had stalled: "How very interesting, Alex, that when you are talking about dear Claire the expression is refined—sleep around—but when it comes to me it suddenly degenerates into a common or garden fuck."

"I shouldn't pursue that line of enquiry if I were you, Vivienne. Anyway, it doesn't matter how you describe it. Just tell me the truth."

Common sense should have told her to keep quiet, but it will be years yet before she learns that confession scenes bring peace to no one, that this sort of trouble shared is more often just a trouble doubled. Like a child lured by the promise of more jam tarts (*tell the truth and you won't get into trouble, lie and you will be found out*) she trustingly told him about Edouard, her grey eyes pleading, sincere as Alex looked at her and through her, saying nothing. "It was only a few times, she gabbled frantically, and he's gone to Paris now."

"So you lied then, when I asked you once before if there had been anyone else. You lied."

"My God, Alex, do stop sounding like an aggrieved Boy Scout. Last time you asked you were drunk and I was frightened. I had to lie."

"Do you still hear from him?" Alex asked, his voice distant, deceptively unconcerned.

"Yes, he writes. He wants me to go and live there. Look," she coaxed, "don't be annoyed, darling. It was you I loved, not him, and after all, there's not much difference between you knowing about Edouard and all I had to put up with, knowing you were sleeping with Claire."

That, she realises, was when we started to use the past tense.

Inevitably, Alex had said it *was* different. He had been quite open and honest about Claire and had thought there was something special between the three of them. Something very rare and very loving. He would have thought, with all there was between them, she would at least have told him she had another lover.

"Oh Alex, it didn't seem important—"

"I see. It's not important who you sleep with?"

"That's not what I meant."

"I can understand, just, you sleeping with this Richard guy, although it is rather ironical that you did it because you were jealous of me flirting with Belinda. At least that's what you say—"

"It's true! And I was annoyed because you and Claire have

been blabbing about me to all your rotten friends."

"Actually we haven't, but never mind that now. The point is that in spite of all your righteous indignation about my behaviour, it now turns out you've been jumping into bed with someone I've never heard of. Very cool, Vivvy, very cool. I wonder how many more men you're going to spring out of the hat?"

"None! I've told you the truth, can't you appreciate that?"

Vivienne pulls out the plug and lets the water gurgle away as she reaches for her towel. It was so important that he should believe her. She had clutched at him across the table, willing him to understand, to tell her everything was all right, tender and secure like it used to be. But his face had suddenly changed, collapsing into lines of tiredness and withdrawal, like that of an actor who, weary of his role, is glimpsed for a disillusioning second hurrying off stage behind the falling curtain.

Seeing her pathetic stare, Alex smiled quickly and said more kindly: "Anyway, we won't talk about it any more now. Poor kid, you've had quite a day, haven't you? Finish your drink and we'll go and eat. Then I shall return you, untouched, to your bed. I'll have to work on my book this weekend, I'm afraid, if I'm to meet my February 4th deadline."

"Oh." Naughty girl must be punished.

"But Claire says you can come over on Sunday afternoon if you like. It's Belinda's birthday, and Joyce and Max are bringing her over for tea."

"Yes, I'll see. I may be busy."

"Well, see how you feel." Then, as he reached the door he said casually, "By the way, Vivvy, are you going to go and live in Paris?"

Surprised, Vivienne heard herself say: "I don't know."

He opened the door and stood aside to let her through

first, saying as she passed: "Well of course, it's up to you entirely, but if you want to go I can't stop you. It might even be best..."

Vivienne pulls on her dressing gown. *It might even be best.* She had expected more than that. "No, no, I love you, I need you Vivvy, please don't leave me." Some bloody hopes. How could such an important decision be taken so carelessly, her relationship with Alex simply fizzling out with no roll of drums, no thunderclaps, no end of the world, just a shrug of the shoulders and five words tossed lightly over her head like handfuls of sand to quench the fire? What a mean, miserable way for it all to end.

For to Vivienne it *is* a decision. Her affair is over.

She has not the experience to regard this time tolerantly as simply a bad patch in her affair with Alex, for Vivienne has yet to learn to accept other people's human weaknesses. She herself is so guileless that if a man she trusts says, I will always love you, then she expects him to do literally that, and if that same man says, it might even be best, she will accept that it is so. Just as it is not yet in her nature to fight for something she wants, so her false pride demands that if she does not feel wanted, she must go.

So she is persuaded that Alex is right. What on earth is the point of it all? "Do you love me?" she asked as he kissed her goodnight. "Of course I do," he replied, as all men reply. For the first time, she had not believed him.

I have been fooling myself, she decides. Deceiving myself in hundreds of ways every day to avoid facing my own lack of purpose; at night lying restlessly awake goading myself into believing in something that really wasn't there.

The flat is lonely and cold. With Stella's room still unoccupied Vivienne misses the friendly sounds of another human being nearby. She looks for the first time objectively round the little room that once meant so much to her. It had always been untidy, but in a warm, cheerful way. Now, she realises, it has an uncared-for appearance, a dull air of neglect.

And so have I, she thinks, reaching decisively for the small leather writing case her parents gave her when she first went away to France.

On the other side of London Alex lies full length on the settee, his head in Claire's lap.

"What really foxes me," he says, "is the way she went to bed with this Edouard creature, and calmly lied about it afterwards. I simply can't understand how she could go and do a thing like that."

Claire looks down at her husband, saying nothing, willing herself not to strike him.

Twenty-two

Hello Vivvy,

Was glad to get your letter, and pleased you have settled in to your flat and are enjoying Paris—it's a marvellous city. News here is that my book is with the publisher and with luck will be out by Christmas. There is even vague talk of a film! Great if it comes off but I don't really hold out much hope.

Claire is very well, spending a lot of time with Joyce who has just announced she is pregnant again. Belinda was so disgusted she left home for a while—you can imagine the uproar—though I think secretly Joyce was quite proud of her for doing it.

Vivvy, I was so sad to see you go. Somehow, I feel we lost our way with one another. We left so much unsaid, and there was such a lot I wanted to say. I feel that I drove you away, and that isn't what I wanted to do at all. Please keep in touch, won't you, or I shall feel guilty wondering what is happening to you. I'm glad you sound so happy. Think of me sometimes, and do write again.

With much love,

Alex.

PS. Claire has just come in with the enclosed note for you.

My dear Vivienne,

We were so relieved to hear from you. It is always upsetting when friends do not part friends and I hope now we will not lose contact again with each other. We think about you a great deal. Your new job with the cosmetics company sounds most interesting and I am sure you will make a success of it.

I also have to tell you that your mother telephoned me yesterday. She evidently found our number through Directory Enquiries, and said she is extremely worried because you have not written.

Best wishes,
Claire.

(2)

... the new hat I wore to Douglas' wedding. Maureen looked a picture, a really lovely June bride but I must say I didn't think much of her relations, scruffy lot they were, dressed more for a jumble sale than a wedding. Your father took some snaps but they came out all foggy. I do think you might have sent a present, I was most embarrassed for you.

Well Vivienne you say you are all right and happy but we worry about you a lot and just hope Edouard is looking after you properly. I am still not clear from your letters what your living arrangements are it all sounds very strange to your father and me. I am sending you a fruit cake by separate post. Remember whatever happens you will always be my daughter and I can't help but wonder if you are really getting on as well as you say. We hope to have another letter from you soon.

From Your Loving Mother and Father.

Paris, December 1st.

Dear Alex,
Sorry I haven't written but v. busy. LISTEN: Edouard and

*I are coming home for Xmas, landing morning of the 23rd.
Can we cadge lunch from you? Claire says your book has been
delayed. Shame, I was expecting a signed copy. Must rush.
News when I see you.*

Love,

Vivvy.

*PS. Please thank Claire for me for the sweater. It's perfect.
Good old Marks and Sparks, why don't we have them here?*

V.

(Postcard)

*From : Mrs Claire Mallender, 31 Ambassador Drive, London
N6. December 6th.*

Vivienne,

Delighted to see you and Edouard for lunch on the 23rd.

Claire.

The road looks shabbier than she remembers it and the
almond tree is wilting in the grey London rain. A broken
plastic gun lies discarded under the new Rover that gleams
wet outside number 31. While Edouard parks their hired car
Vivienne takes her hand mirror out of her bag and checks her
hair: it is short now, shaped to her head in the classic French
style, making the big grey eyes look enormous. The pale tense
appearance she had when she left London has gone, replaced
by a self-assurance that shows in her simple, well-cut clothes
and her walk, now a graceful stride instead of the coltish lope
of a year ago.

As they walk up the path she studies the house, surprised
that it can look so ordinary. With her capacity for endowing
the inanimate with human passions Vivienne had always
imagined the house set apart from the rest of the road and

like a woman in love, magically aglow with secret charmed memories, almost visibly vibrating, so that had she reached out to touch a single brick she would have held her breath, in anticipation of a delicious shock sparking through her.

But this house, with its white plaster, soaked khaki by the rain, has the same shuttered look as all the others in the row, and has obviously forgotten her, like a woman who remembers her first and current loves, but prefers not to be reminded of the ones in between.

As Alex opens the door Vivienne waits hopefully for the sinking feeling which will tell her that he too, is ordinary, that although she may have wasted a year of her life shredding up her heart like cabbage at the feet of someone who is merely a fallible, average man, at least now she will know the agony is over. That, really, is what she has come to find out.

He is smiling and drawing them in out of the rain, taking coats and offering sherry sweet or dry. He has put on weight, grown his hair a little longer but otherwise looks the same. Vivienne tests her reactions, waiting for flutters in her stomach, weak knees or a trembling hand round the sherry glass.

Nothing. Nothing, nothing. She is free.

Elated, delighted with her liberty she walks buoyantly into the kitchen, her face alive with happiness which she sees at once the wary Claire misunderstands.

Well, let her think that, Vivienne tells herself. Let her suffer.

"Hello Vivienne. How well your hair suits you, shorter like that. We can see the shape of your face now."

Typically, Alex has not noticed. For the rest of his life he will remember Vivienne with long hair.

Claire finishes setting the table, telling her the problems

that have cropped up in getting Alexander's book published. Vivienne, relaxed in her new-found confidence, is content to sip her drink and listen, say nothing. Less eager than the Vivienne of a year ago, she is no longer desperate to be liked, so the electrically alert look she used to assume with people when she wanted them to approve of her is replaced now by one of quiet appraisal. She lets Claire talk on until suddenly the older woman runs out of words.

For the first time, Vivienne takes the initiative: "Come and meet Edouard."

After lunch Claire, as usual, refuses all offers of help with the washing up, and Vivienne and Alex find themselves alone in the sitting room while Edouard tactfully excuses himself to go to the bathroom.

Vivienne places a cushion on the floor near the fire, watching Alex, in a moss green sweater she hasn't seen before, spend a long time choosing a record, meticulously dusting it and fussing with the controls on the stereo. Alex, your nerves are hanging out, she thinks. But why? It isn't just the fact of meeting her again. There is something else bothering him. They talk in short bursts as ex-lovers do when they meet again as strangers, not looking directly into one another's eyes for fear of what they will see there, each slightly agitated in case the other should blunder with an embarrassing reference to their past intimacy. Vivienne's earthy instincts translate this into an appallingly ludicrous vision of Alex suddenly whipping his dick out and waving it around in front of her in a frantic attempt to recapture the good old days.

"I must say, you're looking very well, Vivvy."

She smiles. "Thank you."

He asks about her plans after Christmas. Is she going back to Paris with Edouard or not? Vivienne explains that she will still be based in France, but her new job will involve travelling round to all the Common Market countries, promoting her company's range of cosmetics.

He looks alert. "So you'll be in England from time to time, then?"

"Oh yes. Quite a bit in fact, because there is a big campaign being planned to launch the stuff over here."

"I see. So you and Edouard aren't..." he waves his hands and she laughs. "No, we aren't. We live in the same flat for convenience, but we have separate rooms and separate lives, really. My poor mother is going round the twist trying to sort out who is living where, with whom and why."

Edouard reappears, carrying the coffee tray for Claire who follows him in and settles herself, in her neat way, in the rocking chair. Vivienne flashes Edouard a grateful glance, for he has obviously been keeping Claire talking in the kitchen, no easy task. They bounce the conversational ball again, Vivienne saying little but acutely aware now that Alex is talking exclusively for her benefit and if he makes a joke it is to her he looks first for the laugh. He is making an effort, clearly missing the unquestioning admiration she used to show him.

Gradually getting used to being with him again, she allows herself the luxury of analysing his attraction. Yes, she thinks, I can see what I saw in you. You are not ordinary at all. You have a lethal animal magnetism, a kind of sexual energy that shows in every line, every movement of your body. It's something not many men have, thank God. Edouard certainly hasn't got it. But I can feel that it is very much alive and kicking in you.

She suddenly catches herself laughing across at him as if there were no one else in the room. *I can feel.* No. Oh no, that way lies danger.

To calm herself she quickly turns and talks to Claire, noticing little things that were never apparent before; the tiny vertical lines appearing above her top lip, the grainy appearance of her skin in contrast to Vivienne's own youthful sheen, and a prominent tracery of blue veins on the hands busy with embroidery. To Vivienne it seems incredible now that she could once have felt so afraid and unsure of herself with Claire, creating ghosts where there were none.

I have been so happy here, she thinks, and also so uncertain and off balance at times. You did that to me, she accuses the placidly sewing Claire. You pretended you cared for me, wanting to be friends and "develop my potential". But all you did was take away what little self confidence I had; you did everything better than me, you talked better, cooked better, dressed better, were more intelligent, your whole projection was better than mine. The only thing I had over you was sex, and in the end you dominated that too. You made a baby of me when I so desperately wanted to be a woman.

And you, she turns to Alex, you just allowed me to be manipulated until you got bored with the performance and my pathetic attempts to please, and seized on the first excuse to shovel me out of the way.

The afternoon sweeps on. It is getting dark, and Alex draws the curtains, commenting that it has stopped raining. Again, Vivienne senses his edginess. They are waiting for something. But Edouard looks at his watch and murmurs that the traffic, you know, perhaps they should make a move...

"Oh, but Vivienne," exclaims Claire, her bird-like eyes bright, "you haven't seen the blue room have you? Do come and look, you'll be amazed at what I've done to it. Edouard, you must come too."

"It's all right, I don't want to crowd the scene. Let Vivvy go," says Edouard, telling Vivienne later that he didn't know what made him so reluctant to see the room, but it was as if when Claire mentioned it, a hundred invisible wires between them all were pulled tight. Vivienne feels it too, and one sharp look at Alex's face confirms that this is what they have been waiting for.

"Claire, I don't really know if we've got time," Vivienne says, but Claire insists and leads the way upstairs, followed unwillingly by Vivienne and Edouard.

"What do you think?" Claire says, opening the door and switching on the light.

It is no longer a blue room, but a brown one. A real brown study, Vivienne thinks, looking with horror at the dark hand-printed wallpaper, matching carpet and bitter chocolate velvet curtains. There is a chaise longue, a chair and a small roll-topped desk, above which hang two sombre Morland prints in dark wood frames. The overall effect is one of overwhelming oppression, the only relief coming from a bowl of white Christmas roses on the windowsill. Uneasily, to break the strained silence, Edouard asks what the room is for.

"I simply wanted somewhere quiet to come and sit, sometimes," Claire says. "Alex has his own study downstairs and as this room was looking so shabby and in need of redecoration, I thought I'd turn it to good use. We have a perfectly good guest room already, I didn't think we really needed a second one."

You cow, Vivienne thinks, you mean you wanted to destroy the only part of this house that was mine in spirit. And stupidly, I thought it would always stay the same, my little blue room. I should have known better. I should have known you wouldn't be able to stand coming in here and remembering me, sitting up in bed looking out of the window at the sun and the birds in the almond tree. So you smashed it up and stamped your signature all over it, making it scream Claire, Claire. It used to be a pretty room, a room for love and laughter. Now its a monstrosity and yours, your very own triumphant retreat.

Saddened, Vivienne walks away, out of the room, down the stairs, shattered that Claire still has this power to deflate her. Edouard and Vivienne put on their coats and they all stand near the front door and look at one another, Vivienne feeling about twelve years old. "Well," says Claire firmly, opening the door, "at least it has stopped raining."

"Many thanks for the lunch, Claire," Edouard says, shaking hands.

"Yes, thanks," says Vivienne. Say thank you for the lunch nicely, and thank you for having me and thank you for stabbing me in the back. Again. "Well, goodbye then Claire. I'll drop you a line."

Claire smiles.

"I'll see you to the car," says Alex.

Upstairs, Claire parts the brown velvet curtains and watches her visitors drive away. The room is in darkness, the only light coming from the sodium lamp outside, gleaming orange through the bare branches of the almond tree. She feels enormously relieved. Claire's first sight of the new confident Vivienne that afternoon had frightened her. But it is a false confidence, she realises, a deceptive maturity that comes to people in their early twenties when they have had a nibble at life. They think now they are ready for a hefty bite, and then they choke themselves, as Vivienne did right here in this room. She smiles, thinking of Vivienne's crestfallen expression with her smart self assurance clearly crumbled. Anyway, Claire tells herself, the important thing is that it is over, and the girl knows it is over. That much was obvious from her face as she left.

When the car is out of sight Claire draws the curtains, picks off some wilting petals from the bowl of Christmas roses, and quietly leaves the room.

As the car moves off Vivienne winds down the window, welcoming the cold air, fresh after the rain, and feeling Claire's almost magnetic influence receding with each turn of the wheel.

It was a good try, Claire, she thinks, and it nearly succeeded. A year ago it would have worked, but not now. You think you've driven me away, but you haven't. You can't get rid of me, Claire, because it's all still there between Alex and me, the difference being that the balance of power has changed. He wants me now more than I want him, which means if I say "come" he'll drop everything and come. The way I used to. We didn't even bother to say goodbye when he saw us to the car; we just smiled at each other and said, "See you soon." He'll never leave you, Claire, in the physical sense of moving out, but spiritually and emotionally, if I want him to, he'll leave you. If I want him to.

"What a strange woman," Edouard says. "Not unattractive, though."

"Do you think so?"

"Yes, it comes from that quality of stillness ... repose in her face, almost like that of a nun. She's not a religious nut I suppose?"

They approach the corner and Vivienne, laughing, looks back down the tree-lined road to the house they have just left.

"No," she says, "at least not in the way you mean. I think for Claire, marriage is her religion."